THE ISLANDS
—OF—
DEATH

PETER STRIDE

ISBN: 978-1-63950-278-3 (sc)
ISBN: 978-1-63950-274-5 (e)

Writers Apex

Gateway Towards Success

8063 MADISON AVE #1252
Indianapolis, IN 46227
+13176596889
www.writersapex.com

BOOK ONE

ST KILDA, THE HEBRIDES

Donald S. Murray – From 'The Dark Horse'

When a man makes love to a St Kildan woman,
her moans and sighs are like the cries of birds –
a cooing and screaming that seems scarcely human...
as a man and woman couple to break free
from an island's bonds and strictures...
as they touched the heights the birds could reach
with their bodies' power and beauty,
arms charged to wings by the tumultuous air.

CHAPTER ONE

ST KILDA

A naked Jacqueline glanced anxiously at the luminous hands of the bedside clock. Anxiety perhaps tinged with maybe a little guilt. Time was getting away from her. George would be doing his key-note presentation in just over half-an-hour. Her husband always expected her to be in the audience, especially now he was the president of the History of Medicine Society. She would definitely need a good shower now before being presented as his trophy wife to his sycophantic colleagues.

She peered around the half-darkened cabin to locate her bra and knickers which Rocky had thrown somewhere a couple of hours ago in his abandoned lust. She had worn her fuchsia *Agent Provocateur* set and hoped they were not torn! Rocky was a psychiatrist, not a real doctor in the eyes of her husband, the top cardiac surgeon in Australia. Certainly, that was George's personal opinion and his expensive fee schedule supported that concept.

Rocky, however had much greater oral skills as she had experienced during the last two hours of wanton pleasure. He seemed to like her expensive underwear. They were definitely provocative. Her cries of uninhibited bliss had hopefully been drowned by the numerous noisy seagull mimics circling the ship for scraps. His manual skills weren't too bad for a non-surgeon either. George figured if he was sexually satisfied,

1

then she should be equally satisfied. No wonder his two previous wives had divorced him. That and his serial infidelities. A bit on the side was only OK for blokes George thought.

He had once suggested a threesome with Jacqui and his ex-wife. Or a foursome with both exes. George had seemed genuinely surprised when all three women vehemently rejected that idea.

However, instead of group sex, both ex-wives had demanded huge divorce settlements but subsequently with no further claim on his estate. There was still plenty in the bank for Jacqui's every expensive need. And she was now her childless husband's sole beneficiary.

Rocky was much more considerate of her visceral needs. He lay back naked in satisfied exhaustion watching appreciatively as she dressed quickly.

'Wake up Rocky, there's a dear, will you put your head out of the door and make sure the corridor is clear,' she asked. Jacqui and Rocky, she fantasised. Sounds like Bonnie and Clyde. Could even be the good title of a Hollywood movie, but there would be hell to pay if George ever found out. No more big private bank account for her. No more fashionable boutiques and swanky restaurants. Just ex number three while George found wife number four. There would be many willing volunteers for that proposition. A missionary position proposition!

A still nude Rocky peeped discretely round the cabin door to ensure the passageway was empty and to protect her carefully preserved if not deserved reputation. Chivalry was still alive, Jacqui thought. But today she did not have to be placed on a Norman-like chivalrous pedestal of chastity and disempowerment. Lots of money and maybe a little adultery if you can get away with it were the current preference for Jacqui.

She gave him a quick kiss and fluttered her eyelids seductively at him before departing. She hastened down the empty corridor and up in the lift to the penthouse suite to shower and change rapidly. She could not join her husband looking a little dishevelled and smelling of Rocky and sex. Oh my God, she thought, first time with someone new is so good. Especially when there was a couple of hours to take it slowly. Especially when their spouses were near-by on board ship, but totally involved with the conference during that time. Guilt was a great aphrodisiac.

Rocky's latest wife had been chairing a parallel session. Apparently some Australian was presenting details of infectious diseases on the islands of St Kilda, in the Scottish Hebrides, their current location. Tetanus and chicken pox, rhinovirus and scurvy, all from his publications in the Edinburgh College of Physicians journal. All exacerbated by the appalling climate. All gloom and doom. Sounded really boring. He kept her occupied, thank God.

It had been lust at first sight for Jacqui and Rocky at the conference in Australia two years ago. Living twenty thousand kilometres apart had not given an opportunity to indulge that hunger previously. They had not even been able to find a discrete moment together during the Paris conference last year, beyond a short kiss in the corridor. Well, shortish, but one with a mutual promise of greater intimacy as soon as possible. Both could see carnal desire in the other's eyes. Separation had only increased their intense craving for each other. They were like two moths circling a candle drawing progressively closer to the flame. Today they burnt with passion. Hopefully this cruise would give other chances.

Jacqui suddenly, surprisingly felt her conscience prick her. An unusual sensation for her. George wanted a child, so she had stopped the pill a month ago. Strangely none of the myriad of ladies he had bedded, some married to him, some married to other men, some single, became pregnant. Secretly he felt an affront to his proven virility. He refused a sperm test. Insulting unnecessary concept!

George fancied a baby conceived in the Hebrides to commemorate his Scottish aristocratic ancestry. She had a condom in her bag but had sort of forgotten to use it. Sort of. Too bad, it would have reduced her erotic pleasure. George won't know. The baby could be even more Scottish than he expected if she fell pregnant to Rocky.

After a hot shower in their luxury cabin, Jacqueline tossed up between the Alexander McQueen, the Carlos Miele or the Caroline Herrera dresses. George had bought them for her at the end of the previous conference in Paris. She settled for the Carlos Miele. George liked her cleavage partially on show to make all his colleagues jealous.

A little touch of Caron Poivre perfume should remove traces of Rocky's aroma. He had liked her cleavage as well.

She headed back down to the Silver Viking's larger theatre just in time to creep in the back and hear the session chairman introducing George. His list of George's outstanding achievements could almost have been written by George. Probably was. Dux of Shore. Captain of cricket and rugby. Top student of the year graduating with first class honours from The University of Sydney School of Medicine. Rhodes Scholarship with a Ph D in medical microbiology at Balliol College, Oxford, and a cricket blue for two years, Fellow of the Australasian College of Surgeons and past president. Professor of Surgery, Companion of the Order of Australia, etc. Blah blah.

Now he was also president of the Global Association of Medical Historians. He never appeared to lose a moment's sleep over the tragedies that befell his two predecessors. Jacqui found her attention wavering and wondering when she could next see Rocky alone. Did he have any more new tricks to try on her?

George was talking this time as president of the association. George was impressed with his new status. George was always impressed by his status and his achievements. He was talking about surgery. He was always talking about surgery, this time his topic was Hippocrates and surgery in ancient Athens. The previous year had been surgery in the Inca Civilisation, the year before that had been surgery during the Wars of the Roses. It was always well researched and fluently, humorously presented. Always a few well-chosen illustrative but gruesome Power Point slides. It always had rapturous applause and Dorothy Dixsers from the captive audience. It all sounded the same each year and increasingly boring each time. Blah, blah, blah.

Yes, afterwards she would stand adoringly by George as he accepted gushing compliments with fake modesty. He usually celebrated with some expensive present for her. Her interest, as false as his modesty, was fortunately unrecognised by anyone and then well rewarded. She could fake it as well as George. She usually did with him.

'One brilliant man talking about another brilliant man,' said one of the attractive young ladies clustered around him. He introduced Jacqui to his friends to show, yes, he had it all. 'Hello darling. Come and meet some of my friends, so they know what a lucky man I am.'

She met James, his associate professor, Annette, his favourite anaesthetist, Susan, his senior registrar, and Carole, his doctoral student, the previous sycophant, Thomas, the association secretary, Emily, his wife and Amelia, the treasurer. Susan only made extremely brief eye contact before looking away. As did Carole. Jacqui had a good idea of the significance of that. She could teach them a thing or two about concealing infidelity. Jacqui had managed adoring eye contact just now with George in spite of intimacy with Rocky but an hour ago What was sauce for the gander was also now sauce for the goose!

It was now midday. The rain had finally stopped. A crew member pointed to a colourful rainbow touching down on the nearby Isle of Boreray, a most unlikely destination to ever find a crock of gold in his judgement. 'Look at yon watergaw, that's the home of the keeries, the beautiful young female spirits that look over us. Ye don't oft see sunlight here. It's usually snow and ice, storm and tempest. Best te get ashore as soon as possible!' he opinioned.

Gloom and doom, Jacqui thought, just like the sound of the Free Church ministers, all gloom and doom. Why they had threatened the poor past congregation of St Kilda with hell fire and purgatory, she could not imagine. Just living here would be purgatory enough for any poor soul!

The evening before when they arrived in St Kilda bay, the hired McCrimmon piper serenaded them over pre-dinner drinks followed by an information session on the island's extraordinary past. McCrimmon then piped in the top table led of course by George, to a fine highland dinner of lobster bisque and venison, raspberry cranachan and whisky.

When Jacqui first heard that the conference was to be at St Kilda, she presumed it to be in the suburb of Melbourne. Her favourite Acland St. Clothes boutiques and shoe shops. Cafes and night clubs. That sounded perfect. Why the hell would you prefer this dreary St Kilda in the back of beyond?

Four bleak little islands, the most western point of UK suffered horrendous weather most of the year round. There was some evidence of Norsemen occupying the island a thousand years ago, and perhaps the ancient Celts a millennium earlier. The island had certainly been home for several centuries to a small impoverished group of islanders living in appallingly basic circumstances. Poor bastards.

Over two-hundred and fifty years previously, prior to the Free Church of Scotland's tyrannical take-over, several islanders were accomplished musicians. The bagpipes, fiddle and flute were the popular instruments. Jacqui thought the bagpipes might be an improvement on no music. Just. Music and laughter, whisky and dancing whiled away their long dark winters.

Even funerals were happy-sad events where a life could be celebrated with precious memories and spontaneous gaiety. There was even a rumour that a priest of three hundred years ago used to give the engaged young women some private spiritual tuition. Extremely intimate personal tuition to educate them into the mysteries of the first night as a married woman. One on one. Literally. That sounded much more fun than the very limited sex education at her Catholic girls' boarding school. Not till you are married girl then only with your husband producing lots of kids for the church till death do you part. Boring!

Her school experiences were actually a marked improvement on the virtuous tuition. At fifteen she had a crush on her biology teacher. A middle-aged married man. An easy victim for her precocious seductive powers, her pretended shyness, her easily available very attractive self-proclaimed virginal body. He was more than happy to give her some private intimate human biology education. Until they were caught conducting a cosy experiment on the laboratory bench after hours. He was sacked and was lucky to receive a suspended jail sentence. She was expelled and completed her education in a state secondary school. A pleasantly co-educational school with many seducible young men to practice her developing manual and oral skills.

The Free Church of Scotland stopped all that sort of fun on St Kilda in the early eighteenth century.

Subsequently their whole existence centred on worshipping the fanatically strict god of the so-called Scottish Free Church. Music, laughter and dancing were forbidden. Children had to carry Bibles at all times. Free? Freedom? It sounded the complete opposite. Jacqui remembered having her unexpurgated copy of *Lady Chatterley's Lover* being confiscated in year seven of her schooldays. Not a bible.

The minister had judged his long dull sermons on the percent of the congregation crying for their wickedness as he finished. Apparently, he disapproved of adultery, and indeed anything pleasurable. Mind you, Jacqui thought, it would be too bloody cold and wet to take any clothes off on St Kilda. Perhaps, however in one of those cleitans with one or two of their woven blankets. You would have to desperate with all Soay sheep watching, but she had been feeling pretty desperate till this morning.

Sex was limited to married couples. To prove a worthy suitor, a man had to stand on the so-called mistress stone with one leg and both arms extended out over the steep drop below. Crazy-brave. Jacqui knew of better and safer ways to prove a man's ability as a lover!

The minister demanded time in church every day, and most of the day on Sunday; the villagers then lacked adequate time to forage for food. As long as the minister could keep then on his chosen path to heaven, he didn't worry if they all starved. And of course, he expected to be presented with a tenth of all the food they harvested. They heard of a Lady Grange imprisoned there for six years for divulging her husband's Jacobite affiliations, who described the place as a "vile neasty stinking poor isle". What a horrendous fate! What an accurate depiction!

Apparently, the Free Church had even closed the cinema in near-by Stornoway some years ago after it showed Jesus Christ Superstar: the dumb bastards had expected a biblical documentary but were confronted by a noisy rock opera oozing sexuality!

Less than a hundred years ago, St Kilda lacked sewerage, electricity and flowing water. Basic developments by now common even in remote areas on the mainland. There were always rainwater streams coming off the high cliffs for fresh water. Gull oil was used for lamps. In a brief moment of attention, Jacqui asked, 'what sort of toilets did they have?' The three local experts looked at each other hoping one could answer. Finally one responded, 'that is a good question, strangely not answered in any books about the island's history. Perhaps they dug latrines outside, perhaps they defaecated down the animal end of the house with the cows in bad weather.'

Great thought Jacqui, YUK, give me St Kilda in Melbourne any day PLEASE!

The island was finally evacuated in 1930 following a young woman's death from appendicitis, a surgical condition by then deemed eminently curable in the big cities. There were only thirty-six unfortunate souls left on St Kilda at that time. Good job the minister left with the evacuation. Jacqui didn't fancy his eyes boring into her soul, her guilt written large on her face. She would feel like a naughty rabbit caught breeding in the glaring headlights of divine judgement. At least there had not been a saint there before as the name was apparently derived from a Norse term, sunt kelda meaning sweet well water.

In recent years St Kilda had been re-occupied as the furthest west point of the UK by the Ministry of Defence for a missile tracking station, and by the Scottish National Trust working parties to preserve the island heritage. Jacqui wondered why the history group wanted to visit such a remote barren rock miles from any civilisation, except those on board their ship which certainly had all imaginable luxuries... and Rocky! It was a third world environment outside without the benefit of a warm climate. Even when occupied the island had no boutiques, no expensive restaurants, no discos and no cinemas or theatres. No shoe shops. Most of the old inhabitants didn't even have shoes!

No discrete little corners for playing up. Everyone knew everybody else's business. Even before they did anything naughty, even when they only thought about it. The minister knew everyone's sins. Jacqui could not imagine why anyone would have lived there. Why the Scots wished to preserve it was another mystery to Jacqui. No wonder it was the unwanted runt of Scotland's Hebridean children. Give me Melbourne's St Kilda any day she thought.

Jacqui had sat through the evening information session dutifully holding George's hand amazed at the audience's rapt attention to all this historical drivel. Her thoughts had kept drifting impatiently to the next morning's planned liaison with Rocky. At least that kept her awake.

It had been bucketing with freezing rain and blowing a gale since they arrived in the bay last night. And this was their summer! Apparently, there were gales every four days with winds of nearly a hundred and fifty miles an hour and fifty-foot waves smashing into the rocks. Surprisingly there looked to be a window of better weather for the afternoon.

After a brief stand-up lunch with canapes, fine wine and French champagne, a big improvement on the locals smelly birds and bird's eggs, the delegates would be ferried ashore to the island of Hirte, the largest of the St. Kilda group in the Scottish Outer Hebrides.

George had personally arranged the Silver Viking as the venue for this year's Association conference. A blue water luxury liner of some six thousand tons. It had accommodation for just over a hundred guests, matched by an equal number of staff to accommodate every guests' every need. A personal butler in the penthouse for George and Jacqui. She could hardly entertain Rocky in her room under his disapproving eye.

He let them all know he had worked as head butler in aristocratic houses in England. A trip to Scotland serving uncouth Australians was clearly not up to his usual standards! Mind you the mansions of the English nobility and aristocracy were known for a little illicit partner swapping! Maybe she could persuade George to find a baronial hall for next year's conference. Perhaps the butler had a trained blind eye. Perhaps he was even a stand-in for some ageing husbands.

The ship had a beauty salon, a French hairdresser, a shop for luxury souvenirs, a library, billiards room, many computers with Wi-Fi, numerous cafes, bars with a variety of best single malt Scottish whiskys, restaurants, an astronomical observatory, a media room and a large heated spa pool

The low draught of under four and a half meters enabled the vessel to anchor well into shallow harbours like the sheltered bay between the islands of Dun and Hirte at St Kilda.

Unbeknown to most delegates, George had subsidised the trip to the extent of a hundred thousand pounds sterling, so all the guests would only have to find half the usual conference and cruising charges. A calculating practical narcissus, he only let a couple of colleagues 'discover' this philanthropy. A couple with known loose lips and minimal discretion. Hopefully his generosity would be whispered widely around the ship.

George knew he would recoup that outlay fairly rapidly with tax deductions for work-related expenses, increased referrals from the grateful and impressed general practitioners among the delegates, and a couple of aortic valve replacement operations at fifty thousand dollars a pop.

McCrimmon piped them ashore, but not before Rocky and George, arm in arm, spun around the deck to the music in an impromptu highland reel. Jacqui watched in amazement. Obviously, they had more than one taste in common! Fortunately George did not know about one of them!

The Association Committee, the most important delegates, went ashore first in the Techno Sea DNA 999 rigid inflatable boat, the liner's fastest and most luxurious tender, though the short distance to the jetty did not permit it to reach its maximum speed of 80 knots. It was too short a journey to be worth cranking up the ship's helicopter. Perhaps if the sea was calm next morning, they could do the run to Boreray and the sea stacks at full speed in the boat. That could be exciting. Alternatively, they could go in the helicopter. The remaining delegates of lesser status followed at a more circumspect rate.

Rocky surveyed the scene discerningly from the jetty with the psychiatrist's sensory appraisal. Funny he thought, the old abodes of Britain were supposed to have the serene tranquillity of an unhurried bygone age. Here the ambience was angry-sad. Angry for imposition of an intolerable way of life under the Free Church. Angry when a progressive mainland society laughed and otherwise ignored them. Sad for the infant deaths and the demise of a family-based strangely contented society.

The small island had a rare dual World Heritage listing both for its culture and history, and for its ornithology. Pre-arranged groups accompanied by knowledgeable local experts offered several choices of interesting afternoon activities.

The enthusiastic ornithologists could walk up the steep slopes to the fourteen hundred feet cliffs at Conachair where the past inhabitants of

St Kilda used to harvest birds and birds' eggs, their staple diet. Some half a million mating pairs of sea birds inhabit the islands. Puffins, fulmars, gannets, various gulls and skuas predominated.

They heard about the uniquely evolved St Kilda wren. Unique to St Kilda. A bird larger than its European cousin, with a bigger beak, heavier barring on the body, and a more grey rather than red general colouring. The island was sufficiently isolated to experience its own evolution. Amazing. They also heard about the unique St Kilda mice. While the house mouse had not long survived the evacuation, the field mouse had evolved to be twice the size of its European counterpart. A response to the absence of predators, and extra layers of fat to deal with the climate. A response the group standing in the cold sea wind at the cliff top could well understand.

They saw thousands and thousands of sea birds nesting in the crags. They could marvel at stories about the climbing skills of the past St Kildan hunters descending death-defying precipices on horse-hair ropes to collect eggs and capture birds. They were amazed to hear about the prehensile toes that appeared to have evolved in the St Kildan rock climbers. They thrilled to the stories of fatal falls and broken ropes. The tragedy of the man who had to cut a fraying rope to save his own life and allowing his rope mate to fall to his death sent shivers down their spines.

The historians sat in the now roofless stone houses of Main Street. An odd name for the only sort of street lined by primitive once-occupied dwellings. Deserted shells now of brooding silence and past tragedy. The morning rain dripped of the dank stones immune to the feeble rays of sunshine. They heard mainly an abbreviated repeat of the morning lectures at the session chaired by Rocky's wife. She thought he had been busy putting the finishing touches to his psychiatry presentation for the next morning. Finishing touches to Jacqui, yes, to the presentation, no!

They heard of the outbreak of chickenpox in 1727 that killed two thirds of the population, leaving only four adults and twenty-six children alive. That left three men and eight boys isolated in a little bothie on the near-by sea stack, Stac an Armin. There were not sufficient strong adults to row a boat the four miles there and back to collect them. They survived eight months through the harsh North Atlantic winter, one of the most extraordinary, though little-known story of endurance in unbelievable adversity in the whole history of mankind.

They survived on birds, birds' eggs and fish. They patched their clothes with birds' skins. They lost weight! The historians shivered, partly due to the cold environment, partly in empathetic disbelief at the horrendous tales of St Kilda.

The delegates heard about the islander's poor diet. Though rich in Vitamin D from seabirds and fish, the thin volcanic topsoil had largely been washed away by the persistent rainfall over sixty million years. It grew few nourishing crops and sources of vitamin C were therefore limited with possible chronic borderline scurvy amongst the inhabitants. They heard that the peat was impregnated with sea water and that burning sodium chloride impregnated peat on St Kilda produced toxic dioxins though there was no evidence of poor health from dioxin poisoning.

They heard how visits to St Kilda from the mainland brought the small population down with contagious respiratory infections. The boat cough they called it. The unfortunate islanders not only suffered from introduced infections because of their low levels of immunity to external infections. Virgin soil as it was known. They also suffered increased sepsis after the evacuation as they again encountered unfamiliar diseases. Several died of tuberculosis in the following years.

They heard how mainlanders cruising out of Glasgow use to stare scornfully at the natives' backward lifestyle in disbelief and astonishment. Natives stinking of rotten fish from their diet. A freak show from two centuries ago to mock mercilessly. Malicious sneering entertainment. Cheaper and stranger than seeing mischievous monkeys performing at the zoo.

By the start of the twentieth century, the younger restless islanders started to migrate, some to the Scottish mainland or at least to the more developed Hebridean islands, some to America. Others joined the army or navy in the First World War and never returned. The Royal Navy was a less hard task master than the Free Church. Reasonable pay and plentiful food. Rum and trips ashore in sunny climes. Exotic available women in colourful far of places. Jacqui fantasised about the pleasure of removing a virile sailor's tropical whites under the palm trees.

Clearly by the 1920s the place was in terminal decline.

The delegates then heard about the awful tragedies of deaths from neonatal tetanus in the late nineteenth century. A preventable disease by now on the mainland with vaccines and sterile birthing measures. A preventable disease with horrific clinical features, especially in the new-born. They heard of the feeding sickness that became apparent around the eighth day after birth, when baby's jaws dropped and breast feeding ceased, Of the heart-rending painful muscle spasms that tore away up to two-thirds of the new-born from their mother's breast and the heart from the community. Whispers of their names could still be heard on the wind and in the cries of distant gulls. The pain of dying infants in the ruined stone home was still palpable in the hearts of the audience.

They heard of the unlikely original hypothesis that anointing the umbilical cord with fulmar oil was the source of infection. Research had found no evidence of tetanus spores in the oil in the fulmar's stomach. On the other hand, tetanus spores were found in abundance in the island soil. They heard of the unclean scalpels used to cut the umbilical cords which probably caused the infection.

George stood up, irritated and bored, 'how stupid, unclean scalpels and tetanus in the late nineteenth century. A thousand years ago in intelligent societies, knives were passed through a flame to sterilize them before cutting the umbilical cord. I am going to see if the birds up on Conachair are more intelligent than these backward people who once lived here.' He walked out never to be seen alive again.

The less active members purchased a few souvenirs in the island shop. Books about St Kilda's history, T-shirts, mugs, cushion covers and next year's calendar with majestic pictures of St Kilda. Then they gathered in the Puff Inn for silver leaf Sri Lankan tea, or to contrast Scotch from the new Abhainn Dearg distillery in Uig on the nearby Island of Lewis, with the classic Talisker Distiller's edition from Skye. The Uig distillery had only opened in 2010, while Talisker had a history of nearly two hundred years.

They did not need to ask if the Puff Inn was there in the Free Church dominated period. It wasn't! They heard that a German submarine had surfaced in the bay in the First World War and shelled these buildings, hence the gun emplacement on the front.

Mid-afternoon, a dense fog came down suddenly, silently on the island. Thick, thick fog rolling in from the sea and descending rapidly from the cliff tops down to sea level. The ornithologists headed briskly back down-hill led by the guides. One of them, Caitlin Gillies, was a granddaughter of an original islander and knew from experience how rapidly the weather could change on St Kilda. The Puff Inn group and the history group were also sent back to the jetty.

Lights were put on inside and outside the Scottish National Trust Headquarters, the Ministry of Defence building, along the island jetty and aboard the Silver Viking. Powerful shipboard search lights scarcely pierced the increasing gloom. Visibility fell to twenty metres. The temperature fell fifteen degrees in half an hour to near freezing point.

The conference delegates assembled noisily, anxiously along the jetty to be wrapped in blankets and ferried safely back to the warm, well-lit security of the liner for the evening. Tea then whisky, dinner and a movie was the plan. The ship's purser ticked them off one-by-one as they climbed down into the ship's ribs. One was missing. It was George!

The ship's emergency plan for a missing passenger swung efficiently into immediate action. This was a well-rehearsed drill never previously used in real life. It was originally predominantly designed to deal with the awful possibility that someone had been lost overboard at sea.

All the passengers were immediately assembled in the main theatre, where George had given his lecture only a few hours ago. Names were checked meticulously again. George was still missing. Jacqueline sat sobbing comforted by Annette, the ship's nurse and a few friends. Rocky had given her a sympathetic nod but discreetly kept his distance. The stewards checked the ship thoroughly from stem to stern, no George onboard.

The engineer's mate, a veteran of fifty-years-experience in the Outer Hebrides recalled the incident over a hundred years earlier when three lighthouse keepers on the Flannan Islands twenty miles to the north just disappeared never to be found again. Strange things happened out here he said. Weird shapes were sometimes seen out to sea in bad weather. Maybe it was the Skerry Giant out wandering he mused. The few who overheard his unwanted bizarre story were even more disturbed.

The ship's captain, Angus Campbell, and his first mate, Mark Dougal, went ashore in heavy weather gear. They sought a more pragmatic answer. Firstly, they went to the National Trust house. It was the original house number three in main street, now weatherproof following extensive restoration. Three young people, one male and two females, were huddled round the open peat and log-fire clutching mugs of hot sweet tea, fortified with more than a little whisky. They were doing their two-week working stint on St Kilda for the Scottish National Trust to maintain and restore the island and its buildings to the condition they were in before the evacuation.

They welcomed the two visitors and offered tea.

'No thanks, I'm Angus and this is Mark. We are from the ship. We have lost a passenger out there. I don't suppose you have seen an individual out there anywhere looking lost?'

The three shook their heads, one of the girls, Mary replied 'No, we were working on one of the near-by cleitans when we saw the fog coming in. Just behind us was a group coming down from the cliffs. We have been in here round the fire ever since.'

She paused looking at Angus, 'are you going to organise a search party in this dreadful weather, you'll end up with more than one lost or dead. Wait till the morning and hope the poor bastard is still alive, assuming he is alive now. Perhaps he will find one of the huts.'

Angus, increasingly worried, replied, 'we will talk to the MOD, perhaps we can organise a search and rescue team with survival specialists. Thanks, and see you in the morning.'

Next Mark and Angus went to the MOD newly renovated building. Half-a-dozen tattooed muscular young men were playing an aggressively animated game of snooker, gambling fiercely and well lubricated by Thorfinn Skull-splitter ale. It was an 8.5% strength beer named after the Seventh Earl of Orkney. His sobriquet had been appropriately earned according to well informed historians.

Silence fell as Angus explained the distressing situation. These men, men of the elite three commando brigade, had recently excelled in an alpine army corps team training course in Snowdonia and had all survived front-line service in Iraq and Afghanistan. They sobered up rapidly.

Sergeant 'Softie' McKimmon only had to look at them and nod. 'Softie' because he held the regimental record for press-ups. 'Softie' because he drove his team to break the previous record for crossing Snowdonia national park in mid-winter with eighty-kilogram backpacks. 'Softie' because he mothered them like little children in Afghanistan, returning with not one casualty in his platoon.

A brief call to HQ in Fort George near Inverness outlining search plans and requesting a surveillance helicopter at first light followed. Within minutes they had changed into survival gear, picked up prepacked backpacks with attached powerful torches, emergency rations, laser beams, CB radio and personal trackers, and headed out.

'OK boys, we will check the cleitans first, then head up to Conachair. Angus, as you probably know, that's the highest cliff here, fourteen hundred feet straight down, not so good for the health! We will rope together before we head up. Angus, can you stay here and monitor the radio. We will call in every thirty minutes. You can call the ship on your CB and keep them in the picture.'

Just before dawn as the fog started to lift the squaddies returned, tired, cold, hungry, disappointed, Softie announced, 'no luck, only Soay sheep in the cleitans, and a mass of messy footprints near the top of Conachair.'

At first light Angus returned to his ship and set out in the Techno Sea DNA 999 with a few ex-RN sailors to circle the island. The ship's helicopter took off to search the island. They had just left Village Bay when an RAF helicopter flew over and also set off to search around the coast of the island. None found a trace of a body. Phil, one of the ex-Royal Navy Chief Petty Officers, said to Angus, 'high tide was about 3.00AM this morning, a body at the base of the cliffs may have been washed off, we should come back this afternoon at low tide to check again.'

The RAF helicopter landed to disgorge a policeman and a detective sergeant McNeill to investigate the disappearance. Only a terrible accidental tragedy was assumed at this stage.

Back aboard the Silver Viking, Angus found the entertainments officer had offered the morose passengers a trip to Boreray and the sea stacks, or another landing on Hirte, or a walk across the island to see the Amazon's well and house, apparently the home of a female warrior hundreds of years previously. None was interested. Morning conference lectures were cancelled. None wanted to see the latest movies in the theatre.

They gathered alone or in twos or sometimes threes in the library, or the internet café, or the panorama lounge. Some tried the connoisseur's corner hesitantly or the beauty salon. Conversations were minimal and stilted.

Jacqui remained in her cabin alone all morning, picked at a sea food cocktail at the poolside grill for lunch, then asked the captain if she could accompany the rib on the afternoon search. Sitting beside Phil, both were scouring the cliff bases with binoculars, when just under Conachair, they saw a body. Angus nosed the boat carefully through the cauldron of seas pounding the rocky coast into a little half-protected crevasse near the grim finding and hopped out accompanied by the policeman.

Despite severe damage from the fall and being in the water for over twelve hours, it was clearly George. The back of his skull was stove in and the odd angles of his arms and legs suggested multiple fractures. The policeman took pictures, discussed the situation with the detective by CB radio and helped Angus put the remains of George in a black body bag. They clambered over the rocks and managed to load the body on board. Jacqui buried her head on Phil's broad shoulder and remained there tearfully for the return trip.

Was this divine justice and retribution for her previous morning's illicit antics? Did the Free Church moral influence still persist here invisibly somehow?

Once back in Village Bay, George's remains were choppered to Stornoway airport, then flown to Aberdeen Forensic Unit for post-mortem examination the following day.

It was all relatively routine, the post-mortem scan of George's body revealing severe trauma as would be expected, a massive occipital head injury, multiple fractured ribs with bilateral pneumo-thoraces, a ruptured liver and spleen with severe internal bleeding, a fractured lumbar spine with a severed spinal cord, and multiple fractures of his pelvis, arm and legs. There were enough injuries to kill a man many times over.

The Silver Viking meantime had returned at full speed to Glasgow and unloaded a sombre collection of passengers. A piped lament had wafted sadly from the stern as St Kilda faded away into the Hebridean mist recalling the evacuation nearly a century earlier. Jacqui thought there would not be another occasion to go to bed with Rocky sadly, but that every cloud had a silver lining, and there were many clouds here in the Hebrides. They had at least been spared two previously planned island visits on the way back.

One was to Iona to see an Abbey, original home of St Columba, and the ruins of a nunnery. Why a woman would want to become a nun with a black robe and white headpiece to conceal one's beautiful hair and to swear eternal chastity and poverty was inexplicable. The other to Craignure on the island of Mull to see the ruins of Duart Castle where there were no boutiques or worthwhile cafes was equally unfathomable.

The conference was abandoned. Jacqui stayed in Glasgow for a week supported by members of the Association Committee, then flew to Aberdeen to await the inquest in the Mercure Hotel.

CHAPTER TWO

THE INQUEST

The coroner's inquest two weeks later was formal and brief. Jacqueline tearfully told of George's irritated departure from the history group to join the ornithologists. The purser described the fogbound dockside check detecting George's absence. Angus, 'Softie' McKimmon and Phillip detailed the overnight land search including the mass of unidentifiable footprints at the clifftop, the helicopter searches and the two cruises round the island with the discovery of George's body. Detective sergeant McNeill outlined the hazardous terrain and his external viewing of the body. The pathologist listed his findings and the Coroner declared death by misadventure and offered his condolences to Jacqui before closing the enquiry.

Hamish McGrath, crime and forensic reporter for the Aberdeen Times was walking out of the building hoping to find something more interesting for the afternoon than an unfortunate accident. Perhaps a gruesome murder. Aberdeen had the second highest crime rate in Scotland after Glasgow. The local hoods were hoping to claim top spot next year. Beating Glasgow Celtic on the football field was too hard, but there was hope for the local crims. It was a matter of self-esteem for them to outstrip the big city on the Clyde. Aberdeen at least could claim a third of prostitution associated crime in the whole country, a topic of considerable local pride. Surely, they could provide a more exciting copy than some toff falling off a cliff?

He overheard Thomas and Susan talking just in front of him. Dark suits and dark demeanours. 'That's terrible,' she said, 'what a tragic loss of a great man at the peak of his career. We will have to find a new president now, though I for one would not want it after three of them have died in just over three years!'

Now that is strange, thought Hamish, his journalist's instincts alerted. He did not believe in coincidence where violence and death were concerned. Hamish remembered the statement by Auric Goldfinger in the James Bond book, *"Once is happenstance. Twice is coincidence. The third time it's enemy action."* So, was there an enemy, and if so who? And indeed why? Thomas and Susan lapsed into a solemn silence. He could scarcely question them at such a time. Perhaps this did merit some more research.

That evening, once his two bairns had been collected from school, done their homework, bathed, fed and read stories before falling instantly asleep, and his wife Cairistiona, settled in front of some amorphous brain-dead American TV sitcom, he opened up both Google and his bottle of Glenmorangie.

The Global Association of Medical Historians website opened with the inevitable mission statement, to promote research into medicine of past times, to better predict the trajectory of future changes. Hamish considered his own job had a missionary statement, that he should lie flat on his back and be screwed by the editor and his administration.

The website had a long obituary for George, a few PowerPoint presentations from the conference from the first morning and details of future meetings.

There was a request for nominations for the now sadly vacant position of president to be lodged with the secretary within the next three weeks. Any details of the society and its presidents in the past were absent, surprisingly erased. Hamish went back to general google entries for the society, there were pages about George, cut down in his prime. Both his career achievements and his personal affluent lifestyle were noted. He was an 'A lister' in Australia. Opening nights at the

Opera House. Always black tie. Member of the exclusive Cabbage Tree Club. Private suites at the Sydney Cricket Ground and the Randwick Racecourse. The best restaurants. The best wines. The latest fashion suits. A glamorous wife. A 'power couple'. Vomit, thought Hamish

Jacqueline was George's third wife. Three in six years! Few details about his two divorces were documented. Tabloid press had a one page spread after his second divorce. About so-called medical conferences on yachts in Sydney harbour with topless waitresses. There were rumours about threesomes with escort agency girls.

His first wife had become suspicious about frequent 'night surgeries'. Apparently, a hired private detective had some revealing pictures caught on CCTV in George's favourite hotel penthouse suite. Pictures ensuring a mutually satisfactory separation without proceeding to an open court. Pictures some of the ladies concerned did not want their husbands to see either according to rumours.

Certainly, he must have made some enemies somewhere along the way. Was it enough for someone to push him off Conachair?

He tried Global Association of Medical Historians – president – 2000-2017.

The first entry was about the murder of a Mustafa Mohammed. He had been the previous president of the society. Last year he had been shot dead while sitting in a swanky Parisian café congenially surrounded by fellow medical historians. The city of love? The previous conference was drawing to a close and he was working on his concluding speech.

A man dressed in black with his head covered by a balaclava with only a narrow eye slit mounted on a motor bicycle, was thought to have shouted Allahu Akbar, fired twice at point blank range killing Mustafa immediately, and roaring off. Post-mortem revealed one bullet through the forehead, one through the heart. A professional hit. The bullets were from a Glock 22 pistol: there were tens of thousands of these worldwide, they were widely used by law enforcement organisations and in criminal circles.

Subsequent CCTV analysis revealed the bicycle to be a French Wakan 1640 with number plates removed. A similar vehicle was found a day later at the Gare de Lyon. It had been stolen two days previously.

There were no fingerprints. No DNA. No gun. Thousands of train tickets had been purchased heading south that day at the station. Painstaking police search had identified just over half of these, none appeared suspicious. Some had left Marseille by ship or plane, some crossed into Monaco or Italy. After months of investigation, police were left with a dozen totally untraceable suspects.

Mustafa had just delivered a paper on the great tenth century Persian physician Avicenna. Avicenna was one of the great brains of all time. A polymath who wrote on astronomy, geography, psychology, mathematics, physics and many other topics. He wrote and thought a lot about theology, he was said to have memorised the entire Koran by the age of ten. However, his religious opinions had offended Sunni scholars who declared him apostate. Hatred of his views had apparently persisted to the present day in some circles of Islam. Mustafa's assassination was ascribed to sectarian violence by a coronial enquiry in Paris.

Mustafa's online bio showed him to be a quite modest man in spite of a most successful career to that point. He had fled a middle eastern country when religious zealots started to tell him how to practice medicine despite their abysmal ignorance. Decision making by non-expert. Sounded just like the NHS to Hamish.

He had moved gratefully to Australia with his much-loved family. His brilliant research and original publications about placental insufficiency, and his natural charm and instinctive ability as a teacher were widely acclaimed. Within two years he was provided with a personal chair of obstetrics at the University of Queensland.

As a journalist Hamish had found ways to access restricted police computer data. Ways and means he kept highly secret. He had agreed in the past not to expose half a dozen corrupt Scottish policemen in return for unlimited access to their confidential data base. He did this via an anonymous middleman probably in Russia, so he could not be traced.

He reviewed the CCTV footage from Paris and saw the events as described, he replayed it several times. His eye was caught by the man's arm touching a small box on the front of his seat before picking up the gun and firing. What was that about? There was no soundtrack. Perhaps it was a recording device of someone else shouting Allahu Akbar, so his voice could not be identified.

Well, thought Douglas, it seemed hard to connect that assassination with a man accidentally falling off Conachair a year later.

He returned to Global Association of Medical Historians – president – 2000-2017.

After several screens about Mustafa and a few interlopers about George, he came across entries about a Dr Gaspard Barbeau. The third death. Enemy action! He had been president before Mustafa. He disappeared two years ago while scuba diving off the Barrier Reef in North Queensland. His body was never found. Not to this day. He went out in a boat from Hayman Island luxury resort with a group of conference delegates to Hardy's Reef. They all swam around the reef for an hour admiring some of the best coral and colourful fish in the reef. They were all in a small area, all experienced scuba divers, but when they reassembled back at the boat, Gaspard was missing. Like George was missing. But never to be found.

His oxygen could not have run out in an hour. The tanks were all full. No sharks had been seen in the area. Gaspard was a maritime survival expert as a sideline to his cardiology specialty. That morning he had also given a paper about the pearl divers in Broome in Western Australia. He gave details of the treatment back in 1915 of a Japanese diver suffering from decompression sickness in a Heinke compression chamber. It was the first one used in Australia. Within four hours the paralysed diver was able to walk out. Brilliant treatment. Brilliant presentation apparently.

Gaspard should have been the last person to run into trouble in the ocean.

An immediate mayday call to Hayman Island brought out the helicopter to conduct an aerial search. Nearby boats were alerted. Gaspard could not be found. The coronial enquiry said probable death by misadventure with an open finding.

Gaspard's obituary described him as a happy family man leaving a grieving wife and three teenage children. His outstanding research into stem cell cures for cardiac conduction defects, many thought, should have gained him a Nobel Prize. He would not get one now.

The tabloid press said that his marriage was in trouble and that he had recently been treated for depression. There were oblique references to romantic trysts in a petite auberge near Nice. Tabloids always said things like that.

So, there it was, two inexplicable deaths, one man lost at sea, one apparent terrorist assassination and innuendos concerning sexual peccadillos. Innuendos in eminent medical men of high achievement in their areas of specialisation. Acknowledged world experts.

Hamish thought he would investigate further. It could be the scoop of a journalist's lifetime. Sex, murders, celebrity lifestyles and eminent doctors. Wow!

He would also need to be incredibly discreet. If there was a ruthless but as yet undetected murderer in the association, he would be covering his tracks carefully. He would absolutely have no compunction with a fourth murder if threatened. Someone who could eliminate three of the world's most eminent medical specialists without even raising suspicion would not lose sleep about wee Hamish McGrath! A hick journalist working for a third-rate paper in a little backward country! Totally expendable!

Enough for tonight. Hamish would need one of his contacts in the morning. He finished his dram of Scotch and went to bed where Cairistiona was fast asleep. Sleepiness did not come as easily as the bizarre plots and sexual misdemeanours filling his head.

CHAPTER THREE

GRAMMAR SCHOOL 'GASTRO

In the morning, first the bairns were fed, dressed and packed off to primary school and preschool. Hamish still called them bairns, though William was now seven and wee Jock was four. William had been wee Wully till Jock was born. Then Cairistiona set off to the local hospital where she toiled as a social worker. Another day of truanting school kids, abused single mothers, violent teenagers high on ice and unloved demented incontinent old folks for whom there were no nursing home places. At least it helped to pay their mortgage till the NHS decided to close the local hospital.

Rumours suggested this was coming in November just before the winter chills and flu's set in. Typical decision making by bureaucrats. Administrators for whom bean counting was the only important factor. People didn't matter as much as money. Quality community service near home, visiting specialists with various essential expertise's, research publications and a long tradition of excellence mattered not a jot to NHS accountants. Everyone would then have to drive twenty miles to the Aberdeen Royal Infirmary. A great hospital but already packed to the eyeballs.

Hamish opened his email account. His contacts were not always on the side of law and order: well theoretically they claimed to be on the side of law and order. He emailed his mate, 'e-litefingers' Mac via his anonymous intermediary. Mac was so named because he believed most of the self-styled society elite, the money people, were actually quite ignorant when it came to information technology, as well as many other things, hence e-lite. Litefingers as he stole online data usually undetected. He was the best computer hacker north of the highland line.

Hamish too thought the self-styled elites were rarely much good at anything. Elite celebrities seemed to be people with bank balances and self-esteem much larger than their IQ.

Some years previously Hamish's painstaking investigative journalism had unearthed evidence that Mac was not guilty of a murder charge. A murder for which he had been stitched up by the local cops. They objected to his ability to hack into their private emails detailing widespread corruption in the Aberdeen police force. The true perpetrator of the homicide was uncovered by Hamish and convicted. A few naughty cops were given a gentle tap on the wrist. Mac remained free and always happy afterwards to help a good mate.

Hamish explained that he needed information from the Global Association of Medical Historians website, particularly the list of delegates for the last three years annual convention and a list of scuba divers at Hardy's reef.

Less than an hour later Hamish's phone beeped. There was an email from Mac in the in-tray. He opened it to find three lists. The delegates to the last three years conferences. Only a hundred in Scotland with limited spaces on the Silver Viking, two hundred and twenty-five in Paris, and a hundred and twenty-one in Queensland. Cross checking against the Scottish list he found seventy-nine had been on all three.

This was going to be painstaking work. He would need assistance to save time. Hamish drove to work where Archibald Brown, the editor greeted him. 'Ah Hamish, the great investigative journalist, always working on the next great scoop. Watergate in Aberdeen! Always late to work. Hamish there has been an outbreak of gastro-enteritis in the Aberdeen Grammar School. Can you get down there now and knock up a couple of paragraphs for tomorrow's edition? You might even get on page three if it's any good.'

Shit thought Hamish. Literally. 'OK boss, I will go now. If it's OK, I'll take Fiona McIntosh with me. Its best to have a female to interview girls about extremely private problems.'

The new apprentice looked as enthusiastic as Hamish. She threw down her pencil, turned off her computer, grabbed her fleece-lined leather jacket and followed him down to the car park scowling.

Once in the car, Hamish explained the much more interesting possible murder investigation he was addressing. They parked in the front of the august, austere ancient school, alma mater of Byron the poet, and John McLeod, Nobel prize winner in medicine. A brief discussion with the deputy head, school nurse and public health medico who was there at the time enabled them to prepare a report.

The problem seemed to have little to do with the school tuck-shop, but much more to do with the local Chinese take-away called Goh Sun! Really? It was frequented by the school's black sheep over the lunch break and after school. Cockroaches and rats infested the pantry. Empty cans of dog food filled the rubbish bin. Handwashing was infrequent in the kitchen as it was in restaurants in their homeland. Money trumps hygiene. No wonder most of the world's epidemics started there.

The absentee group of the school's rough kids from the toughest suburbs found it a useful discrete rendezvous for buying and selling drugs. Dope and Ice. The Chinese owner and chef would deny all knowledge. Ten percent for ignorance and silence. Hamish often thought the kids would be learning astute business principles in their school days. Perhaps more useful than Latin or physics.

They repaired to Hamish's house where he gave Fiona hard copies and emailed lists of the three-time delegates. They agreed she would check-up on the females, and he would investigate the males. They agreed there was something fishy in the business. Something overlooked by the coroner as the two previous independent enquiries had taken place in Paris and Townsville, North Queensland. No one seemed to connect the three deaths. There was no mention of the Barrier Reef death in the Parisian coronial enquiry. There was no mention of the deaths in Australia and France in the Scottish coroner's inquest.

He dropped his report about the school gastro' into Archibald, who seemed impressed at the efficiency, and left Fiona back at her desk. A Fiona with a new zest about her manner. They set about searching for details of the seventy-nine delegates. Forty-two were male, thirty-seven were female. Twenty-five of the males were general practitioners. They lived in twelve different countries, mainly Europe or the Anglosphere. Their practice opening times were the main information Hamish could find. They seemed largely united by an interest in history, and probably Doug guessed, Harris tweed jackets.

None had held association committee positions. None had police records beyond traffic offences for infrequent speeding or parking illegally. They had a few unremarkable publications in the medical press or history journals between them. Three were divorced having been caught traditionally in flagrante delicto with the practice nurse or secretary or both together! Quite a low percentage for the medical profession, Hamish thought. Perhaps the interest in history made them more aware of problems with infidelity.

That left seventeen. One was obviously George. Unless his death was an unlikely suicide, that left sixteen. It did not seem likely that George was depressed or had low esteem! Thomas Seaman, the man he heard talking outside the coroner's court, was a close associate of George's. He was the previous secretary, now acting president and the man most likely to get the full-time position. Did that ambition alone give him the motive to murder three people?

He had a high profile in medicine. Thomas was an acknowledged international expert in microbiology. He was involved in the preparation of the first effective vaccine against malaria for which he had won international academic awards. Another potential Nobel prize winner. He had co-authored papers with George. They seemed close associates. Close friends? Thomas had previously presented a paper on the possibility of Robert the Bruce having leprosy. Could that have antagonised one who claimed royal descent from the Bruce?

Thomas was overtly happily married with children, but also rumoured to be gay with the same sex partner for twenty-five years.

Longer than his marriage to Emily. Bizarre! Thomas seemed an unlikely suspect, a maybe for the moment. That left fifteen.

Next name he encountered was Richard Rockingham, a psychiatrist from Aberdeen. He was known as Rocky to his friends. Some said it was because his first marriage had been rocky. Hamish remembered reporting on his salacious divorce five years ago, apparently for serial adultery. It was the talk of the town for weeks. He had only recently remarried. Otherwise he seemed to have a low profile as a hospital-based psychiatrist. He appeared every now and then as an expert witness in the Aberdeen law courts or local TV news. Drug and mental health problems were common problems in Aberdeen. His memberships included the Physicians against Nuclear War Association. Sounded mainly a peaceful fellow. An unlikely suspect, except men having affairs often had enemies. That left fourteen.

Now here was an interesting one. Akshay Patel, an obstetrician from the north of England. He was once sued for negligence. Mustafa Mohammed appeared against him as an expert witness for the prosecution. Akshay was duly found guilty of negligence. Damages of five million pounds were paid to the complainant. That might be a cause for Dr Patel to hate Mustafa, but what about the other two deaths. Here was a possible. That left thirteen.

Nine of the remainder were other health care professionals. Nurses, social workers, wardsmen and physiotherapists. None appeared in google or Wikipedia. None had police records. None was on the association committee. One was a physician from somewhere called Kalgoorlie, a mining town in Western Australia. Home of many miners, was that why Australians called each other diggers? That did not seem a place for an ambitious person. That left four.

James Harvey was associate professor on George's surgical unit. A man with an honours degree from Oxford during a Rhodes Scholarship, a higher doctorate from Queensland, a string of publications in peer-reviewed journals, and some novel surgical techniques. A quite modest man apparently happily married for nearly thirty years with three children. The man expected to succeed to George's professorial chair. That would be a motive. On the list of possibles.

Two others were career university-based historians with an interest in past medical issues. One had been caught smoking dope in an Oxford University college party. What was wrong with the other guy? Aberdeen police would have demanded a drag and the rest of the dope, then ignored the problem. Otherwise neither academic had police records. Not even a scandalous divorce. Both were on the committee. Either might become president of the association. They would be the first non-medico to achieve that. The doctors seemed to have the voting sewn up.

The last one was an Australian physician. No police record. Not on the committee. Married forty-eight years with three children and many grandchildren. Many academic publications on medicine and history. Main interest, contract bridge! Sounded a totally boring person.

So, his list of 'persons of interest', were firstly the three victims. George Hamilton-Bruce, Mustafa Mohammed and Gaspard Barbeau. George with his claim of distant linkage to the royal Bruce line. He would claim that. Something about the three of them made them a target. Secondly Thomas Seaman, Richard Rockingham, Akshay Patel and James Harvey. Well that was an interesting list to be going on with. He emailed his summary to Fiona and would see what she had discovered tomorrow.

CHAPTER FOUR

FATAL HEROIN

On their arrival at the newspaper offices, Archibald sent Hamish and Fiona to report on a sudden death from drugs in town. An eighteen-year-old male found deceased behind a disused warehouse near the docks with multiple puncture marks in his arms. The scene was taped off pending the police investigation to exclude foul play. It was always hard to distinguish the idiots who overdosed unintentionally from the idiots who hadn't paid for their fix and were given a helping hand by their unforgiving dealer. Or the idiots injecting contaminated infected drugs.

His weeping parents and presumably younger sister in school uniform were standing nearby. She would know much more than the parents. More than she would divulge without a little forceful digging. Little miss innocent. One of Hamish's police contacts at the scene confirmed that the young man had a police record for breaking and entering to fund his drug habit. Hamish suggested talking to the sister, but his contact merely winked and said, 'we are on to that, Hamish.' The forensic pathologist was collecting blood samples pending the body's transfer to his autopsy room.

The two dashed off a brief report with some statistics on the number of heroin addicts and unfortunate deaths in young people in Aberdeen. Then they repaired to a café for a couple of mugs of flat white and a comparison of notes. Hamish was impressed that Fiona didn't have some skinny milk or turmeric latte like so many young trendy ladies these days.

She opened her tablet pulled up a file and emailed him a copy.

'First, I looked at Jacqueline Hamilton-Bruce. They had been married just over three years, the time frame of the crimes. She is his third wife after messy divorces. She is a stunner, look at these pictures. Beautiful long blond hair and surgically augmented lips. Perhaps a boob job. A director of every man's universe. Wow!'

Hamish nodded appreciation.

'When she was fifteen, she had a relationship with her school biology teacher. Initiated by her rather than him apparently. Well that's what he said in court. When she was eighteen, she was Miss New South Wales. She dropped out of an arts degree in Sydney and took up modelling. There are suggestions she worked for an escort agency for a lot more than journalist's wages. Apparently, George saw her first modelling at some A-list fashion event and was totally smitten. He spoils her rotten, buys hugely expensive clothes and jewellery and she is always draped over him. Or was! Lucky bastard, or too good to be true.'

'Secondly Justine Barbeau. Only of interest as the widow of the lost Gaspard. She still attends the conferences as she has many friends there. And just in case Gaspard turns up. No police record. Not on the committee. Spends most of her time looking after her grandchildren.'

'Third, Emily Seaman, wife of Thomas. She is a dermatologist with a quiet but busy practice. She is always at Thomas's elbow in social functions singing his praises. She is as pushy as he is modest. Apparently believes that she can eliminate the gay interest in his life. Rumour is that she encouraged him to stand for the committee and in the past, apply for a position as associate professor.'

'Fourth, Jasmine, Mustafa Mohammed's widow has not been heard of for a year.'

'Next is a Clarissa Windsor. She is a forty-five-year old matron of one of the big teaching hospitals in Sydney; an academic high-flyer with a doctorate and numerous publications about the brilliance of the nursing profession throughout history. She has stood for the committee for the last four years but been unsuccessful each time. She believes, probably correctly, that she should at least be on the committee, and preferably the president.'

'Clarissa has been on bad terms with the last three presidents. Many bitter arguments have been heard in the conference corridors. She hates most doctors, hates men and has been in a stable relationship with a female medical doctor for some twelve years. She wears the trousers metaphorically and literally. A potential suspect.'

'Amelia Moore, the current treasurer, is a fairly newly-appointed nephrologist working in Townsville. That's kidney disease Hamish.'

Hamish scowled at being thought ignorant.

'A brilliant driven young lady. She was dux of her school year, graduated with honours and was top candidate for her college specialist exams. She did not attend the conference in Townsville two years ago, though she has been a member of the association for a decade. She has a low profile in her private and professional life. She appears to have no ambition beyond her current roles. She is unmarried and appears to have no current partner. She lives with her aging mother; an unfortunate lady with early dementia.'

'There is a GP in Alice Springs, Clare Jones who was on all three conferences and in the scuba diving group. Otherwise there is nothing untoward on her record. A society member for six years, but not on the committee.'

'Annette Smith, George's recent favourite anaesthetist, only joined the society last year. Susan Hennings, his senior registrar, and Carole Parsons, his doctoral student, are not yet members of the society. They appear to be personal 'guests' of George. Just there for the interest in medical history!'

'So, of that lot I always suspect the wife, Jacqui, Clarissa and Emily. The other thirty were unremarkable.'

'Thanks, Fiona, that must have taken a long time' said Hamish, 'next I would like a list of those on the scuba diving trip, and a picture of Mustafa and delegates in the café where he was shot. However, a delegate sitting there may have arranged the hit. Presumably you would prefer not to be too close! Looks like we will need a trip to Australia as most of the witnesses appear to be resident there. Maybe we could visit Rocky. He is the only one living here.'

They adjourned to the excellent pub next door, strangely, appropriately, known as 'The 21 Crimes' for the twenty-one crimes that once resulted in deportation to Australia. The place was clearly still the location for the criminal classes. Several small groups sat furtively around tables speaking softly and keeping a careful eye on newcomers.

Hamish ordered a bridie and a pint of heavy while Fiona ordered a second coffee and a toastie. 'We better get back to Archie or he will wonder what we are doing,' said Fiona between bites.

'OK, excellent work Fiona, we will resume this tomorrow,' replied Hamish.

CHAPTER FIVE

Like the previous day, Hamish collected the bairns from school and encouraged their homework activities with bribes of food and their favourite TV show. Cairistiona arrived soon and after dinner, baths, bedtime stories, and some chewing over the day's events, Hamish pulled out his tablet and the Glenmorangie. A tot or two helped concentration. The bottle, however, was nearly empty. The angel having his share again thought Hamish.

Hamish's second requirement was easily solved. A Parisian newspaper had a picture of the conference group just before the drive-by shooting. The caption included everyone's names. There was Mustafa beside his wife appearing relaxed and happy. On one side posed George and Jacqui, a power couple. On the other side were Thomas and Emily Seaman, a would-be power couple. On the fringes of the group were a scowling Clarissa, a smiling Annette, a vacant looking female, Clare Jones according to the caption, and a wistful Justine.

The first requirement appeared more difficult. A call to e-litefingers Mac, requesting a trawl through the Hayman Island trip bookings was unsuccessful. They erased such information after six months.

Hamish texted Fiona for suggestions. By return she suggested the coroner's report. Idiot, thought Hamish, how come his apprentice thinks of the obvious when he doesn't. He is supposed to be her mentor.

Yes, the coroner's report listed those on the boat. It was the usual list of the inner circle of the association members, Mustafa and Jasmine

Mohammed, George and Jacqui Hamilton-Bruce, Thomas and Emily Seaman. Justine and Gaspard Barbeau, Clarissa Windsor, James Harvey and eleven others.

Cross-checking his lists, eight of the passengers had been on all three conferences. The Seamans and the Hamilton-Bruces. Clarissa and James. Bruce Dundee, the consultant physician from outback Western Australia, and Clare Jones, the general practitioner from Alice Springs. She had been in the Paris café photo when Mustafa was shot.

Neither of the last two had any blemishes or indeed much on their profile. Surely the likely suspect would be in this select group. Those who had been scuba diving and attended all three conferences. Except the victims of course.

According to the Townsville coroner's report, they were all experienced scuba divers, and all went swimming except Clarissa who stayed on board helping everyone with their oxygen equipment; a fact that aroused some suspicion. She was apparently quite horrified when asked if she had tampered with Gaspard's equipment.

Next morning Fiona and Hamish completed their drudgery for Archibald and repaired for coffee across the road. Further progress online seemed improbable. The next step would be surveillance and interviews. And to see who ended up as the next president. The only relevant witness in Scotland was Rockingham. Justine was in Paris, Jasmine probably in Dubai, and the rest in Australia.

Fiona phoned the Aberdeen hospital, left a message for Dr Rockingham, who was busy in a public psychiatric clinic, requesting an interview to prepare an obituary for George. They returned to their offices. A few heads turned wondering why they spent so much time together. A few others didn't look as they thought they knew the answer.

Shortly Fiona received a text from Dr Rockingham suggesting they met at his house tomorrow at nine am for half an hour before he had to go to his private rooms. The big money-spinner for psychiatrists. Wealthy widows with self-diagnosed depression. Lonely widows with big cheque books and an eye for a toy boy with a record of affairs on the side.

He would be happy to talk to them about his friendship with George.

CHAPTER SIX

THE PSYCHIATRIST

D r Rockingham lived in Rubislaw Den North in the west end of Aberdeen. Fiona and Hamish arrived half an hour early in his ageing Ford Escort. He like to 'scope out' the property in advance of an interview. Rocky owned a huge old grey stone mansion. It was surrounded by luxuriant trees and was scarcely visible from the street. It was probably heritage listed. Hamish drove round the block. It was even less visible from the street behind. It had a U-shaped driveway and a triple garage. It was the most expensive street in the whole city. Probably the most expensive house in the street.

'You wouldn't get that on a journalist's salary,' mused Hamish.

'Or on most NHS doctor's salaries,' added Fiona.

At ten minutes to nine, a bright yellow Lamborghini suddenly shot out of the driveway. A young female camouflaged by large dark glasses and a head scarf was at the wheel. Hamish's dashcam would note the number.

At nine precisely they rang the large ship's bell at the front door. An Iberian-looking maid welcomed them into the study where Rocky was waiting. He was a tall casually dressed middle-aged man with a natural smile, a bouffant hairstyle and probably an impenetrable emotional screen.

'Welcome, come and sit down, I am Richard, you can call me Rocky if you like, everyone does.' he turned to the maid, 'Beatrice, there's a dear could you bring some coffee.' Turning back to his visitors, he said, 'my wife has had to go down to London to arrange a nursing home for her grandmother, poor lady is ninety-five and recently broke her leg.'

So, wondered the two journalists, if Rocky's wife was away, who was the lady leaving in the Lamborghini?

Hamish and Fiona introduced themselves and sat down.

Fiona started, 'we are sorry to invade your privacy at a difficult time, we gather you knew George fairly well. What can you tell us about the man as a person, his career is obviously up in the public domain?'

Richard blathered on for five minutes about what a sterling chap he was, about his brilliant career etc etc. How they had become close friends through the association. How they many interests in common. What a good raconteur George was etc etc.

Fiona taking notes asked, 'could he have had any enemies?'

Rocky was surprised by the question. 'No, none that I could think of. Everyone loved him, his patients for his prodigious skills, his friends for his charm and modesty.'

'Is the history association a happy one, we have heard there is one lady, a Ms Windsor who objects to the male dominance on the committee?'

Rocky was surprised. 'Oh Clarissa, her bark is worse than her bite, she would like to be the first female president. It's not a big problem. We would have to call her seigneur then!'

'Why seigneur?' asked Fiona curiously.

'Oh, it's been the title of the president since, well I don't know how long. Since before I joined.'

Hamish looked casually around the room. One wall was plastered with books, medicine and history, psychiatry and philosophy and the classics of British literature. Expensive objects d'art and modern pictures by trendy artists filled the room.

At a pause in the conversation, Hamish asked, 'do you know how Mrs Hamilton-Bruce is managing, does she have much family to support her?'

Rocky paused and broke eye-contact. 'I think she is heading back to Australia any day now when she has completed arrangements for the repatriation of George's body. There is going to be a big funeral service for him in Sydney Cathedral. I believe Jacqui has a sister, but they were orphaned when fairly young. Apparently, both her parents were killed in a terrible car crash.'

'And doctor, can you tell me which group you joined on St Kilda on that fateful day?'

'Oh yes. I sat in the Puff Inn testing whisky. Great whisky! One from the new Abhainn Dearg distillery in Uig on the island of Lewis, and the classic Talisker Distiller's from Skye: the nearby largest islands in the Outer Hebrides. Exquisite. I never saw poor George after he went with the history group. Such a terrible loss to us all. Can I pour you more coffee?'

'No thank you doctor, you have been most helpful,' replied Hamish and they departed.

Back in the Ford, they headed back to the office. 'An enigma of a man. Typical psychiatrist. They avoid telling you anything about themselves. We didn't learn anything new about George and little about Rocky. He seems bland and sociable. His personality was not on show.'

Once back at the office, Hamish reran the dashcam, detecting the Lamborghini's registration plate. A little delving into the confidential police information files revealed it to be owned by a local car hire company. Hamish knew the secretary well. A phone call would reveal the driver.

'Hi Allie, its Hamish, is it true you have a yellow Lamborghini for hire for special events? Aberdeen must be moving upmarket.'

'Hi Hamish, its way beyond your pocket. It's out till tomorrow anyway.'

'So, Allie dear, can you tell me the name of the person renting it?'

'I shouldn't do this Hamish. Bring flowers next visit. A Dr Richard Rockingham hired it with two registered drivers, himself and a real blonde beauty, a Mrs Jacqueline Hamilton-Bruce. She's out of your league, like the Lamborghini Hamish. You stick with Cairistiona and your lovely kids.'

'Allie, you're a beauty too, flowers and wine next visit!'

'Well Fiona, that bland affect Rocky displays is definitely hiding something! Even if it is only a remarkably recently widowed lady, an exceptionally beautiful widowed lady visiting while his wife is away.'

Hamish sent an email to Mac. Could he see if Rocky had a phone app to monitor the CCTV cameras around his house and check the last twenty-four hours. A reply came within twenty minutes. Sure enough a yellow Lamborghini drove into his garage at about six pm and did not emerge till the following morning.

Fiona was stunned, impressed. 'Well, how about that! Amazing! Hamish, you are teaching me a lot about investigative journalism. You seem to need a wide collection of dubious contacts and very flawed friends. I don't suppose for one minute you will pass them on to me. So, Jacqui stays overnight with Rocky while his wife is away. Perhaps it was for a psychiatric consultation or perhaps even a game of chess. They certainly have something to hide. It may just be some old-fashioned adultery rather than a murder. Looking at her pictures, I reckon any bloke would want to get his hand in her knickers.'

She paused and continued, 'what now?'

'Good question,' replied Hamish. 'I would want to meet all the other suspects. That will not be easy with so many in Australia.'

Hamish jotted down a list of suspects which they perused together.

All attended three conferences and were on scuba diving trip

Jacqui Hamilton-Bruce*
Thomas and Emily Seaman*
Justine Barbeau
Clarissa Windsor*
Bruce Dundee
Clare Jones
Richard Rockingham*
Akshay Patel*
James Harvey*

* = motive, Jacqui and Rocky having an affair. Patel, a medico-legal grudge Seaman, Harvey, Moore and Windsor seeking presidency or promotion

Others

Amelia Moore *, only attended two conferences, perhaps would like to be president.

Jasmine Mohammed, only attended two conferences, husband murdered

'Well Fiona, there are three not too far away. Akshay in Leeds, Jasmine in Paris and Jacqui in Rocky's bed. After that we will need to take a few weeks in Australia. We would need to go to Kalgoorlie to see Bruce Dundee, Alice Springs to see Clare Jones, Townsville to see Amelia Moore, Sydney to see Clarissa Windsor and James Harvey, and Melbourne to see the Seamans. That would be great fun. I wonder if I can persuade Cairistiona and the kids' school to let us all go driving in the outback for a term.'

'Wow, I hope there would be a fifth place in the car for your apprentice. It's your duty Hamish to take me to learn the ropes!' enthused Fiona.

'I would love you to come, so much because we will have to go on our gut feeling with these people. We are journalists not police. We cannot interrogate as police can. Your impressions will be important.'

'Hamish, you may be surprised to know I have an older brother in the Queensland Police. He migrated to Australia about five years ago. At the moment he is some wild west place, I think it is called Mount Isa. He says it is the best place in the world because the politically correct turmeric laté drinkers haven't found the town yet,' added Fiona.

'Fantastic, we may need his support! Now we have to run the idea past Archie! First, we should email the three nearby seeking an interview, nominally about George's career and tragic death. I will do Akshay and you do the women. Also, we need a list of who went bird watching, who went to the pub and who did the history bit on St Kilda. Yes, I worked it out this time Fiona. Try the coroner's report!'

Hamish struck lucky first. Akshay was in Glasgow for two days at an obstetric conference. He was giving a paper on placental insufficiency, Mustapha's specialty.

Fiona and Hamish went to see Archibald and revealed the details so far. 'So,' said Archie, 'we all knew in the office you two were up to something. We were sure it was just some routine office affair, a bit of boring adultery, but this has huge possibilities. Much more exciting! Well from an editor's viewpoint.'

'You can work on this in your own time, I will pay you while you are on set assignments. You may take two months off in Australia on half pay with economy travel expenses paid. I will pay standard rates for an article in the travel section from wherever you are. An interesting article for Scottish people mind you, preferably twice a week.'

'Finally, if you nail me a story with an identified murderer and at least a pair of high-profile medical adulterers, I'll pay your reasonable economy rate expenses in Australia, your full wages for that period and a bonus of twenty-thousand pounds. I own the copyright of the story for all forms of income including TV interviews and books. And Fiona, you will become a permanent member of staff having passed your apprenticeship.'

'What do you say?'

Hamish and Fiona leapt up, shook his hand vigorously, and headed out for coffee. If they had thought a bit more, they would have asked for a bigger bonus should they find a murderer. They then went to find Cairistiona in her social work office and put the situation to her.

'You mean I can spend some time lazing on a sunny beach. You mean I can buy some suitable summer clothes in a Sydney boutique. You mean Fiona can babysit sometimes while we have dinner on the sand in the balmy tropics. You mean we can drink some delicious Australian wine. Sauvignon blanc with calamari. Shiraz with rare steaks. You mean I can avoid wet grey Scottish skies for a few weeks and see the outback gold fields and rain forests. I can go on a cruise round Sydney harbour and climb Uluru,' replied Cairistiona.

Hamish and Fiona nodded encouragingly.

'Maybe, I'll think about it,' answered Cairistiona evasively, 'ask me tomorrow when I've slept on it.'

'That's great Cairistiona, thanks so much, I'll talk to the school.' Hamish gave her a big hug and a kiss.

'I haven't said yes yet,' came back Cairistiona, 'but YES, YES, DEFINITELY YES!'

CHAPTER SEVEN

THE OBSTETRICIAN

Next morning Hamish and Fiona took the early train to Glasgow. It would take them close to the conference centre without the worry of driving and parking. They walked the eight hundred meters to the hotel wondering if they would find evasion again like Rocky.

Akshay's conference was in the Bythswood Hotel. A highly select hotel for an especially select small group of obstetricians. The Big Pharma had a new dreadfully expensive biologic drug that prevented ninety-five percent of eclampsia and placental problems. At around twenty-thousand pounds per pregnancy, it would be for expectant mothers in the top end of town. The very top end. Potential heirs, male heirs of course, of aristocratic titles, shipping lines, oil fields, huge estates, fabulous fortunes. For treble the price it could be done with some IVF to guarantee a baby boy.

The Big Pharma expected plenty of obscenely rich customers from India, China, the Middle East and USA. They wouldn't bother with the National Health Service in UK.

Fiona and Hamish were ushered courteously into the luxurious saloon where a smiling Akshay, a smiling Akshay in a Stuart Hughes Diamond suit donated by the big pharma, was waiting for them. 'please sit down and have some coffee or better still the house whisky, I'm told its exceptionally good. I have a half hour before my next talk, how can I help?'

Fiona said, 'we know so much about George for our article, what did you think of him as a private friend?'

After five minutes about his modesty, brilliant conversation, surgical skills, blah blah, Doug stopped him and said, 'do you know how Jacqui is coping?'

'Sorry, no. I heard she is returning to Sydney shortly with the body for a big memorial service. I do not know her well. They have only been married a few years.'

'Do you know how George got on with his previous wives?'

'No, we never spoke of that.'

'Did you see George the night he disappeared?'

'Yes, I went with him and Jacqui to the history talk. I was fascinated to hear about the chickenpox episode, and especially fascinated as an obstetrician on the tragic neonatal tetanus story. George walked out saying the medicine and the people on St Kilda were unbelievably backward. We never saw him again. It was absolutely awful.'

'Did anyone else leave that group?'

'No.'

Hamish changed the topic, 'Did you know the previous president Mustafa?'

'Yes, we were close friends.'

'Yet Mustafa appeared as an expert witness against you in a medico-legal case.'

Akshay laughed, 'Look I don't tell many people this, Mustafa was my brother-in-law, he was married to my sister. He was my best friend. Friend and professional colleague. One of the reasons he migrated to Australia was because of disapproval of him marrying a Hindu. A serious offence in the eyes of some bigoted political and religious leaders. We were working together on the same area; we have published papers together.'

'Why did he appear against you in court?'

'There had been an error in my unit, and I carried the responsibility. A lady having her third Caesarean section, all done by me, had severe intra-operative bleeding and I was forced to do a hysterectomy to save her life. She had acquired an antibody to clotting factors sometime after the second Caesar, and the laboratory did not detect it before surgery, even though we ordered a routine pre-operative coagulation screen. We gave blood and clotting factors in theatre but that did not stop the bleeding. My hand was forced.'

'She was not unhappy, she had three healthy daughters. However, her husband desired a son more than anything, more than his wife's life. He sued me. He was planning to divorce her now she was no use to him! I was going to plead guilty and pay the costs. However, my defence organisation thought I could reduce the damages by pleading not guilty and going to court. The prosecuting council asked Mustafa to appear as an expert obstetrician against me. We were both amused by this. No one knew of our relationship,'

'Prosecution asked Mustafa if elective Caesars often ended in a hysterectomy, he said no, rarely. They asked if a coagulation screen should be done preoperatively, he said yes, always. Prosecution asked if preoperative therapy with clotting factors would have avoided bleeding and a hysterectomy, he said probably, yes.'

'He asked if the mother would be able to have another child, the much-wanted son, he said no, it's hard to have a child after a hysterectomy. The court was amused, but my goose was cooked, and damages were awarded. My professional indemnity company had a large bill to pay. Once the court was empty and everyone gone home, Mustafa and I and our wives shared a laugh with a glass of champagne and shook hands, there was no ill-feeling. We still grieve bitterly for poor Mustafa. His murder was truly awful.'

Finally, Fiona asked, 'are you going to stand for the presidency of the association?'

Akshay laughed again, 'me be the seigneur? no that would cause too many difficulties.'

'What difficulties, and why is it called seigneur?' continued Fiona.

'I don't know why it's called that; it always has been since I joined, and why, I am terrified of Clarissa Windsor, I don't want her as my enemy!'

The journalists thanked Akshay, downed the remainder of their double tots of The Glenlivet Archive Distiller's limited-edition malt whisky, shook hands and left. Not bad for 'house whisky' Hamish thought. If he had been smarter, he would have done medicine at university, rather than journalism. And then become an arrogant obscenely rich surgeon. George and Akshay lived the life of Reilly in the big smoke. Amelia and Bruce, the physicians maybe academically smarter, lived in Hicksville apparently.

On the return journey they looked at each other quizzically. Fiona said, 'I am inclined to believe everything he says, but he seemed a bit coy about becoming president. Nobody will tell us how the president became known as the seigneur. Also, I think we have excluded any motive for him to have been involved in any way with Mustafa's shooting.'

Hamish nodded. 'I could get used to that whisky, that's about twenty-one years old and about four hundred pounds a bottle!'

'Paris and Justine next?' asked Fiona. Hamish nodded.

CHAPTER EIGHT

THE WIDOW

Fiona booked a long weekend in Paris. She was quite excited about her first visit to the city of love. However, she came back a day early. Hamish picked her up at the Aberdeen International Airport.

'Well I saw Justine in her little apartment in Paris. She is totally overwhelmed by grief. She can scarcely speak of Gaspard. She was in floods of tears the whole time. She has no idea what happened. She is not certain that he is dead. She has no closure. He had no enemies; they were happily married with three teenage children. His life insurance company will not pay out his life policy for another three years if there is no answer for his disappearance in the meantime. They say he may have gone into hiding to claim his life insurance. It is for twenty-five million euros. They probably think she knocked him off!'

'She attends the conferences in the hope that she may see him there. She was upset about the deaths of Mustafa and George, especially since Mustafa died in her home city. She wonders if she brings bad luck to the association. It is only her children that prevent her doing something silly she says. Maybe she would catch up with Gaspard then. No, she never heard him being called seigneur. Justine has not ever returned to her job as a senior nurse at the Hotel Dieu Hospital.'

'She made me feel so sad that I could not enjoy seeing Paris, so I came home. I tried your remedy for all ills. I had a double scotch on the flight and feel a little better. Yes, I believe she is sincere. I think we can take her off the list of suspects as well as Akshay.'

'Thanks for doing that Fiona. Next plan is finding Jasmine.'

'No problem, I have been looking her up on the internet. She is now a famous fashion designer in New York would you believe. Just under the name of Jasmine, she has dropped the Mohammed. And she has a fashion display in London next week. You should see the prices. No wonder I haven't even heard of her, let alone buy some of her stuff. If we get that twenty grand, I shall buy one of her dresses, well perhaps half a dress!'

'A dress Fiona, I won't recognise you!'

'She has a partner Barry and the clothesline is called 'Jasbar', apparently like Kasbah where she came from. They are in a relationship.'

'Hm,' mused Hamish, 'I wonder for how long?'

Fiona emailed Jasmine explaining that their newspaper was planning to publish a whole page spread on George, noting his stellar career, Scottish aristocratic ancestors and tragic death in the islands. She appeared happy to oblige with an interview.

Next week they were ushered into the penthouse suite of St James Lodge in London by an awfully superior butler who looked askance at their Scottish working-class clothing.

Jasmine ordered coffee all round and sat them down.

'Are you recording this?' she asked.

'No.' Hamish and Fiona responded simultaneously.

'What I say I want to be completely off the record, or this interview ends right now.'

'OK, no notes, no recorder,' promised Fiona, putting down her pen.

'Has everyone one so far told you what a wonderful man George was?' Both nodded ascent again.

'Well that's from all his boot-licking toadies. Gaspard was all those things; he was a delightful man. I try to keep in touch with Justine, but she shuts herself away from everyone much of the time.'

'George was an arrogant, patronising, boastful, conceited, superior, pompous, narcissistic, misogynistic womanising bastard. There I bet you haven't heard that. He seemed pleased when my husband was shot.

That is once he got over his fright. He was first out the café back door when the shots were fired. No concern for his new beautiful wife.'

'The only consolation he offered me after Mustafa's death was to fill in for the poor man and screw me in my hotel room. It would cheer me up he said. That was a few hours after the shooting! I had just been widowed so traumatically and three hours after he wants to screw me for my benefit! If you find this hard to believe, ask his previous wives. He used to bring home some of his female students and junior doctors for some private tuition in his study. Well that's what he told the wives! That's not what both of them found when they walked in unannounced once. Surgery wasn't his specialty, adultery was.' Jasmine paused reflectively, 'I suppose I shouldn't criticise though.'

'What do you mean by the last comment?' asked Fiona curiously.

'Well again don't publish this. I suppose it doesn't matter too much now. Barry and I have been designing clothes together for nearly five years. We were sleeping together occasionally for a year or two before Mustafa was shot. I am fairly sure Mustafa had no inkling of this. One night when working together, but otherwise alone quite late, Barry asked if I would model a bikini he had just finished. Just to tease him I undressed slowly and completely in front of him. He watched curiously while I put on the bikini, then amorously when I took it off. It was an hour later before I finally got dressed again. That was our first time. Mind you Mustafa had a few lovers on the side. He didn't particularly try to hide them. He expected me to tolerate it. It was a normal part of his background culture.'

'I tell you all this in a degree of confidentiality because I couldn't bear to see an article saying George was a saint. There is another side which deserves exposure.'

'Thank you,' said Hamish, 'Thank you for taking us into your confidence. We will respect that. We suspected something like this. No man is so perfect. We will have to rethink our obituary. A balanced article will pose some difficulties. Tell me, are Rocky and Jacqui good friends?'

Jasmin smiled insightfully, 'Well what a surprise, you would not ask that if you had not discovered something, fancy that! They avoid being seen together in public. Serves George right getting a dose of his own medicine. Perhaps he couldn't deal with his wife being unfaithful and jumped off Conachair.'

'Hm, interesting thought. Finally,' asked Hamish, 'the association seems to be an organisation covering a lot of infidelity. Would you agree with that?'

'You might believe that, but I could not possibly comment!'

'Finally, from me,' asked Fiona, 'did Mustafa have any enemies?' 'Barry did not shoot him if that is what you are asking, Barry was already getting everything he wanted before Mustafa died! No, I don't think he had enemies in the association or in the medical profession. A religious extremist was thought to have murdered him, but every sane person is their enemy.'

On the train back, Hamish and Fiona looked at each other thoughtfully.

Fiona started, 'so Jasmine may have killed George, she hated him and had some grounds for killing him. She may have arranged Mustafa's death because of her affair with Barry. She was fond of Gaspard she says. I felt however, she was being totally honest with us. She did not hide her own misdemeanours. I think our villain is going to be down under, where they sent all the convicts, bushrangers did they call them?'

Cairistiona paid a visit to the boys' school. As usual an overseas trip was deemed to be of enormous educational importance. William and Jock were asked to keep a travel diary, a picture book of the places they would visit, any animals they saw and of experiences in general. William was asked to write some notes in his. They had the head's blessing to take a term off.

CHAPTER NINE

CAIRNS

Cairistiona, Fiona and Hamish agreed to stay in Australia from the start of October for up to two months. It should be pleasantly warm, but avoid the cyclone season, heavy tropical rain and high humidity. Fiona's brother, Robert arranged to meet their flight in Cairns in North Queensland. He had managed to borrow a Toyota Land Cruiser for the duration of their stay from a friend who would be away on an around the world cruise.

Touch down in Cairns just before midday was exceedingly welcome. Willie and Jock were going stir crazy after eighteen hours confined to a small seat on a plane with only a short stopover in Singapore. None of them had much sleep. Fortunately, their baggage collection and customs checks were fairly quick. There waiting for them in the arrivals' lounge was their new 'Uncle' Bob. He gave Fiona a bear hug, then shooks the hands of the two boys gravely. Then he greeted Cairistiona and Hamish.

'Welcome to Australia, I have a car waiting for you all. I have booked a motel close by as agreed. You can have a shower, a change, a swim in the pool, something small to eat and a short sleep. Only two to three hours sleep max, or your body clocks won't adjust. I will be back at six. We can have a beer or two and a steak while you tell me what this is all about. I can tell my little sister is holding something back!'

A few hours later they were sitting in the motel restaurant under some palm trees in the balmy tropical dusk. Scottish tweed and Fair Isle wool had been exchanged for cotton t-shirts and shorts. Beers and lemonades were delightfully welcome as the adults awaited the steaks and the boys their chicken and chips.

'So, Bob,' began Hamish, 'it's great to meet you, thanks for all your arrangements. We all fancied some warm sunshine and tropical beaches. My editor wants us to run a twice weekly column on Australia in the tourism section. Your outback as well as your big cities. Fiona is my apprentice at the Aberdeen Times, and she couldn't turn down a chance to catch up with her big brother.'

'Also, an Australian man called George Hamilton-Bruce was on St Kilda in our Hebrides on a conference a few months ago when he fell to his death. A terrible tragedy as he seems to have been a leading cardiac surgeon. We also wanted to find out about his innovative work at the hospital in Sydney where he worked. We hoped to catch up with his widow as well. We plan to talk to his closest colleagues around Australia. We are planning a whole page spread in the Aberdeen paper about his life and death, and especially about his innovative cardiac surgery.'

'So here we are!' smiled Fiona disarmingly.

'Funny, our work seems to overlap,' replied Bob suspiciously. 'two years ago, I was involved here in a search for a missing scuba diver. Gaspard Barbeau was his name. He had been staying at Hayman Island at a medical history conference and went diving with a group of delegates. He disappeared without a trace to this day.'

'Strange to relate he was the then president of the Global Association of Medical Historians and the conference was their annual meeting. Strange because that was George Hamilton-Bruce's position when he died. And even more strange was that the president between their tenures was a doctor named Mustafa Mohammed. He was assassinated a year ago in Paris in an assumed terrorist attack'

'Now I'm a bit of a James Bond fan Hamish. I remember Auric Goldfinger in the book Goldfinger, saying *"Once is happenstance. Twice is coincidence. The third time it's enemy action."*. Have you heard that

Hamish? Are you conducting a murder enquiry, a police enquiry in my cabbage patch Fiona?' asked Bob.

Fiona looked at Hamish inquisitively. Hamish nodded.

'OK Bob, you are on to us before we start,' confessed Fiona. 'We do plan to write a eulogy for George. We do plan to write for the travel section. However, we noted the three deaths. Hamish has read Goldfinger as well. We suspect enemy action too. We have unearthed a short list of people who attended all three conferences and went scuba diving at Hardy's reef. We have found most people, certainly most men, think George was the greatest thing in medicine since Hippocrates, and some women think he was the greatest philanderer since Casanova. We have also discovered some affairs going on among the other members which may provide motives.'

'We were going to interview them under the guise of the eulogy,' apologised Fiona.

'OK,' said Bob, 'I am grateful that you alerted me to the connection. You may have pointed a finger at perhaps three currently undetected murders, where the possible murderer has got away scot free thus far. Totally unsuspected. I am going to investigate this myself, so I have some rules for you. Police Rules. You will contact me if you discover any suspicious behaviour. You will not intimidate any witness or even suggest a crime has been committed. Do we have an agreement? If so, I can use police channels to investigate any unexplained facts and help all of us. If not, I might get you deported even though you are my little sister!'

'Fiona, the last two years, I have been working in the detection department. Your big brother is a detective-sergeant and hopes to be a detective-inspector soon.'

Fiona and Hamish agreed to the terms, progress seemed more likely with Bob's aid. They had little option.

They had previously agreed they would drive all the way to Kalgoorlie first, then to Alice Springs, down to Melbourne, up to Sydney then finally Townsville and the flight home. Bob looked critically at their itinerary from an Australian perspective.

'Do you have any idea how far these places are? Do you know how much bigger this country is than Scotland? You will spend many days on the road. May I suggest you fly from Cairns to Alice and hire a car there just to drive around the town. Then fly to Kalgoorlie via Adelaide and hire a car there. Then fly to Melbourne, probably via Adelaide again. I will get this car to Melbourne for you. From there you can drive to Sydney and up the east coast. That will take a week or two out of your schedule and give more time seeing the sights of Australia apart from the beautiful but harsh and endless outback.'

'I have a little present for the boys. Children's iPads. You will be grateful for these on your long car trips. They are loaded with some Disney movies, songs and games. If you have Wi-Fi access, I have loaded some maps and some websites of Australian geography, history, archaeology, animals and indigenous culture.'

'Ooohhh, thank you Uncle Bob, they are so cool!' enthused William, 'yes I know Mum, only an hour a day maximum and we hand them over to you at bedtime.'

CHAPTER TEN

ALICE SPRINGS

The flight from Cairns arrived in the remote town in the south of the Northern Territory. Through the plane windows, they had seen mile after mile of red desert with low scrub but no trees. Then suddenly a small town in the middle of nowhere came into view. There was no land bridge to greet the plane once it came to a halt near the terminal. Instead they descended stairs onto a dry blazing hot forecourt. Luggage and the hire car were rapidly collected, and they headed out of the forty plus degree furnace into town to their pre-booked air-conditioned motel units.

Jock and Willy had their swimming togs at the top of their luggage and couldn't wait to find the motel pool.

Dr Jones had suggested a late afternoon appointment when she had completed her afternoon surgery. After a quick refreshing dip, they had time to visit some historic building including the Overland Telegraph Station, the old Court House and Adelaide House which was the town's first hospital. In the courthouse the boys stood in the dock while Fiona sentenced them to a chocolate free day if they misbehaved.

They saw some indigenous art in the galleries. Fiona purchased and posted a picture home to her parents. A hopefully appreciated striking change from the scenic pictures of the Scottish Highlands and Islands that adorned their walls. Jock said in a less than flattering assessment,

'Auntie Fiona's picture looks like Willie when he had chicken pox! It's all covered in spots!'

They learnt about the early days of the flying doctor, and about the aboriginal culture before the Scots arrived in Australia. William wrote and pasted pictures to fill several pages in his journal for school and Jock found lots of pictures to stick into his. Then they returned to the motel. The boys wanted another swim. Fiona and Hamish drove to Dr Jones surgery.

Clare Jones' last patient departed at five-thirty and an inquisitive receptionist ushered them in. 'Are we going to be on the television or in the papers?' she hoped.

Clare Jones was an attractive thirty-something business-like lady. 'Welcome to Alice, it's a bit hotter than the Hebrides! How can I help you?'

Fiona explained they were planning a newspaper page eulogy about George and some travel notes about Alice for the Aberdeen Times.

'Hmm, I did not know him especially well. He seemed to be always surrounded by adoring fans, male and female like a pop star. I was not part of his inner circle of devotees. Some people hated him. Clarissa Walters despised his popular aura. Justine Barbeau and Jasmine Mohammed avoided him. Something about inappropriate offers after their husbands died. His cardiac surgery results and new innovations appeared outstanding. A few of my patients have been under his knife in Sydney and are progressing brilliantly.'

'The accident on St Kilda was awful. I went up the cliffs with the ornithology group, but we never saw him. Mind you, we had only been up the top for a short while before the fog blew in and we could scarcely see anyone a few yards away. How terrible that we should lose three presidents in such a short space of time. I was scuba diving with the group when Gaspard disappeared. Funny, I thought I saw one of our group, I think it was one of our group, swim towards another boat nearby. There were a few others in the water around us. I couldn't see if it was Gaspard behind the mask. It was probably a male, but I couldn't be sure of that either as the person was wearing a wet suit.'

'Thanks Doctor Jones, did you tell the coroner's court about the other boat?' asked a surprised and curious Hamish.

'Call me Clare please, and no, I was not called as a witness. I don't know if that was important,' answered the doctor.

'Can you describe the boat at all?' enquired Fiona.

'Just a big white speed boat with two large outboard motors and a wide blue stripe down the side. I couldn't see a name. Perhaps a thirty-footer.'

'Thanks Clare, perhaps we could talk to your patients that you referred to George about him if you wouldn't mind.'

Dr Jones provided names, addresses and mobile numbers having obtained their permission.

A couple of Clare's patients, one a successful heart transplant recipient told them nothing new. Just what a wonderful surgeon and modest man he was.

Dinner at the 'Red Ochre' restaurant in the Todd pedestrian mall saw Hamish choose the 'Alice Springs mixed grill'. Portions of camel, crocodile, emu and wallaby adorned his oversized plate. Large portions. Hamish, Cairistiona and Fiona washed their meal down with some lifesaving deliciously cold 'Almost Summer' beer from the recently opened Alice Springs brewery. Willy looked surprised. 'You mean this is only almost summer! How hot is real summer?'

The boys shivered at the thought of eating a crocodile. A picture of Dad's mixed grill went into their albums. Only a short way out of towns in the northern part of Australia, crocodile reclaimed top position on the food chain.

That night Hamish phoned Bob to tell him about the other boat. 'That's exceptionally interesting,' mused the detective curiously. 'That piece of information hasn't surfaced before. My God, there are hundreds of boats in the area. It would be amazing if we knew which it was. I could spend weeks wandering around the local boat harbours looking for a white speed boat with a blue stripe.'

'Hm,' ruminated Bob, 'I do have a thought of how to solve that question. Tell you later.'

Hamish and Fiona dashed off an article about 'The Alice' for the tourist page of the paper before heading to bed.

Next morning, they went to Alice wildlife park. Not only did they see venomous snakes, they saw many native Australian animals of which they were totally unaware, quokkas and quolls, bettongs and bilbies, even a barking spider and a thorny devil. Alien creatures from another planet. Pictures to fill pages of their travel logs. The boys' eyes sparkled with amazement and fascination.

'Definitely not,' announced Cairistiona firmly, when the two boys turned to her, 'you can't have any of them to take home for 'show and tell' at school! Do take some photos though.'

In the afternoon they drove out to Hermannsburg. A hundred-and-fifty-year old Lutheran mission, it was now home to a gallery full of Albert Namatjira's paintings. The boys were unimpressed by the old building and the indigenous art. Fiona purchased herself a painting of bush tucker man showing witchetty grubs and edible native plants. Willy and Jock were horrified at the thought of digging up and eating a still wriggling grub. Much worse than eating sheep's guts! As good Scots, they favoured haggis over wriggly worms! They were however delighted to have a cold chocolate milk shake and a slice of apple strudel with thick cream in the Kata Anga tea-room.

CHAPTER ELEVEN

KALGOORLIE

The next morning, they were back at the Alice Springs airport. The flight down to Adelaide and then across to Kalgoorlie was uneventful. William and Jock had an invitation up into the cockpit to look over the captain's shoulder. The plane's crew seemed delightfully naïve about any possibility of high jacking. Again, there was no land-bridge at the airport, just steps down into the inferno that was Kalgoorlie.

Cairistiona drove their hire car into the historic gold mining town as the sun was setting. The dashboard thermometer was still reading thirty-six degrees. They found their motel, the 'Lucky Nugget', unpacked and leapt into the motel pool. That felt like a hot bath. It was however, still refreshing after a day on planes and the short dry dusty hot drive from the airport.

Ready for a beer and a meal the five went to the Miners' Tavern. It was one of the original hotels opened in 1889 on the corner of Boulder Road and Hannan Street. Passing though the bar, William and wee Jock stared at the barmaids in unconcealed astonishment. The orange glow of sunset through the window highlighted their bare breasts. Hamish noticed them in passing.

'Mummy, mummy,' burst out Jock, 'why are those ladies not wearing bras?'

Cairistiona hustled them upstairs to the restaurant, 'must be because it's damned hot Jock.'

Turning to Hamish, she hissed, 'you can find somewhere else for dinner tomorrow night, what bloody century is this place living in?'

The next morning Hamish and Fiona went to the Kalgoorlie Hospital to find Bob Dundee as arranged. The individual specialty wards were separated by corridors in the gardens. They had roofs but no sides, so were at the already high shade temperature. Dundee was sitting in the air-conditioned doctors' offices pouring over a huge leather-bound dreadfully tatty ledger. After introductions, he waved at the volume with enormous enthusiasm.

'Look at this will you, these are the hospital records going back nearly a hundred and forty years. It goes back to the early days of the gold rush. 1886. Most of the patients had typhoid because there was little clean water here. Some were working in the Kalgoorlie hospitality industry so sadly spread the disease amongst their clientele in the town taverns and restaurants. There were no drips or antibiotics so twenty percent died, isn't that fascinating.'

Hamish and Fiona were bemused by the doctors morbid absorption into deaths of yesteryear.

'About twenty years after the hospital opened, still over a hundred years ago Charles O'Connor constructed a thousand-kilometre pipe-line to bring water from Perth. It remains the source of the town's water supply at the moment. It is getting worn out and will be placed soon. They will probably change the name to that of some useless politician, unfortunately.'

'Today is sadly not much better in many places in the world than Kalgoorlie was during the gold rush days. There's still lots of typhoid in south-east Asia. Several hundred thousand deaths every year. It costs four dollars per person to drill a fresh water well in a third world country. However, we prefer to spend money on dumb celebrities.'

'Sorry, you did not come to hear that. You wanted to know about poor George. What a tragedy, he was a top bloke, great fun at parties, such a storyteller with an endless supply of jokes. Pretty good opening batsman. I reckon he could have got a baggy green playing for Australia to add to his Oxford blue had he wanted to. He scored a century opening in successive varsity matches, brilliant.'

'He was the best cardiac surgeon in Australia. I am especially grateful to him because he arranged the last conference in Scotland at my request. You see from my name; my origins are there. My ancestors include Viscount 'Bonnie Dundee', John Graham of Claverhouse, the victor at the Battle of Killiecrankie. However, he died in the battle. I went to the battle site and also to Sir Walter Scott's home at Abbottsford where Dundee's pistol is on display. What a fantastic trip to Scotland. What a sad ending.'

'Sorry, have I answered your questions...?' Dundee faltered.

Fiona finally managed to get in a question, 'so do you think he may have had any enemies, someone who benefitted from his death?'

'Absolutely not, everyone loved him and respected him. Jacqui will inherit a lot of money, but she was quite besotted with him. They were all over each other. Desperately sad! Everyone thought most highly of him.'

'Look at this old page of admissions here, even doctors, nurses and clergy in Kalgoorlie caught typhoid!'

'Sorry to interrupt your flow of thoughts,' Hamish interrupted, 'did you see him, George that is, on the island of St Kilda?'

'No, my heritage is Scottish, obviously I had to go to the Puff Inn for the whisky tasting. Wow, they were delightfully good. I never saw him again after he headed off with the history group to the old houses in Main Street.'

'Last question, were you with Gaspard when he disappeared at Hardy's Reef?'

'We all dived in together, but I never clearly saw him in the water. He was gone when we reassembled on the boat. Terrible isn't it, we change association presidents faster than this country changes its bloody Prime Minister! God knows who wants the job now, we might end up with a leaderless committee. It will be like our parliament with a rabble of pompous egos sitting on the crossbench blocking the elected government's mandate!'

Fiona and Hamish shook hands with Bob and left. The air outside felt like a blast furnace. The temperature had reached forty-seven degrees.

Fiona said, 'either a good actor or more probably a typical doctor. Obsessed by medicine and past medical history with little insight into his colleagues' flaws. Funny, all the men think George is quite special. The ladies are less convinced.'

They caught up with Cairistiona and the boys for a late lunch. Willie and Wee Jock were full of excitement. A quick glance at Cairistiona suggested nothing as inappropriate as last night.

'We have been down the super pit where they mine for gold,' said Willie. 'Its two miles across and five hundred yards deep,' added Jock. 'We sat in the front of this humungous truck,' said Willie. Jock in turn said, 'its wheels are twice as tall as Daddy.'

'And boys,' asked their mother, 'what else was special about the truck?'

Blank faces.

'What about the driver?'

'Oh,' responded Willie, 'nothing much, it was a lady driver.'

Cairistiona cast her eyes to heaven. The importance of equal opportunities had been lost on her sons.

Jock bubbled, 'then we went to the swimming pool, it was nice and warm!'

Willie said, 'I swam a whole length and Jock did half a length!' The boys' swimming was coming on brilliantly.

After a light lunch, they had a wander around the town. They went to the original town hall with its golden dome. The boys collected a few books and some respectable post cards amongst many unsuitable offerings to send back to their school. They went to see the mining museum and were amazed to see the wooden wheelbarrow pushed all the way from Perth by Russian Jack at the time of the original gold rush. Ten minutes in the heat was enough for them.

Fiona took the boys for an ice-cream and to play in the park. Cairistiona and Hamish did a tour round Questa Casa, the town's remaining active brothel. Only when she assured that there would be not untoward exposure or activity. It was open for tourists to see in the day, and for business as usual at night. Night visits cost ten times the cost of the afternoon tour. With benefits!

They visited the domination room. In spite of being a journalist in Aberdeen for a decade, with a wide experience of the seamy side of life, some of the equipment was quite puzzling to Hamish. He did his best to describe his experiences for the travel section of his paper. An expurgated version. The Free Church puritan streak was alive and well in Aberdeen. At least in public view.

The Golden Indian served dinner. Mild curry for the boys. Demurely dressed waitresses in saris for Cairistiona. A bottle of Boulder Gold from the local Beaten Track brewery for Hamish and Fiona.

Wee Jock asked, 'Mummy, these waitresses don't seem to be too hot.'

'No darling, they have the air-conditioning on,' she replied with a scowl at Hamish.

What would Jock say at show and tell back in Aberdeen?

Cairistiona waved some tourist brochures at them, 'there is so much to see in this area, brilliant wineries at the Margaret River, Gormley's sculptures at Lake Ballard, a whaling museum in Albany and golden beaches at Esperance. And then all the attractions of Perth and Freemantle. Are we coming back next year?'

The next morning, they caught a flight out of Kalgoorlie to Adelaide.

CHAPTER TWELVE

THE GARDEN OF
UNEARTHLY DELIGHTS

Having saved time flying around Australia, they all agreed to spend a couple of days in Adelaide. They spent the next morning walking up the North Terrace, visiting the Adelaide Art Gallery and Museum, before ending up in The Garden of Unearthly Delights for lunch.

The ever-inquisitive William asked, 'Mummy, what are unearthly delights?'

'Ask your father.'

Jock and Willie looked at Hamish, who replied, 'er, I'm not sure, perhaps it the big hamburger and coke you are eating.'

Immediately opposite was the National Wine Centre of Australian where they did a little tasting. Then purchased a couple of bottles especially selected for the evening amongst hundreds of South Australian wines. Langmeil Barossa Shiraz and a Hahndorf Hill Gruner Veltliner. Gorgeous!

Later the boys and Hamish went to the Adelaide Oval to see a Sheffield Shield game, Australia's first-class cricket championship, in progress. The boys were impressed to see the ground where Don

Bradman made a century on his debut in first class cricket. The ladies headed off for a shopping spree to ensure enough stylish casual clothing for the Queensland coast.

The next day, Fiona, now definitely the favourite 'Aunty Fiona', took the boys down to Victor Harbour. They took the horse-drawn carriage to Granite Island to see the faery penguins, and the old Cockle steam train to see the mouth of the mighty Murray river. Between there were stops for burgers, chips and ice-creams. Several stops.

Hamish and Cairistiona hired a second car for the day to visit the Clare Valley wineries. They were enchanted to find the Scots and Irish were well represented at the Claymore, Robertson, McNeill and Stringy Brae vineyards. Another couple of selected bottles complemented their dinner. Cairistiona complained there was not enough time to visit the Barossa valley wineries, nor the raw beauty of the remote places in outback South Australia like Wilpena Pound or the painted desert road. She was working on a longer trip maybe next year.

Both journalists were able to send articles for Archie back in Aberdeen about their day's experiences. Scots liked articles about alcoholic indulgence.

CHAPTER THIRTEEN

MELBOURNE

They caught the early flight to Melbourne and settled into their hotel in the centre of town by lunch time. Thomas Seaman had suggested they should meet in his club around five o'clock.

They were welcomed at the door of the Melbourne Savage Club in Bank Place by Emily Seaman who ushered them politely up to the lounge. It was a most elegant place, a lounge of leather and timber in an old sandstone townhouse. It reminded Hamish of the Whisky Club in Edinburgh.

Thomas was a middle-aged ascetic looking man. He gave them a brief almost effeminate handshake and summoned a waiter. Double scotches were clearly the standard order of the day. Hamish thought the place was a bit up itself, so as an Aberdonian, he ordered a Glen Dronach. He was pretty impressed when the waiter said smoothly, 'will that be a double of the Parliament Glen Dronach sir?'

Hamish had drunk the eight-year old Hielan before when feeling affluent, but never the twenty-one-year-old Parliament. That retailed for around a hundred and fifty pounds a bottle back home.

Yes, that's the one thank you.'

'Same for me please,' added Fiona.

Fiona explained their task and looked at Thomas.

'Such a tragedy,' came from Emily, 'he was such a brilliant surgeon and such a convivial person. We all loved him to bits.'

Fiona continued, 'that's what we hear from everyone. He seems to have been universally popular.'

'Yes, that's right. My husband wrote some brilliant articles about infectious diseases with George as the second author. They had so much in common. You know they had articles published in the Lancet and the New England Journal of Medicine. The two most prestigious medical journals in the world.'

'The Global Association of Medical Historians is lucky to have such an outstanding man to take over as president as my little Tommie here. We are planning next year's meeting in Istanbul. There's so much of historical medical fascination, particularly infectious diseases in the city. Tommie will be the keynote speaker of course.'

Thomas spoke, 'Emily dear, you are jumping the gun, Clarissa Waters may be elected.'

'That harridan, she hates everyone,' flared Emily, 'She would be hopeless at organising any social event!'

Hamish asked Thomas quietly, 'did she hate George?'

'She hated anyone who became president ahead of her God-given right to the job in her opinion. It wouldn't surprise me if she pushed him off the cliff!' fumed Emily. Thomas obviously did not need an opinion or a tongue for the most part in this relationship.

'Quiet, dear, these two want to hear nice things about George for their newspaper article. Not baseless accusations. People will start to suspect someone of these horrendous accidents. We were both with the history group on St Kilda in the old stone houses. The infectious diseases on St Kilda interested us. We saw George walk out but never saw him again. I say Hamish, may I call you Hamish, this is not bad whisky, thank you for introducing us to this one. I must make sure the club gets a few more bottles in.' placated Thomas.

'And my little Tommie, I'm going to look after you especially carefully so nothing nasty happens to you like poor George, Gaspard and Mustafa when you are the president!' continued Emily.

'We heard about Gaspard; has anything more been heard about him?'

Emily shook her head.

'Did you two go scuba diving with Gaspard Barbeau?' asked Fiona.

'Yes, we did. What a terrible, terrible event. Poor Justine is so lost, she has no sort of closure. You know Clarissa was fiddling with the oxygen cylinders on the boat, would surprise me if she fixed Gaspard's', crimed Emily.

'Shush dear,' begged Thomas.

'Were there any other boats nearby?'

Thomas looked up peering acutely at Fiona, 'there was one not far away, some sort of big white speedboat. I say, this is all awfully morbid, why don't you stay with us here for dinner and tell us all about Scotland? We could have another of your GlenDronach whisky's.'

'That's most kind of you Dr Seaman, but I'm travelling with my two young sons and I must get back to them. Can I ask you one last question, have you heard how Jacqui, George's wife is managing?'

'Poor Jacqui,' Emily answered as usual for her husband, 'we saw her of course at the memorial service for George in Sydney. Hundreds of people turned out. It was desperately sad. We told her to come and stay with us in Melbourne any time she felt lonely or depressed. She loved George to bits, and he spoilt her rotten. They were a totally devoted couple. She must be absolutely devastated.'

'We heard on the grapevine that she had gone back to Scotland. Funny, you would think she would want to avoid the place!'

Perhaps not so surprising, perhaps not so devastated, thought Hamish and Fiona.

They shook hands and departed.

'Hm, 'Fiona said thoughtfully, 'Lady Macbeth. She would do anything for him to bask in reflected glory. She is keen to suggest that if there was a crime, then it must be Clarissa. Certainly not her, certainly not the saintly Thomas!'

'The history group on St Kilda all alibi each other. The Puff Inn group do the same. We need to find out who was on the ornithology group. Would that be in the coroner's report or the Silver Viking's data base.'

Back at the hotel, Jock and Willie were full of exciting stories about Hardrock climbing and the Aquatic Centre. Both had climbed the children's wall attached to a safety harness. Wee Jock had slipped once, but Willie got to the top without slipping once. In the aquatic centre they had gone down in the shark tank in an enclosed water-tight chamber to get a close-up view of the shark's teeth.

'They were humungous teeth,' announced wee Jock baring his baby teeth with a snarl.

William complained, 'Aberdeen are playing Celtic tonight, but it's not on the TV. Spurs against Chelsea is on one sports channel. The others have some funny Victorian sort of football game on four channels! It looks a bit like rugby with an oval ball, but they do forward passes, are always offside and can't tackle. Will that be better in Sydney? Will we be able to see Scottish football?'

Hamish shrugged. Sounded a bit like America with their own parochial form of football. Never to be seen on the world stage. No ambition to play for their country in an international let alone in a world cup. Mind you, reflected Hamish ruefully, it was quite some years since Scotland had appeared on the world stage. The FIFA World Cup finals.

Scotland also appeared regularly in the rugby world cup but never with much success. The southern hemisphere teams had a near monopoly on that.

Cairistiona said, 'Hamish, you can have the boys tomorrow, I am going to find some shops, some nice safe shops! Fiona, why don't you come with me?'

Hamish sent a message to Mac, asking about the three groups on the ground in St Kilda. Within half an hour, he had the lists. Only two delegates were in the St Kilda bird watchers and the Hardy's reef scuba divers. Dr Clare Jones and Dr James Harvey.

'That's disappointing,' said Hamish, 'I can't see her as our murderer. Maybe its Harvey. I had the impression George was his mentor and best mate. Maybe we are seeing a murder mystery that does not actually exist. Perhaps Goldfinger is wrong. Perhaps it just a journalist's wishful thinking for the scoop of a lifetime.'

'No Hamish,' replied Fiona, 'there are secrets, affairs and hatreds in this group. We will surely find a killer.'

CHAPTER FOURTEEN

THE OPEN ROAD

Bob, as good as his word, arrived at their hotel in Melbourne at nine in the morning the following day with the Land Cruiser. They spent half-an-hour over coffee comparing notes and discussing routes to Cairns. Bob sounded as though he had a secret, but he would not talk about his progress. Then the five Scots loaded up the 4WD and Bob took a taxi for the airport.

The three adults took turns at the wheel for the over four-hundred-mile trip. The National Highway 31 and the Hume Highway allowed a steady seventy miles an hour. With only short stops for toilets and refreshments, they entered Canberra, the National Capital around six pm. They followed the usual routine of a cup of tea, a quick dip in the hotel pool, then a shower, followed by a beer and dinner with local wines.

The next day in the national capital, Fiona took the boys to the National Dinosaur Museum in the morning and the National Zoo and Aquarium in the afternoon. Cairistiona and Hamish visited the old and new parliament houses in the morning, went up the Telstra Tower on Black Mountain for lunch, then spent a fascinating afternoon at the War Museum.

Exchanging notes on the day over a beer or two and after a dip in the pool, they all agreed they needed to come back to Australia again. And again.

Willy was puzzled, 'Canberra is so much smaller than Melbourne or Adelaide, why is it the capital of Australia Daddy?'

'Well son, Sydney and Melbourne are the two biggest cities here. When all the states, like our counties, decided to combine in a federation, neither would allow the other to be capital, so they chose a place in the middle. It's a bit like Scotland, when neither Glasgow nor Edinburgh would agree which should be the capital, they made it London! However, now we are independent from England after the Brexit debacle, Edinburgh has become the capital, but Glasgow want their turn sometime in the future. Perhaps they will choose Aberdeen to keep both cities happy!'

Willy thought about that as Fiona choked on her beer.

CHAPTER FIFTEEN

SYDNEY

The nominal three-hour drive to Sydney was prolonged by a stop in Oberon where fortuitously, the National Cool Climate Wine and Food Festival was in full swing. The adults enjoyed the wine, the boys enjoyed the food, and all enjoyed the bands playing exuberantly in the dazzling sunshine.

They only reached Jenolan that night. Canberra to Sydney was further than Glasgow to Aberdeen, further than they could drive in daylight with a long stop for lunch. The next morning was spent exploring the nine limestone caves and their underground rivers in Jenolan. Willy did his best to spook Jock about cave monsters and being trapped underground. Jock's ancestors had been in the death or glory charge at Culloden. His genes were made of unyielding stuff. He was not frightened. Not with an imaginary claymore in his hands.

After a brief lunch they drove to Katoomba for a ride on the Scenic Cableway with its breathtaking views as the sun set. William had to start a new exercise book to accommodate his latest amazing pictures. 'Is that what sunset usually looks like?' asked Jock somewhat to the adult's surprise. A sad reflexion on the Aberdeen weather.

Their experiences thus far in Australia had been quite incredible and most educational.

An early start took them into Sydney as the rush hour was concluding. Cairistiona took the boys on the ferry across Sydney harbour to Manly for a swim. The boys thought it was pleasantly warm in the sea compared with Aberdeen, though the locals thought it a bit chilly still. Meanwhile Hamish and Fiona somewhat regretfully returned to their original objective. The diversity of food and wine, scenery and wildlife, forests and deserts, all in warm sunshine had become much more fun than a murder mystery. So different from Scotland.

Hamish and Fiona were ushered into the matron's office in Sydney's major cardiac surgical hospital on the dot of 11.30, their appointment time. A petite middle-aged lady with a winsome smile welcomed them to a trio of armchairs overlooking the harbour. A formal desk and chairs sat on the other side of the room.

'Hello, welcome to Sydney. I am Clarissa Windsor, please call me Clarissa. Can I pour you a cup of tea?'

Both nodded ascent.

'I gather you are from Aberdeen. I have done post-graduate courses in Glasgow and my PhD in the history of medicine is from Edinburgh. I went through Aberdeen once disembarking off a ferry from Lerwick. The place was in thick fog, so I have never actually seen Aberdeen.'

'I love your country, its grandeur and rich history, the tartans, the bag pipes and the whisky. But you haven't come to hear me prattle on about your home, you want to hear about poor George.'

'George graduated from Sydney Medical School top of his year with honours. He went to England on a Rhodes scholarship for a couple of years. He sailed through his surgical fellowship again top of the year in Australia. He did a year's post-doctoral fellowship in Boston and they begged him to stay. George was a brilliant technician with a scalpel in hand. When I was charge nurse in theatres many years ago, I assisted him often in theatre. He was the most proficient surgeon I ever worked with. Some of his cardiac procedures were ground-breaking. He took on cases others refused and still succeeded almost all the time.'

'His private practice attracted the extremely wealthy from all over the world. He was exceedingly knowledgeable about the medicine in history and gave meticulously prepared lectures. He often unearthed facts that others could not find. He could be an amazingly generous man. He sponsored half the costs of the last conference to St Kilda.'

'Have I told you all you want to know?' she beamed at the pair and poured them another cup of tea.

They looked at each other, having heard all these platitudes more than once. They seemed to have to listen to this every time before they could ask some more pertinent questions. Questions limited by being journalists not detectives in the police force. 'Well yes and no,' said Fiona probing gently, 'did everyone love him, was he a saint, rumour has it that you two did not get on?"

Clarissa's smile faded. 'Are you recording this? Everything else I say is off the record. OK?'

'No, we are not recording this,' Fiona responded as she put her notebook and biro away.

'George was a pants man. He expected me as his favourite theatre sister to go to bed with him often. When I refused, I was replaced on some petty professional trumped-up accusation. He seduced his female junior doctors on a regular basis leading to the breakup of his first two marriages. He enjoyed adultery. He loved adulation even more. Actually, he probably enjoyed adultery and adulation equally. Funny they both begin with a-d-u-l, the combination must addle your brain! He would then display the most false modesty.'

'We had words recently when he persuaded many members of the Global Association of Medical Historians to vote for him to become president. Dinners, opera and theatre tickets, a dozen bottles of his favourite wine for his dear colleagues. A weekend in his luxury penthouse on Bondi Beach or the other one at Port Douglas. He said it wasn't bribery, he was just being social. And a not-so-quiet word in the ear that the matron was a lesbian or on drugs, had bipolar disease, suicidal depression and HIV, but don't tell anyone.'

'That's how he operated, so no he wasn't a saint and I would be upset to read your eulogy saying he was. Your job will not be easy to compose an accurate eulogy for poor George without being sued!' Clarissa spoke in an unemotional measured tone. There was no rabid hatred. 'I shall stand again for the presidency and I hope it will be a level playing field.'

'How did you feel when he died?' asked Hamish.

'I was not upset, but I didn't push him off Conachair if that is what you were asking. I stayed on board ship that afternoon in St Kilda and prepared my talk for the next day, a talk that never happened. And I had nothing to do with the deaths of the two previous presidents. I hear Emily Seaman whispers about me tampering with Gaspard's oxygen at the time of his disappearance scuba diving.'

'We heard about that too. Was there another boat in the vicinity?' asked Fiona.

'I don't really remember, there are obviously thousands and thousands in the area.'

'Well if you will excuse me, I have a lot to do. It was a pleasure to talk to you. Next time I am in Scotland I will expect you to introduce me to your boys and the whisky from around Aberdeen.'

The pair headed across the hospital to the University of Sydney offices to meet James Harvey. Another affable immaculately suited gentleman welcomed them into his office.

'Yes, George was my role model, I followed him as surgical intern and then surgical registrar. Every job I had the staff told me how good my predecessor was. It was a bit intimidating. Eventually we were appointed to the same unit. Me as training registrar, he as senior advanced trainee. We became good mates, he taught me a lot of surgical techniques and practical skills. He taught me about fine wines and opera singers.'

'We had weekends away at his parents' unit on the beach. Good job they were not around. He was always surrounded by available young ladies. Don't quote me but he seemed to have the energy to shag all night and surf all day. Or operate all day and shag all night. He rose rapidly to become one of the youngest consultants here ever after a surgical fellowship in USA. He leaves a huge gap in this hospital. He was a good lecturer, a delightfully affable organiser, and most knowledgeable about history.'

Hamish tried to concentrate. 'Did everyone like him, did he have any enemies?'

'Not that I know of, he had some disagreements with Clarissa Windsor, a most objectionable woman. You know her? Unfortunately, she is matron here.'

'Did you see him the night he disappeared on Conachair?' asked Hamish.

'No, I was with the ornithology group, but he was not with us. I never saw him after landing on the island and heading separate ways. Mind you, the fog became so thick, it was hard to see anyone. Apparently, he tried to join us, but I never saw him on the top of Conachair.'

'Will you be standing for the role of President of the Association?'

'God, no! they all die and are replaced faster than we replace our Australian Prime Ministers! No, I have no ambitions that way.'

Same joke, thought Hamish, mind you not surprising. No wonder someone called the place a banana republic! A nice sunny banana republic mind you.

'Did George ever speak of his past wives?' asked Fiona, as tactfully as possible.

'Not in my earshot. You must know he is, or rather was married to a most beautiful woman, poor Jacqui, she must be heart broken. They were completely devoted to each other.'

'Well, thank you for your time, it has been most useful. By the way, were you on the swimming trip when Gaspard was lost?'

'I was, I was a relative novice compared with the others, like Jacqui, so the three of us stayed close to the boat under George's eye. I never saw where Gaspard went or what happened to him.'

The family joined up for lunch in the Sydney Tower where they enjoyed the amazing view of the city and its magnificent natural harbour. Fortunately, Hamish thought, Jock and Willy were too young to be permitted to do the outdoor Skywalk. Hamish hated heights.

That afternoon they went to the Maritime Museum where Willy and Jock went on an old Russian submarine to imagine they were Robert the Bruce heroically attacking London. Then an old replica sailing ship to imagine they were unjustly accused Jacobite convicts sailing to the penal colony of Australia two hundred and fifty years ago. Next, they went around the Sydney Rocks area to learn the early history of British colonisation.

William was looking puzzled. 'Mummy, when the Bastard English came, did they clear all the indigenous people off their land and out of their houses?'

'More or less Willy.'

'It was just like the Highland Clearances our people suffered at the hands of the Bastard English wasn't it?'

Willy had an unfortunately retentive memory for everything his teacher said, especially controversial opinions and language.

The following day they managed to see the dinosaur skeletons and life-like models in the Australian Museum. William could identify all the skeletons by name. Hamish and Cairistiona had an education lesson. Next was the flying foxes and sky walks at the Treetop Adventure Park with a snack lunch, followed by a visit to IFLYDOWNUNDER, where they all floated in space on a cushion of air above massive wind generators.

'I'm a wedge-tailed eagle and you're a mouse for my dinner,' announced Willy to Jock, displaying his new-found knowledge of Australian birds.

'I'm a Scottish sea-eagle, I'm bigger and stronger than you. I'm going to eat you for breakfast,' replied Jock, displaying sibling rivalry. And his bloody-minded Aberdonian birth right.

'They are both huge and very fierce eagles, but about the same size,' placated Cairistiona. 'More importantly the females of both species and bigger and stronger and fiercer than the males, so watch out!'

Willy and Jock looked at their mother with total disbelief.

Two extremely tired boys went to bed early under Fiona's watchful eye while Hamish and Cairistiona managed a quick meal in the Sydney Opera House Bennelong restaurant before a stunning performance of Cinderella by the Australian Ballet.

CHAPTER SIXTEEN

NOOSA

The next two days they drove for many hours with an overnight stop at Glen Innes, a centre of Scottish culture in northern New South Wales. Unfortunately, the annual Celtic Festival was many months ago, but they all experienced some nostalgia listening to a lone piper playing laments in the middle of the standing stones. A replica of Stonehenge.

William asked, 'if this is a Scottish town, why didn't they build a replica of the Ring of Brodgar, or the Callanish Stones, instead of Stonehenge. Did the Bastard English make the Australians do that?'

'Probably son,' responded Hamish, 'if you go to England, don't call them Bastard English all the time. You might end up in a fight!'

'Good! When I go to England, I'll go with an army of the old Highland Regiments. I'll raise the Gordon and Seaforth Highlanders, the Black Watch and the Argyll's, and we won't stop at Derby like Bonnie Prince Charlie, we will attack London! I'll put a Stewart back on the throne.'

'Me too! I'm killing Bastard English!' announced a ferocious Jock, vigorously waving a pretend claymore, leaving imaginary beheaded Sassenach bodies all around.

Cairistiona thought she might have a few words with the boys' teacher on return about anger management and peace studies, as well as gender issues.

Finally, they reached the coastal resort town of Noosa for a couple of days rest. The boys had a wonderful time playing in the turquoise blue transparent warm waters of Laguna Bay. The adults enjoyed the sea and a selection of the many beachside cafes and restaurants. Fiona and Cairistiona enjoyed the fashion boutiques lining Hastings Street: as many as possible over the two days. Unfortunately few items of clothing there were suitable for the climate in Aberdeen.

Hamish penned a couple of articles about the last two stops inspired by a couple of beers from the local Eumundi brewery.

There was still a thousand miles to their final destination. The next brief stop was at Mon Repos turtle hatchery where the boys were entranced to see turtles laying eggs.

Bright eyes asked, 'how do they know how to get back here at the same place every year?' and 'please, PLEASE, can we come back next year to see them being born?'

Overnight stops at Airlie Beach and Mission Beach with quick splashes in the patrolled beaches with more warm turquoise sea, saw them reach Cairns with three days before their flight home was due. The iPads from Bob had ensured tranquillity in the back of the car. The boys either slept, ate, watched the scenery or played with their iPads. Not just for an hour on the days when they drove for six hours. Squabbles were largely avoided. Rotating an adult in the back sitting in the middle between the boys helped. The middle seat however was not especially comfortable.

CHAPTER SEVENTEEN

CAIRNS

After breakfast, Hamish and Fiona wandered down the corridor where the senior doctors had their offices in Cairns Hospital. At the end was a sign, Dr Moore. Fiona tapped gently, no response. She knocked a little louder, no response. She opened the door and peeped in. There was a lady asleep on the desk. Her head cradled in her arms.

'Excuse me,' Fiona whispered. No response.

'Excuse me,' she said a little louder.

Dr Moore raised her head. She was pretty, she would have been a real beauty but for the tears running down her face. She had obviously been crying for a while. She also looked to have put on a lot of weight since the pictures of the group at St. Kilda.

'I'm so sorry, I've had a few problems,' she said as she wiped the tears from her eyes. 'Are you the journalists from the Cairns Gazette or from Scotland?'

'We're from Aberdeen, should we make another appointment?'

'No, no. sit down and make yourself comfortable. You wanted to know what I thought of George? Well he was a fantastic surgeon. Although hearts were his specialty, he helped me set up the renal transplant unit here. He could manage any operation, especially linking up blood vessels. The first few kidney transplants that he did here are still doing well. He was a fantastically sociable fellow. We had a few dinner parties before he left. He presented some fascinating papers to the Historical Association.'

'He arranged the conference in St Kilda. I had hoped to do some cold-water scuba diving there but the whole social program was cancelled after his death.'

'Thank you, Dr Moore,' responded Hamish. 'so, everyone thought highly of poor George?'

'Yes!'

'Did you see him on St Kilda?'

'No, I was in the ornithology group and he was in the history group. I heard he walked out to join us, but we never saw him. The fog came down so quickly, we were worried about finding our own way back. Visibility was under fifty metres.'

'Have you heard from Mrs Hamilton-Bruce?'

'No, I have sent her messages saying she is always welcome in Cairns.'

'Did George ever speak of his previous wives?'

'No, he avoided the topic, perhaps he felt guilty.'

'Why guilty?'

'Well his reputation was well-known; fidelity was not his thing. The title of seigneur suited him.'

'Why seigneur, what was the origin of that title?' asked Fiona

'No idea, just some tradition,' responded Amelia.

Hamish and Fiona both felt she was keeping something back; a feeling they had with most of their interviews. They felt obliged to obey Bob's quite reasonable terms rather than alert people to possible murder charges. Back home they would have had no hesitation in applying the verbal thumbscrews.

'Well, thank you Dr Moore, are the local journalists writing about George as well. Do we have competition?' concluded Hamish.

'No, sadly they only want to talk about our last three kidney transplant patients who all died.'

They shook hands and murmured thanks and apologies again.

As they passed the secretaries room, Fiona nodded Hamish to keep going out and went in.

'Who is Dr. Moore's secretary?'

A young coffee coloured lady in the corner, perhaps indigenous, put her hand up. 'I am, I'm Rosie.'

'Thanks, poor Dr Moore seems dreadfully upset. Perhaps she would like some tea or coffee.'

'I'll take her some coffee, thanks for telling me. It's the hospital's fault, they put so much work onto her. They won't get another nephrologist, so she is on call all the time. She is director of physician training and academic head for the students. She has had almost no holiday for two years. She got to some oddball group in Paris and then Scotland for ten days only in the last two years. She works fifteen hours every day including weekends. She is always at the end of her tether.'

'She loves scuba diving and fishing but hasn't been out in her new boat since she bought it nearly two years ago. She has nobody to talk to except me. She lives with her aging mum who has early dementia. Now the administration is blaming her for three deaths in the transplant unit! Poor Amelia, I'll get her some coffee and a nice piece of my home-made chocolate cake, would you like a piece dear?'

'Thanks, it looks yummy, Amelia is lucky to have your support.' Rosie gave her a beaming smile.

Fiona went back downstairs and found Hamish in the front hall.

'Poor girl,' said Hamish, 'sounds like working for our NHS, long hours, no support, no time off, then blamed if something goes wrong!'

'Funny though, she had a picture on her desk of herself and a lady friend scuba diving. Her secretary says it's her favourite activity, but she hasn't been out for a year and a half because she is too busy, even though she has a new boat. If she did like it and likes medical history, why did she not join the association meeting here two years ago? It was on her doorstep. Nowhere near as far as Paris or Scotland.'

Fiona phoned her brother with details of their interview with Amelia and to arrange the venue for dinner.

Later that night the five Scots sat down with Bob to detail their progress. That was when they could get a word in edgeways while the two boys regaled Uncle Bob with all the myriad of activities and sights and odd animals.

Jock asked, 'uncle Bob, is it true there are crocodiles in the sea here? Willy says they are waiting to eat me. If I had a claymore, I would kill them all!'

Bob smiled, 'its true Jock, best to swim in the motel pool or the enclosed sea pool. Mind you, if the crocs heard that you were coming with a claymore, they would all swim away in fright!'

'See!' Jock announced to his big brother.

Fiona reverted to their main problem and said, 'well I don't know if there is a villain. I don't know who it is. It could be the Seamans, or Akshay, or Rocky, or Clarissa, or Clare, or Jasmine or James Harvey. None of them quite fit the bill.'

Bob looked at her in amusement, 'Fiona, I think we should both stick to our day jobs. Tonight, please write about Cairns and a little plug for the Isa. We have the best rodeo in Australia. Tomorrow come to the Cairns police station about 9.00am and I'll have something for you to watch.'

CHAPTER EIGHTEEN

DETECTION

Fiona and Hamish sat down in front of the one-way mirror to watch brother Bob at work.

Amelia Moore and her solicitor were ushered in and sat down.

'Thank you for coming to talk to us Dr Moore, we all know how busy you are. My name is Detective Sergeant McIntosh, this is my senior colleague, Detective Inspector Barnaby.'

'I have taken the liberty of asking your solicitor, Anne Francis, to sit in on this as she may be needed as your representative in next month's coronial enquiry into the deaths in the renal transplant unit.'

'Thank you, Sergeant, I doubt if I will need a solicitor for a routine coroner's enquiry. The deaths were unfortunate, most unfortunate. However, these things happen at the advancing frontier of medicine in an era of increasing antibiotic resistance. Antibiotics should be controlled by medical people only, not given to animals to make them fatter for the benefit of greedy business types. All three men died of Klebsiella septicaemia. The bacteria were resistant even to colistin. The deaths need an inquest, but there was no evidence of less than the highest level of care from the medical, surgical and nursing staff.'

'Dr Moore, first may I ask you about the past history of sexually transmitted disease. All those three men had documented past infection with gonorrhoea, and one had previous syphilis. Would that have increased their risk of Klebsiella or other infection?'

'No, those sexually transmitted infections would have been cured long ago.'

'How would those infections have been acquired?'

'Well, sergeant, you don't look as though you came down in the last shower. They all would have been having sex with an infected person, illicit sex.'

'Dr Moore, we have spoken to their wives or partners at the time of infection. Apparently, they all had been unfaithful, two in local brothels and one with a series of other women. Two ended up divorced, and one had some sort of rapprochement.'

'So, there you are sergeant, you managed to work it out. Well done! They were just your average promiscuous male. They got what they deserved.'

'Dr Moore, do you mean they deserved a sexually transmitted disease and divorce, or to die of a different infection.'

'That's a silly question sergeant.'

'Dr Moore, I understand you live with your ageing mother?'

'Correct. My poor mum has early dementia.'

'And Dr Moore, I understand your father died some years ago, but that you were estranged from him from when you left home to go to university?'

'Correct, he was a violent bastard, he abused my mother and me. I hated him!'

'OK, Dr Moore, let us change direction. You are the treasurer of the Global Association of Medical Historians, yes?'

'Correct, though I may have to resign that position as I don't have time for that or indeed this interview, the purpose of which bemuses me.'

'So, Dr Moore, two years ago, Dr Gaspard Barbeau, then association president disappeared while scuba diving not far from here at Hardy's Reef.'

'So, I understand. I did not attend that conference as my workload is too heavy.'

'Yet you had time to attend the conferences in Paris and St Kilda?'

'Correct, I finally persuaded the hospital bean counters to arrange a locum for the last two meetings.'

'Dr Moore, you had clinics and dialysis sessions to attend every day during that conference here including the day when Dr Barbeau died?'

Amelia looked at her watch and yawned, 'correct.'

'And yet, Dr Moore, when I look up the clinic bookings for that day, I find you had cancelled all the patients?'

'Oh, I can't remember that, I probably had a sick day, you know 'flu or perhaps women's problems. We have a lot to deal with you know, or you probably wouldn't as a mere male.'

Anne Francis frowned; she was getting an inkling of where this was going.

'OK Dr Moore am I correct that you owned a Cobalt 323 twin engine cruiser two years ago at the time of the conference. A white speed boat with a big blue stripe down the side?'

'Of course, sergeant, even a novice policeman could look up the Queensland boat registrations!'

'But you do not own it now?'

'No, I have a Bayliner 285 SB as you would also know from the registrations.'

'You got rid of the Cobalt and purchased a Bayliner just after the conference?'

'Some time a year or two ago, I can look up my records for you if it would help your bizarre questions.'

'Dr Moore, what happened to the Cobalt, it is no longer registered in Queensland.'

'I sold it to a man who took it away on his trailer. I think he was from the Northern Territory. Check the register there if you want to find it.'

'Dr Moore, do you know the NT does not have a state government boat registry?'

'No, why should I, backward place, probably run by men!'

'Do you remember his name?'

'Yes, he introduced himself as Bob.'

'Bob who?'

THE ISLANDS OF DEATH

'Just Bob.'

'Did he pay you by cheque or bank transfer?'

'No, he pulled out this huge wad of hundred-dollar bills and paid cash, two hundred thousand dollars. Probably a drug runner or brothel owner.'

'Did you pay that into your bank or something?'

'No, I kept it in my safe to buy a smaller boat, the Bayliner.'

'Yet your bank records showed you had a bank loan to buy that and it is not yet paid off.'

'Oh, is that right, I must have spent that on something else.'

'OK, Dr Moore, a different scenario. The terrible day in Paris when Mustafa Mohammed was shot. Do you recall where you were?'

'I was with the conference.'

'Can I show you this picture from the CCTV taken just before the shooting. All the committee members are sitting with Mustafa except you. The conference records show you were not presenting, nor chairing a meeting that day. Do you remember what you were doing that day?'

'That was a year ago, I may have been in the audience for one of the talks.'

'Tell us about it.'

'Well I remember George talking about surgery during the crusades or something. If I had no duties that day, I may have gone shopping. Inspector, what woman would not want to go shopping in Paris?'

'Yet, Dr Moore, your credit card does not show any purchases that day. Your mobile phone appears to have been turned off as we find no calls made or received that day.'

'Well there you are, sergeant, I must have been in the meeting with my phone turned off. Obviously, we are all required to turn our mobiles off, or at least to silent mode during presentations.'

'Dr Moore, on the day on St Kilda when George fell to his death, where were you?'

'I was with the ornithology group. It was fascinating, we saw gannets and puffins and skuas and lots more, until that fog came down.'

'Did you see George?'

'No, I was told he was with the history group.'

'Dr Moore, do you possess a motor-bike?'

'Yes, it's easier for a single person to get around the city. I don't need a big gas-guzzling European car to demonstrate my importance. I am not a high and mighty surgeon with a personal registration plate. Global warming will ruin our beautiful barrier reef. Every citizen in the world should be reducing their carbon emissions.'

'Dr Moore, am I correct that you are a member of the Cairns gun club and a member of the pistol shooting team, one of the best shots in the team?'

'Yes, a girl has to look after herself these days. These days the streets of once-sleepy Cairns are full of aggressive males high on ice and alcohol. It is not safe at nights for a single woman. And I have my mother to protect from home invasions.'

'You know Hitler's male doctor fed him on testosterone and cocaine. You men were responsible for fifty-million deaths in the second world war!'

'Dr Moore, can I take you back a few years when you helped to establish the renal transplant unit here, a most worthy achievement if I may say. The people of Cairns are most grateful to you.'

'Yes, thank you.'

'I understand that George came here for a few weeks to assist. He even did a few transplants?'

'Correct.'

'The City records show he stayed in the Shangri-La Hotel.'

'It's possible, its popular with vastly wealthy visitors.'

'And you went there to his suite to make arrangements for the opening of the unit?'

'Yes.'

'And Dr Moore, that is where he raped you for the first time?'

Amelia's poised honest demeanour suddenly collapsed. The assured confidential professional image disappeared. Her head went down on the table cradled in her arms and she started sobbing. 'Yes, yes.'

Anne Francis stood up, 'I demand some time alone with my client. Stop this interview now!'

'No,' said Amelia, 'we may as well keep going.'

'Have a glass of water, tell me when you are ready to continue.' consoled Bob.

'OK,' sobbed Amelia.

'Were you sexually abused by your father?'

'Yes,' sobbed Amelia.

'So, George, brilliant surgeon George was a promiscuous sometimes violent man?'

'Yes, I couldn't believe it. Once we had solved a few problems in the unit he gave me some wine and started taking my clothes off. I could not believe it. I was quite bewildered. Here was an eminent married surgeon about to screw me. I was so dumbfounded I did not resist. He thought I was compliant and that I enjoyed the privilege of being screwed by an eminent man. Lucky me!'

'The men who became president were known as seigneur?'

'Yes.'

'Is that from the French term *'droit de seigneur'*?'

'Yes.'

'Tell me how that worked?'

'The committee was like a medieval men's club. They believed that the president could have sex with the other members' wives or any female on the committee. I was once an attractive young woman, would you believe. They preyed on me. Gaspard, Mustafa and George came to my room on many occasions after the first time with George when we had gatherings of the committee. They took it in turn to have sex with me. Sometimes two at once, if you understand me.'

'If I had gone to the police, would you have believed me for one moment. A little small-town female nephrologist against three of the best known highly regarded male doctors in the world. My father was a violent man. He bashed my mother and sexually abused me. My childhood innocence taken by a rapist who was supposed to protect me. I vowed it would never happen again, but it did. I swore revenge!'

'Did you kill Gaspard?'

'Yes'

'Did you kill Mustafa?'

'Yes.'

'Did you kill George?'

'Yes.'

'That was your boat at Hardy's Reef?'

'Yes, the day before I messaged Gaspard. I told him he could come on board for a quick screw. I stuck a knife in his heart while I was on top of him. Then I went out to sea and tossed his body into a pack of sharks. I weighed his wet suit down with his oxygen cylinders and threw that overboard. Although I scrubbed the boat to get rid of the blood, I was aware that forensics could find small residual traces of blood, so later I towed the Cobalt into deep water with my new boat and sank it.'

'And Mustafa? Let me tell you how you shot him Dr Moore.'

'You stole a bike, got a recording of a male shouting Allahu Akbar, stole a pistol, and shot him. Then you rode to the Gare de Lyon, left the bike there and got the Metro back to town in time for the last lecture, though that had been cancelled. The pistol went into a river and you burnt the black clothes and balaclava?'

'Yes, all correct.'

'Then you surprisingly bumped into George near the top of Conachair on St Kilda. He had lost his sense of direction in the fog. It was easy to lead him the wrong way and push him over. Then you caught up with the group and nobody had any idea.'

'Yes.'

'And the three transplant patients, they were unfaithful evil men who deserved to die. You injected them with a culture of Klebsiella taken from the pathology laboratory.'

'Yes.'

'Dr Moore, I arrest you for the murder of the six men, the murders to which you have confessed. Anything else you say may be taken down and used in evidence against you.'

Dr Moore looked surprised. 'Why sergeant. I imposed punishment for crimes just like you do. I exacted justice for violation of my body by three of them and infidelity in marriage for all six. I merely jettisoned the detritus of society. You should be grateful. You know that is what appealed to me about nephrology. The kidneys remove the impurities. I see myself as society's dialysis machine. I have removed the impurities.'

'If we had lived in the country in which Mustafa was born the state would have done the job for me. Beheading or stoning for adultery for all six men. I was just filling in for a weak legal system. The Free Church of Scotland would have condemned George to burn in hell for eternity as a fornicator and an adulterer. I just gave him a nudge in that direction. You should be grateful that I eliminated some undesirable male specimens from the earth.'

Bob, Anne Francis and DI Barnaby all thought she had a point. A guilty plea and mitigating circumstances might reduce her sentence. The psychiatrists would need to check her sanity first. She appeared not to be entirely of sound mind, even though she managed the renal unit with considerable skill and dedication.

CHAPTER NINETEEN

D I Barnaby looked at Bob after Amelia had been removed to the cells in handcuffs.

'That was a brilliant piece of detective work and a dazzlingly clever interrogation Bob. You had done a lot of investigation beforehand. Wow, the information you hit her with was extremely thorough. You caught her not telling the truth three times, softened her up a bit, then when you hit her with the big question, the one I suspect you didn't know for sure, the one with a huge amount of emotional baggage for her, she crumbled.'

Bob smiled modestly, 'no I did not know for sure, but it was a pretty good guess.'

'We were both in on the original investigation of Gaspard Barbeau's disappearance two years ago. Why did you investigate that again?' Barnaby asked.

'Let me introduce you to two people to answer your question, come with me,' replied Bob

They went to the observation room.

'This is my boss DI Barnaby, boss this is my sister Fiona and her associate, Hamish McGrath from Aberdeen. Both journalists with their Aberdeen Times. A couple of months ago, she said she was coming here to investigate the life's work of a man who died in Scotland. George Hamilton-Bruce. I looked that up and found that he, like Barbeau had been president of the Global Association of Medical Historians. Then I found that a third one, Mustafa Mohammed had been assassinated in Paris a year ago.'

'Hamish and I both on hearing that immediately recalled a bit in Ian Fleming's book Dr No, when Auric Goldfinger said, *"Once is happenstance. Twice is coincidence. The third time it's enemy action."*

'Hamish and Fiona came here to file reports in the Aberdeen Times, in the travel section as well as a report on George. Hamish and Fiona also suspected there was a connection between the three deaths. If there was a perpetrator it was most likely to be someone in Australia once they have excluded a few Europeans. I had to drag it out of them that they were going to investigate a murder in my cabbage patch. Naughty, naughty. Once over that we pooled resources most effectively.'

'Their interviews with men about George appeared to reveal a brilliant faultless enormously popular modest surgeon, a fantastically wealthy 'A-lister'. On the other hand, three women described him as a sexual predator, not above using his status to coerce women into his bed. They said the president was known as the 'seigneur', an odd title. None would tell or knew where that came from. My first thought was from the movie 'Braveheart' in which the English imposed the 'droit de seigneur' on the Scots. The right to the first night with a new bride before the husband slept with his betrothed. Prima nocte.'

'Could that be what the presidents did? Were they all sexual predators? That could create many men or women with motives to kill all three. I thought about your list of people who had been to three conferences. Nobody had been to all three, been scuba diving on Hardy's Reef, walking with the ornithology group on St Kilda and was missing from the photo at the Paris café where Mustafa was shot. I thought about Dr Clare Jones telling Fiona and Hamish about the other boat that was seen nearby. About someone boarding the other boat. I thought about the picture you said was on Amelia's desk and that she was living close to the Queensland conference site. That was the critical piece of information that pointed me in the right direction, thanks little sister.'

'I checked to see if she had a boat on the register. I found she had a Cobalt 323, a big white twin engine speedboat with a blue stripe down it at the time of the conference diving trip. I found she had got rid of it somehow shortly after and replaced it. I checked the guns register and found she had a pistol licence. I phoned the gun club and found she was an expert on the club first team. A dead shot. It's all falling into place. I checked her bank accounts and found she had taken a loan for the replacement boat but had nothing paid in for the Cobalt 323. I went to the hospital and checked the clinic lists. She had cancelled her bookings on the day of the diving event. I checked her vehicle registration and found a motor bike.'

'The rape was a guess.' Bob finished explaining

'Brilliant Bob, I shall sign and support your application for the detective inspectors job in Mt Isa.'

Hamish looked at his watch, it was 10am, midnight in Aberdeen.

'Come on Fiona, we have work to do, see you at lunch Bob!' Back in their unit, Fiona started typing, while Hamish phoned Archie.

'Hold the press, we have it all, a murderer, details of how three men died, details of rape and sexual predators in the medical society. We have it all. It will be with you inside thirty minutes.'

Fiona had been creating a draft report as they progressed around Australia. Ten minutes was sufficient to add all the new developments.

Bob joined them over a glass of champagne.

'I phoned Justine Barbeau and told her that her husband had been killed on the day of the dive. I said his body had been buried at sea. That sounded better than being thrown into a pack of sharks!'

'I told her it was a revenge killing by a female. She said, was it Clarissa, so I said no. Then she said was it Amelia, so I said yes. She said she was not surprised. Although she loved her husband dearly and he was a brilliant doctor, he seemed to have the same attitude to women as the current national French president. And most of his predecessors. A few women on the side, possibly with 'gentle' coercion was OK by him.'

'Then I phoned Jasmine and told her that Mustafa's death was not a terrorist assassination. She immediately asked was it Amelia. She said her husband was fairly westernised but still had a penchant for polygamy from his native culture. Somehow, she got the impression that he had wronged Amelia. So, no surprise there.'

'I tried Jacqui's number in Sydney, but there was no answer.'

Hamish laughed, 'don't worry, I'll find her.'

He rang Dr Rockingham's number in Aberdeen.

'Is Jacqui there please?'

'There's no Jacqui here you must have the wrong number. Do you know what the time is, you bloody idiot!

'Settle down Rocky, this is Hamish McGrath from the Aberdeen Times. Jacqui Hamilton-Bruce had stayed with you the night before we had an interview a few months ago. In case you don't remember, she was the beautiful blonde lady in your bed overnight with the yellow Lamborghini. We know who killed her husband. Could I speak to her please?'

Some mumblings followed for a few moments, then a sleepy female voice said, 'yes.'

'Mrs Hamilton-Bruce, I am Hamish McGrath from The Aberdeen Times. I am sorry to break this news to you. The police in Queensland have been trying to contact you. I am sorry to say that a person in Australia has confessed to the murder of your husband and also Mustafa Mohammed and Gaspard Barbeau.'

'Was it Clarissa?'

'No.'

'Then it was Amelia?'

'Yes. She has admitted to pushing him off Conachair.'

'I am not surprised. She hated him. I suspect it was a revenge killing and she had good reason. Please don't ring here for me again. I am only here on the rare occasions when Rocky's wife is away. We were all lucky with your timing of this call!'

'Yes.'

'Thank you, Hamish and good night.'

Once Hamish finished that call his phone rang.

'Hello, Hamish, this is Archie. I have some news you may like. Your article, yours and Fiona's is front page news here. Papers in London, Paris, Manchester, Berlin and Tehran have run it with our title along with theirs on page one. It will be front page in most Australian papers in a few hours. We are publishing before the television news has heard the story. It has various headings.

Doctors' society a cover for sex orgies

Droit de seigneur leads to murders of three doctors

Brilliant Scottish journalists uncover sex killings of eminent doctors

'I think we will have at least ten to twenty million front pages world-wide. Also, I have arranged a publisher for your book. You must have it ready for proof reading within one month. You have pre-sale orders of five million copies. As a result of that I have already three million pounds in the paper account to be split a million each at this stage with probably more to come. Much more. I will transfer the money into your accounts when the banks open.'

'Congratulations on your efforts. I look forward to sharing a wee dram of GlenDronach President's whisky with you.'

Hamish awoke Fiona the next morning. 'Fiona, we are staying here a little longer. I have booked the three-bedroom luxury penthouse on Hayman Island for four days including a scuba diving trip to Hardy's reef. Bob is joining us with his fiancé. He did not tell us about that, but she answered the phone! They got engaged yesterday after his successful interview and promotion. The boys don't mind staying here a little longer as you may imagine! Did you see the Cairngorms had the first snowfall of winter yesterday?'

'And by the way, I have upgraded our return flight to Scotland to first class. Is that OK with you?'

'And Fiona, I hope you feel happy with your apprenticeship. I hope my news will not upset you. I hope you feel you have learnt something, maybe enough, about crime writing from me. I have been offered positions as chief crime writer with papers in Sydney and Melbourne. The boys asked for Sydney as it is warmer and has more proper club and international football. We have downloaded migration papers and are giving it incredibly serious thought. I hope you don't think I am deserting you.'

'Well Hamish McGrath, you don't get rid of me that easily. Bad luck. I have been offered a position as crime writer in Brisbane! Like you

I have downloaded a migration application form and I too am thinking about it seriously. You can send the boys to Aunty Fiona for holidays in sunny Noosa!'

'And Hamish, what a fabulous apprenticeship you gave me, the impossible unsuspected cold case we cracked so brilliantly, well with a little help from my brother, the places and things we have seen. A best-selling book! Awesome. Amazing. Beautiful. Fascinating. I need you to put in a good word for me now with e-litefingers Mac! Now I will only visit Aberdeen in their so-called summer to catch up with family.'

'I hope Hayman has some deliciously smooth single malts!'

BOOK TWO

THE ORKNEY ISLES

....

George Mackay Brown. From 'The Dwarfie Stane'

The hermit and one lonely star
The hermit and the bountiful sun – the moon masks -
The hermit and the snowflakes
All created lights to lighten the soul
The road from birth to death
Yet the soul must dwell in its darksome house of mortal clay
The better to understand the light of the first world

CHAPTER ONE

Douglas bubbled internally with excitement while strapped into his airbus window seat. His trained poker face did not reveal his innermost feelings. A long career of unspeakable tragedy alternating with outstanding success had taught him not to betray his own emotions overtly. His role was always to support others dealing with their own overwhelming sentiments, be it joy in overcoming adversity, with grateful relief, always thanks only to god, or with grief beyond words when there must be a doctor to be unfairly blamed. No one considered for a moment how a doctor felt. Life taught him to be an internaliser.

After many years of fascination and captivating study he was about to land at Kirkwall Airport in the Orkney Islands. The bleak windswept ruggedly beautiful historic islands to the north of the Scottish mainland: forgotten jewels of British history and scenery. Once home perhaps of King Arthur. Once home of the ancestors of William the Conqueror. His first visit: Doug was aware that preconceived images of new places usually turned out to be fallacious. It would be an absorbing exploration and experience.

The islands were home to a close-knit community accustomed to tragedy but with the inner strength to start again. And again. Like the story of Robert the Bruce's spider. Climbing up and falling. Again, and again until final success. Orcadians claimed that story for one of their remote caves.

Home to the legendary Norse Earls of Orkney and their womenfolk described in the Orkneyinga Saga. Men and women untroubled by fratricide or matricide to satisfy greed or lust. Power and gold beat kinship. Animals obeying the law of the primal Orcadian jungle. Where Hell and Purgatory were actual place names on the map: names of irony designed to offend the self-proclaimed righteous. Had there been offender-activists a thousand years ago?

The Orkneys according to legend were once the home of mermaids, wizards and seal-folk, the predecessors of the little-folk and then humans. In a land where the countryside holds its memories closely the little folk are thought to live on in the mounds and tumuli way from the bright lights of the towns. Orcadians are careful not to offend them for fear of ill-fortune.

Such stories are children's rubbish in town on bright sunny days. But myths inexplicably develop an alarming aura of plausibility out in the lonely wilderness. Shapes moving close by in the swirling mist on dark and stormy nights could be anything. Shapes from today or perhaps from yesterday. Shapes of living men and animals or the undead.

Doug had just finished reading that Orkneyinga Saga on the plane. A blood-thirsty tale of the Viking overlords of the Orkneys a thousand years ago. A blood thirst not apparently diminished by the conversion back to the Pictish Christianity in that time, the conversion, not always a gentle intellectual persuasion. Jarl Sigurd, held at sword point with his son by King Olaus, could see that Christ trumped Odin when the blade was then held to his son's throat.

Many grisly events were commemorated in original verse. Runes of Viking culture; runes of Viking violence. A paradox today, one and the same thing a millennium ago. Doug was happy to believe that those times were just fascinating memories swirling around the ruins of past days. Memories of gruesome murders, but not for today. Memories awaiting his arrival. None of the undead mentioned in social media lurking at night in dark corners of ancient ruins seeking vengeance. No thank you.

Doug read of one Ragnhild, the daughter of Eric-Bloodaxe, who married Arnfinn, the first son of Earl Thorfinn. She didn't like him as much as the second son, Harvard the fecund, so she arranged Arnfinn's death and married Harvard. Perhaps she liked the fecund bit. Anyway, Harvard turned out to be a bit of a dud too. She persuaded a nephew to kill Harvard with a promise of marriage, but had that poor fellow murdered by another nephew before finally marrying Arfinn's third brother, Ljot.

A dark age Norse female praying mantis devouring the unwanted males after sex. Not more to her than grubs before a medieval insect spray. Hopefully Ljot was more fecund than Harvard. Hope he had a lot.

Some Earls co-existed, others fought though closely related. When Earl Thorfinn and his nephew Earl Rognald Brusason met in battle, a poet wrote *'Ill-fortune followed when the Earls fought, many a hard lesson learned, many a life lost: when the spear shower fell.'*

As Earl Rognald wrote, *'many a bond broken by the best-born of men.'* Treaties broken with dark treachery was standard behaviour. Friendships broken by unexpected attacks and murders in the dark. Life was cheap in the Orkney Viking's cut-throat world.

Orkney was also home to Thorfinn Skull Splitter Ale, the appropriately dubbed rich malty, chocolaty powerful beer named after the seventh Viking Earl of Orkneyjar. Eight and a half percent alcohol, yet a deceptively light taste of exotic spices the label claimed. Thorfinn, who became earl when his two elder brothers met with 'misfortune' on the battlefield: by splitting skulls, not by eating crustless cucumber sandwiches at tea-time with his pinkie extended.

Home to the smooth peaty honeyed single malt whiskies of Highland Park and Scapa. He had read of the recent release of the Norse God or Valhalla series of Highland Park whiskies, Thor, Loki, Freya and Odin. Apparently, they cost around two hundred pounds a bottle. Perhaps he could have a wee dram to taste. Maybe the Freya, Norse goddess of love would be appropriate.

Home to Earl Ragnvald, perhaps son of Ragnar Lodbrok, hero of the TV series, 'Vikings.' Ragnvald and his wife Ragnhild were parents of Hrolf, a man so big, no horse could carry him. Hrolf who conquered Normandy and fathered the line of the Dukes of Normandy. He was the great-great-great grandfather of William the Bastard and the tyrannical

Norman line of English Kings. The original home therefore of medieval English history.

So many pleasures in store for the month.

Orkney was also once the cherished home of the mighty Royal Navy, sadly Scapa Flow was now just another memory. And a timeless centre of courageous and highly skilled fishermen and of delicious platters from the bountiful ocean. The treacherous sea was, however, a demanding mistress, sometimes reluctant to yield its abundance. Huge waves pounded ships and shore alike. Howling winds tore apart homes and vessels if not well crafted and handled. The Orkney Sea-Gods demanded a blood sacrifice every now and then in return for sustaining the populace.

Orkney also looked to the future: a Janus island. North Sea oil in the later decades of the twentieth century had greatly increased the local economy. Surprisingly or perhaps not, it is not a backward technological culture either. Orkney was the leading centre in the world for tidal generators, home to two-thirds of the global tidal energy producers. The European Marine Energy Centre had been established in Orkney back in 2003. The isles were now a net exporter of electricity.

Home to men and women for nearly seven thousand years. The site of buildings older than the Egyptian pyramids. Maybe not as grand. Certainly not as well known. No informative hieroglyphics. The site of ringstones at Brodgar and the village at Skara Brae. The location of the ancient tomb at Maeshowe and of the six-thousand-year old stone house of the Knap of Howar on the little island of Papa Westray.

What ceremonies had occurred there. Rituals happening thousands of years before the documentation of the Viking era. Fertility rites? Symbolic deflowering of virgins? Human sacrifice? Beltane festivals? If only the stones could reveal their secret memoirs. So many mystic sites to ponder.

How did those ancestors live and survive? What food did they eat find? How did they keep warm through the long dark cold winters? How did they manage to raise thirty-ton slabs of stone in their constructions? Thirty tons! What happened to their society that apparently made them leave the Orkneys four thousand years ago? What happened that they apparently left the place deserted for a millennium and then returned?

Douglas had arranged a whole month to flavour all these and the ancient mysticism of the isles. A month of combined conference and sabbatical leave. A spirituality so well encapsulated in the poems of George Mackay Brown. Mysticism that perhaps included the origin of the legends of King Arthur and his knights of the round table.

And a month in which he would be unfaithful for the first time after over twenty years marriage. He had that tingly genital sensation of anticipation, the one he felt all those years ago when his wife agreed to go to bed with him for the first time a few months before their marriage. Perhaps there was a lingering influence of Sir Lancelot and his illicit pleasures with Guinevere in the Orkneys. Perhaps like Orcadian men in the past, he could have a human wife, his one in London, and a mermaid or fairy wife, the one for tonight in Orkney.

Sadly, the airline hostess was totally unimpressed to hear he was staying for a month. She muttered something quite hostile about bloody tourists. No apology for splashing his glass of wine on his trousers.

Doug had been reading 'the Orcadian' online for a couple of weeks. Brexit and new expensive Spanish visas had seen the advent of unwanted holiday makers from south of the border arriving in increasingly large numbers. 'Costa del no sun' or Costa del rain' they referred derogatorily to it. Still they came. Drunken supporters of London and Lancastrian football teams battled continental counterparts at the sea front in Kirkwall.

Orkneyinga brutality had returned. Heavily tattooed thugs redolent of the Vikings. England versus Germany. England versus France. England versus Holland. Manchester versus Munich. Chelsea versus Arsenal if the continentals stayed away. Any mob of equally intoxicated idiots. Hatefun events prearranged on social media with ubiquitous brain-dead adolescent screens for the current post-goodwill, post-civility generation.

Attitude, preferably backed by aggression, was the new knowledge, the new courtesy. The odd death or critical injury enhanced the subsequent drunken boasting in the harbour pubs.

Only rarely was it England versus the Scots. The locals stayed away in the English holiday season. Caution and common sense. The newly independent Scotland remained in the EU and Scots preferred to visit the Mediterranean.

The legalisation of cannabis by young 'trendies' in some English city councils had increased the number of violent psychotic schizoid youth arriving in Kirkwall. The 'trendies' of course were too busy having congratulatory selfies for their superior sophistication and wisdom to read the evidence based scientific medical press detailing increased driving fatalities and admissions to emergency and psychiatric departments.

Bloodstained glass fragments were strewn over the foreshore many nights of the week. Every ambulance in Kirkwall was there to treat ungrateful victims of violence. Even though Kirkwall's new forty-eight bed hospital had only been open a year or two, it was under-resourced in typical British NHS style. The inside story of Kirkwall hospital was whispered discretely around UK clinical units.

A very different version from the smug congratulatory statements issued by the ministry spokespersons. Carefully selected data. Numbers that sounded like outstanding progress. Bureaucrats who had been in the front entrance and the offices but eschewed the wards and clinicians for fear of public contradiction before the media and their cameras.

There was only staff and equipment to open thirty-three beds at the maximum. The administration office on the other hand had so many staff that they had moved into one of the empty wards. Long coffee breaks between drawing up documents of strategic strategies. Networking, teamwork, equal opportunities, gender equity, racial equity, climate change and clinical decision making by non-experts filled their time. Origami for the next meeting's data-free agenda. Origami for snail-mail. Communication by email to the next office substituted for face-to-face encounters.

An under-staffed emergency department meanwhile struggled to deal with so many injuries. With so many offensive and aggressive still inebriated patients high on ice and alcohol. Few had been vaccinated against tetanus, or indeed against any of the optional infectious diseases now becoming commonplace again. Thanks to the trendy anti-bigpharma pseudo-intellectuals, diseases like measles and whooping cough with inevitable deaths had become as frequent again as they were a century ago.

The forty-eight beds squeezed into two-thirds of the wards were soon full of intoxicated hooligans, significant head injuries and other trauma. Violent pack rapes of young women foolish enough to come here. The modern fashion for tattoos amazed the medical profession. Significant doses of heavy metals, toxic colouring chemicals banned from food, and dangerous bugs in tattoo ink.

Medical and nursing staff worked extra unpaid shifts, often eighteen hours a day. Administration were gone by 4.30 pm every day. Senior specialist staff took over organisation after hours. It was the easier part of their job compared with clinical management.

The new CAT scanner was able to triage the head injuries and the ones with cerebral haemorrhages were flown as soon as possible to the neurosurgical unit in Aberdeen. Pilots risked life and limb in appalling weather for the ungrateful. The ungrateful who wanted to get back immediately for the next street brawl. It was hard to distinguish the brain-damaged from the new normal.

Unappreciative patients and their despicable friends usurped the children's play area for cigarettes, illicit drugs, more alcohol and even unashamed sex in public. Disgusted hospital staff noted that gender discovery was sometimes a surprise but rarely inhibiting. The area was searched twice daily for discarded needles and more broken bottles. Children were kept safely locked in their ward. The treatment and storerooms on the wards and the hospital pharmacy were fitted with stronger locks. Visitors stole meals from the trays of the few elderly patients left in the hospital, but unable to fend for themselves. The visitors complained then about the quality of hospital food.

The more elderly residents with chronic degenerative diseases waited too many hours to have their strokes and heart attacks treated. Death, pain and organ damage occurred when urgent standard protocols could not be implemented in a timely fashion for Orkney's old and sick. Golden hours were often lost.

Dialysis machines were reallocated to young people with renal failure from toxic, so-called recreational drugs. Young people who paid good money to swallow unidentifiable but dreadfully poisonous unlabelled white tablets from shonky dealers in the post common-sense era. Cuckoo for intellect. Cuckoo for usurping another's nest in the dialysis unit. They expected the already overworked hospital pathology department to test their recreational drugs free on the NHS. Doug was not surprised to read research showing a childhood of screens and social media impaired frontal lobe neurological development and self-control.

Doug could remember an era when strongly held views were supported by debate not violence. When druggies were spaced out gentle people. When feminism and religion encouraged peace not aggression. When environmental greenies opposed war not starting one of their own. The last half century had been a great place to live till now.

Police and hospital staff were spat upon and punched in return for good natured professional care and unbelievable restraint. God's angels, the nursing staff, ironically claimed the same motto as the Hell's Angels bikie gang. The good we do is forgotten, or attributed to God, the wrong we do is remembered.

Violence was the standard anger management approach. Complaints about police brutality and incompetent hospital staff appeared frequently on social media. Occasionally the comments had correct spelling and reasonably correct grammar. Occasionally there were no expletives. Gratitude was lost from the post-civility world of youth, a world of hatred. A world where some thought love and justice was promoted by hate and violence. A world where most didn't think.

Very, very occasionally they were valid complaints. All complaints about the doctors and nurses, however, were received joyfully by administration. Although usually vexatious and erroneous, it gave administration a cheap shot at those with much better qualifications and skills.

Spray-painted graffiti defiled the ancient stones of Brodgar and Skara Brae. Maeshowe stank after a visit by defaecating youths. A close colleague of Doug's air hostess had been raped and bashed in the airport car park by two balaclava-wearing unidentified tourists after her late shift only two weeks before. A similar episode had occurred six months previously. Recently installed CCTV had not provided protection. The under resourced and over stretched police force did their best to maintain law and order. The once important and welcome tourist industry had seriously palled in the eyes of the Orcadians.

Douglas banished his gloomy thoughts and peered out of the window at the grey heaving sea as the bleak green coastline came into view. An emerald haven in an unforgiving sea. He had a brief glimpse of the grey granite buildings of Kirkwall through the low rain clouds before the plane touched down tugged sideways by a strong crosswind then came to a reassuring halt.

Here in Kirkwall were the docks where King Magnus Barefoot disembarked ten centuries ago to found the city and install his son Sigurd as King of Kirkwall. Here were the docks where Sigurd later departed for Norway and then east to Istanbul and the Holy Land, becoming fabulously wealthy. Doug reflected sadly that his travels only left him poorer.

Here was the St Magnus Cathedral built nearly nine hundred years earlier. A glorious building with massive red and yellow sandstone pillars. A change from English granite. Home not just to church attenders, but the Kirkwall centre of music and culture, habitat for flower arrangements and even agnostic meditation. A place where an Orcadian could sing or pray or just sit in exactly the same spot as his ancestors did nearly a millennium ago. A site where he would feel their presence.

Apparently, it now leans a little at one end, Doug looked forward to seeing that. The cathedral was dedicated to the pious Jarl Magnus Erlendsson, Earl of Orkney, who was murdered by a rival. Magnus who preferred to sing psalms rather than fight in the Battle of the Menai Straits. Unbloody Viking like! He would not be a football fan today. When he was murdered, his mortal remains were placed over the altar in St Olaf's Kirk.

They soon became a site for pilgrimages and miracles. The blind regained sight, the cripples walked, the lepers were restored to health.

Beatification followed. The remains of Magnus were later transferred to the cathedral.

Here was the Bishop's Palace, now a ruin, once the home of Jarl Rognald, nephew to St Magnus. Rognald promised to build a cathedral dedicated to Magnus. It took eight-years to build and remains today almost unchanged still in service in the middle of Kirkwall.

Was it only imagination that could see time as a concertina that could merge and separate? Some days' time seemed to be the only dimension that separated Doug and other tourists in the city of today from that of Magnus Barefoot and Sigurd, from St Magus and Rognald. Some days it felt that dimension shrank to nothing. Chapters of the history book blown backwards and forwards through the sands of different ages. Some stormy nights in Kirkwall today one could hear the wind howling across the harbour and shrieking through the rigging of the Viking longboats. Or the screeching of Valkyries with their body armour and swans' feather wings escorting the fallen warriors to Valhalla after a heroic death, sword in hand, on the battlefield.

The town remains full of character and other ancient buildings. The court and castle upheld the law. Laws developed from the old Norse 'bjarkoyrett' governed trade, shipping and marketing, as well as the rights of the inhabitants both permanent and temporary. Laws enforced by the 'gjaldkeri', twelve major landowners led by one of the leading nobles, to administer the town. Old ways and traditions were still seen as important in Orkney.

Even the library was old, having provided continuous community service since being founded back in 1683. Thanks to an Evan MacGillivray, it now had archives, a family book service for the outer islands and a mobile library for the mainland. A book in the hand was worth two on the kindle here. MacGillivray, born in 1908, rose during the second world war to command a ship during the D-Day landings. The ghosts of the Viking longship warriors sailing beside him.

He also established the museums of Tankerness House and Corrigal Farm, and organised conferences of the Orcadian archaeology and history. So much history and such pride in the Orkneys to ensure it was not forgotten.

Doug thoughts returned reluctantly to the twenty-first century. It should be a pleasant stay in the Orkney summer. Perhaps he would hear the lark ascending and smell the honey-scented white blooms of the Parnassus grass on the warm breeze. Perhaps he would hear the waves lapping on the beach rather than winter storms pounding on the rocks. Certainly, he expected he would enjoy some extra-marital sex for the first time.

He collected his suitcase from the carousel and his hire car. He exchanged a few words with car hire assistant of his plans to visit all the ruins before heading to his hotel, the Ring of Brodgar Lodge.

The verges and adjacent fields were full of Orkney's colourful summer wildflowers. The uniquely Scottish primrose with purple petals and yellow centre. The grass of Parnassus with white petals streaked with purple veins and a yellow centre. Pinks thrifts and the purple and white heath spotted orchid. White eyebrights with yellow centres. Doug stopped to collect a mixed posy. Scottish wildflowers for Carolyn, his wild Scottish flower.

On checking in he discovered he was in room twelve. It overlooked the standing stones of the Ring of Brodgar. Wonderful. He texted his wife, Susan, to say, 'arrived safely.' He sent a text to Carolyn on his spare phone. One he proposed to use only for next week before discarding it. It read '12'. Nothing more.

CHAPTER TWO

Doug and Carolyn had met at work six months previously. Their professional association had been highly competent and appropriate until two weeks ago when she had slipped on some undesirable body fluids in a dimly lit ward at night to land in his arms as he grabbed her to prevent her falling heavily into the same brownish offensive fluid. They looked into each-other's eyes before their lips met in the split second of a relationship changing moment. An awareness of mutual undisclosed, unsuspected passionate desire for the other emerged suddenly.

A discrete drink in a neighbouring pub saw them agree to spend a week together. A secret illicit week in Scotland at a meeting of the Edinburgh Royal College of Physicians on cardiac diseases. He flew from Heathrow via Edinburgh to Kirkwall. She flew from Watford via Aberdeen to Kirkwall. She hailed a taxi to their hotel and a few minutes after checking in and letting her husband know she too had arrived safely, she tapped discreetly on door twelve after checking the corridor was empty. She had never done anything like this previously either.

Doug felt that anticipation again. When desire overcame any shyness at exposing their naked bodies to each other for the first time. When lust exceeded guilt. But not by very much. When the unparalleled euphoria of imminent intimacy, of first-time intimacy, of illicit extra-marital intimacy, banished all other thoughts of morality, or indeed anything else. When a naked woman's body just prior to making love is the most beautiful sight on Earth.

Formality, fidelity and female fashionable items were despatched rapidly before a couple of hours ecstatic discovery of each other. Doug felt he was the luckiest man on the planet. However, they had crossed that irretrievable relationship threshold. Adultery could not be undone. Not even St Magnus could restore the adulterer to fidelity.

That evening they registered separately for the conference, equally distantly they met others with similar professional interests at the opening cocktail party and dined apart with their respective new-found colleagues. Doug failed to find like-minded antiquarians interested in visiting Neolithic ruins. No matter. He was happy exploring alone. He did however find many who shared his interest in the island's whisky.

Half-an-hour after final whiskies and conversation ceased, the hotel fell silent. The last rays of the late setting sun shone down the corridor. Doug crept quietly to room twenty. Carolyn had read the Orkneyinga saga too. 'Welcome Doug Bare-legs, welcome Doug Bare-balls,' she parodied as she watched him undress.

'Thank you and greetings my Queen Fine-hair,' Doug responded as he assisted her to disrobe. 'You can be my Orkney mermaid wife. You know if they sleep with a human man, they retain their great beauty like you, but if they marry a fin man, they become ugly old crones. I might be doing you a favour!'

He spent the remainder of the night there surprised to find his vigour and recovery time had returned to that of a quarter of a century earlier, but one tempered by control and patience to ensure mutual satisfaction. Guilt was less second time around.

As Doug crept out around 5.00 am having had a couple of hours sleep, he said, 'I hope you did not read about Ragnhild in the Saga.'

'Oh yes I did,' responded a sleepy Carolyn, 'she disposed of three lovers because of their inadequate performances. But don't worry. After last night I definitely, definitely won't be doing that to you! You have a Ljot! Tonight can't come soon enough.'

Keynote lecture on the second day was the effect of mental health on the heart. Grief, depression and guilt damaging the heart. Professor

Wendy Saint was the perhaps appropriately named speaker. Doug found it difficult to concentrate on the rest of the content. He saw Carolyn across the other side of the auditorium. Their eyes met briefly with shared shame as Wendy spoke about guilt. It was too late to stop now.

Doug recalled the story of the godly Earl Magnus. In spite of marrying a beautiful young lady from a noble Scottish family, they lived a life of chastity for a decade. When lust and temptation came upon Magnus, he plunged into the cold water of the Orcadian sea or lakes. Ouch! That would have shrivelled Doug's illicit desire. Rapidly. Too late now.

Doug could also recall reading that historians and archaeologists were supposed to make good spouses as their interest in their spouse increased as both aged. It had not worked for him yet. Maybe when he was older than today.

On the third day of the conference, July 22nd, a month after the summer solstice, Doug awoke early at 4.00am. Carolyn's naked breasts rose and fell against his chest. Rhythmically and soporifically. Romantically and enticingly. Reluctantly he tiptoed out of Carolyn's bed. In retrospect he would have encountered less problems by staying in bed. Again, they had slept little.

Back in his own room, he dressed in some warm clothes and crept out of the front of the hotel intending to watch the sunrise from the ringstones of Brodgar. Stones more enduring than the memories of men.

Had this been a month earlier on the date of the summer solstice, the site would have been crawling with would-be neo-druids who thought white robes and some dope would give them a spiritual connection with their ancestors of over five thousand years ago.

Doug was excited to have a chance to see the ring alone at sunrise which he expected to be just after 4.30am that day. The stone ring was thought to have been built in the late Neolithic period around 2500BC. He would share the site and view of sunrise with the original Orcadians. An unchanged view at a predominantly unchanged site for four and a half millennia. Doug didn't need dope and a white robe to feel a connection, an aura of past ceremonies.

Sadly, he could see that only twenty-seven of the original sixty stones in the hundred-meter diameter circle were still standing. Silent sentinels hearing and seeing all without comment.

In the summer-dim Douglas could see and hear a large collection of large black birds, probably crows, a murder, attacking something in the centre of the circle. Perhaps they were attacking one of their own. As Doug approached squelching through the wet grass, Alfred Hancock's film, 'The Birds', ran anxiously through his head. Would they attack his eyes?

However, they all took off noisily, gronking grumpily as he approached. Their wedge-shaped tails and cries showing them to be the less common ravens, not crows. A lump was left underneath. Once twenty yards away the lump took the form of a prone human body lying in a pool of blood. A male body naked above the waist. The chest looked to have been attacked by the ravens initially.

However, as Doug stopped by the body, it was clear that the mutilation had been caused by human hand. The posterior chest wall had been chopped away from beside the spine on both sides and opened up like bird's wings allowing access to the lungs. These lungs had been removed, ripped out, and were sitting near the body having been further scavenged by the ravens. Oh My God. Recognition hit Doug like a sledgehammer.

It was the old Viking dreadful process of killing their enemy with the most horrendous pain, the blood red eagle. No wonder the ravens were there. The battlefield scavengers of Norse mythology. The takers of dead sightless eyes. The battle-flag emblem of merciless scavenging Vikings. Doug had read of this in period history books. It had been done on Orkney before. Earl Einar of Orkney, a blood-thirsty ruthless man of his time did that to Halfdan Long-leg, a son of King Harald of Norway. Einar dedicated the poor bloody victim to Odin. Odin would have been pleased.

But Doug never for one moment expected to see a victim. A person who had been alive and breathing not long before. His career had exposed him to many gruesome sights but never an unbearably painful murder.

He retched a few times and pulled out his primary mobile to call the police as the sun peeked over the horizon. He might have imagined a human sacrifice at sunrise several millennia ago, he had not expected to see one. As he waited the flagstone sentinels observed him in silent disapproval. Centuries of seeing and hearing. Centuries of knowing and remembering. All with a locked in syndrome. If there was a way a releasing those memories, a website to logon to, it would shed light on today's murder as well as the past culture of the Picts.

Within minutes an approaching siren announced their arrival. A young policewoman and an older police male sergeant emerged. He took one look and said, 'Oh my god, it's the Njuggel come back again!'

His younger colleague looked blankly, but Doug, well reread in Orkney and Shetland mythology, explained, 'the Njuggel is a shape-shifting devil creature. Mostly it appears as a horse with hair growing upwards. If you ride on it, it will drown you in a loch. However, it can take any form even human and murder people. But it's only a myth, mainly from Shetland, like you,' Doug guessed looking at the sergeant. 'This was human hand.'

Strange the way the old beliefs persisted amongst the older islanders Doug thought.

The area was cordoned off and kept under police guard. A temporary shelter was erected over the corpse as rain was approaching. It was always approaching in Scotland if not currently raining. A preliminary statement was taken from Doug, including his identity, current and home address and phone number. He promised to attend the Kirkwall police headquarters during the conference luncheon interval to give a full statement.

Doug returned to his room, made some coffee, shaved and showered, then headed to Carolyn's room to let her know he had stumbled across a body, a murder victim in the ringstones. Then he returned to his room to notify his wife and his hospital administration. He preferred to give them advance notice of seeing his name in a paper, even if he was blameless. He toyed with some breakfast. Haggis and black pudding were his favourites in Scotland. Somehow today he only managed coffee. After sitting through several talks with his mind elsewhere he headed for the police station.

CHAPTER THREE

Doug was ushered into an office to be confronted by an exceptionally thin tall bearded Orcadian.

'Ah, Dr Douglas Larsen, come and sit down. I am Detective Inspector Rob Olsen. Perhaps we share a Viking ancestry considering our names. Thank you for coming. You may be interested to know the deceased male you found was a Swedish tourist, aged thirty-two. His wallet was still in his pocket with over three hundred pounds in notes. Clearly theft was not the motive. He had only been here a few days with his male partner. His time of death has been estimated as being between midnight and 2.00 am. I understand that you found the body just after 4.00am. A search of the area failed to find any vehicle tracks or footprints other than yours. Hotel CCTV shows you leaving the hotel at 4.05am so you are not really a suspect.'

'I am glad to hear you know that!'

'The gruesome procedure that killed the unfortunate man was known as the Viking blood red eagle. I gather you recognised that?'

'Yes, I have read about it. Not that you expect to see it in the flesh, literally in the flesh,' responded Doug.

'Would you be able to do the operation Dr.?'

'Goodness! What a question! Well in theory, I know how the anatomy works, though I am a physician and my days as a house-surgeon in the Middlesex Hospital in London were long, long ago,' said Doug, somewhat surprised by the inquiry.

'So, Dr, what sort of person would commit this murder? I thought you might have some interesting ideas considering your medical knowledge and historical interests. Was it Earl Einar of Orkney come back to haunt us?'

'Gosh, that's your job. Ghosts seem unlikely even here. Someone or more than one who is pretty strong, so perhaps male? Perhaps someone who doesn't like Swedes, or tourists, or a previous lover. Half the people on Orkney at the moment don't seem to like visitors.'

'And Dr, someone with a knowledge of Viking history?' asked the DI.

'Wouldn't that be most people here, it's such an integral part of Orcadian history and DNA. Perhaps someone who doesn't like gay men, perhaps the partner. I'm sure your psychological profilers, if you have such people like the TV shows, would have a better idea. Why are you asking me these questions? Am I a suspect?'

'Well Dr, I understand you have an alibi anyway, so no, you are not a suspect.

Doug, a little surprised at the alibi concept, said, 'yes well up to nearly eleven I had dinner and a few whiskies with some newfound colleagues. Then I went to bed alone and slept till I got up early to see the sun rise on the stone ring.' He did not think he would need an alibi and certainly would not offer it at this stage.

'Um, Dr, you will be surprised and embarrassed to know the hotel not only has CCTV at the front entrance, but also in the corridors. My detective sergeant discovered you were in room twenty during the hours of half-darkness. It seems you have an alibi. A female work colleague. It is not my job to preserve your marital integrity nor to publish salacious facts unless demanded by our investigation. I am a policeman, not the old Shetland Rancelman who was once a guardian of moral and religious behaviour here as well.'

Doug was dumbfounded to be discovered.

Olsen laughed and continued, 'don't worry, adultery has a long tradition here, even amongst the supposedly moral citizens. One of the ministers on Sanday had a long-term affair with a parishioner's wife till pursued back to the church by the devil out for his evil soul. He went inside and slammed the door shut just in time. To this day there are scratch marks on the church wall caused by the frustrated devil's sharp fingernails. Careful he doesn't find you doctor.'

'I understand you will be in the Orkneys for at least three weeks longer. Are you planning to visit more ruins?'

'Oh God,' Doug swallowed and continued shakily, 'well, I would like to see all of them, perhaps Skara Brae tomorrow afternoon.'

'Please let me know if you plan to leave Orkney. Thank you for coming. If any other facts come to mind, please come and see me. Here is my card with my private mobile number. Ring anytime.'

Doug left feeling dreadfully agitated and anxious. He texted Carolyn on the second phone to arrange a meeting in the back garden and explained the situation to her. She burst into tears. 'Oh my God, we are going to be found out by our spouses, we have been found out, what shall we do?'

'Nothing,' he said, 'we might as well carry on in bed together and if we are to be hung, it might as well be for a few sheep than a single lamb. We stay together discreetly till the end of the conference. I would love to have more time in bed together with you.'

That night in room twelve, she sobbed naked and distraught in his arms for ten minutes before intimacy gave way to transient relief. Unfortunately transient relief with tears of mixed ecstasy and shame.

CHAPTER FOUR

The next morning it rained. Scottish fashion. Incessant. Heavy. Plowetery was the current local term for bad weather. Wolf days had been the old Norse term. It seemed to be the standard conditions here. No honey scent of wildflowers. No lark ascending into sunny skies. The nearby hills appeared dark and barren apart from stunted heather. The more distant and scarcely visible hills shapeshifted in the whirling mist and rain, perhaps bizarre shapes of the walking dead depending on one's imagination. No wonder Shetlanders could conjure up the little people. None of it was like the tourist brochures showing purple heather-clad slopes bathed all day in bright sunshine.

Doug sat through the morning lectures somewhat absent mindedly. He was distracted by current events and lack of sleep. The afternoon session was of limited interest. Doug had already decided he would visit the Neolithic stone village of Skara Brae. Carolyn planed a trip to Kirkwall to check out the smart female fashion boutiques. Retail therapy for guilt. Doug was surprised to discover there were quite a few classy ladies shops in town.

Doug had consulted his well-thumbed Orkney tour guide. Older than the Egyptian pyramids and Stonehenge, the eight little buried houses of Skara Brae would have been a cosy home to some four dozen original Orcadians about five thousand years ago. Men, women and children. Families. Rediscovered after severe storms in 1850 that killed over two hundred people on Orkney as well as stripping the topsoil from the ruins, it was now a world heritage site under the Scottish National Trust.

He drove about eighteen miles east past the settlement of Voy to the coastal Bay of Skaill, the site of the old ruins. This was a truly amazing place. In the ringstones one could only imagine the ceremonies of five millennia ago. Probably incorrectly. Were there human sacrifices, initiation ceremonies, fertility rites? Was there music and dancing, spiritual gatherings? It was anyone's guess. Imaginary events. The echoes of time were palpable rather than audible.

Here in Skara Brae the constructions were so similar to those of today. The ancient lifestyles could be easily visualised.

The village of eight interconnected stone houses was sunk into an old midden for warmth and security. The predecessor of the semi-detached style of today. Seven rooms appeared for private family accommodation. The living rooms had a welcoming central hearth, a large bed to the right thought to be for the male or husband, and a smaller bed to the left for the wife. Doug wondered if the right-hand bed might be for mum and dad, Doug and Susan. Or Doug and Carolyn? A threesome? To keep each other warm, and then the left-hand bed for the kids.

There was a dresser against the wall for family mementos, treasures or objects of importance. Not graduation photographs and rugby medals. No wedding pictures of faithful couples. Nevertheless, trophies important at the time. Perhaps the skull of an eagle, or a sealion, or even another human's skull, an enemy. A trophy of combat. Perhaps leather clothing or dried fish or weapons. Archaeological findings here included killer-whale teeth, lumps of ochre perhaps for body paint, and even the earliest discovered human flea!

It was just like home. A home where the family cuddled around the hearth for dinner to keep warm in winter. A home where the roof once kept off the driving rain still pounding on his umbrella. A home that even had a primitive sort of toilet. A home Douglas felt with guilt, like his own where he lived with his faithful betrothed wife. Not where he had fantastic but illicit sex with another woman. A woman who was another man's wife.

The eighth was different. Not buried in a midden but free-standing with two-meter-thick wall. Doug entered through the porch and was struck dumb, suddenly overwhelmed with confusion. He sagged at the knees in shock and revulsion.

In the middle of room eight was a supine body. An awfully dead body! A swarthy skinned male naked from the waist up with a wide deep incision in the left chest wall and something sitting on the chest. When Doug approached and collected some of his wits, he realised it was a heart, a human heart sitting on the chest. A rain-washed body sitting in a large pool of lightly blood coloured rainwater. Oh My God. It looked like an Aztec sacrifice of a millennium ago. A broad blade used to be inserted between the ribs on the left side and rotated to spread the ribs. The now visible beating heart was then torn out to appease the pitiless Aztec Gods. Not just once sacrifice, but hundreds at a time.

Doug was an expert in resuscitation. Cardiac massage and defibrillators. There was not much he could do with this externalised heart.

Doug's trembling fingers dialled DI Olsen's mobile to explain the situation.

Greyness. The stones of Skara Brae, the wild sea and the sky. His mood. All matching greyness. It reminded him of Heathrow, the décor, the people, the sky. At least here there was no M25. The twenty-first century flying Dutchman would be condemned to drive round and round the M25 for all eternity.

London, a city of twelve million people with limited facilities for perhaps only ten million had to keep two million quarantined out of the inner metropolis driving round and round the M25 to function adequately.

Greyness. Was it the end of days predicted by the Vikings? According to one legend, Yggdrasill, the Norse tree of life had one root growing in the heavenly pool of knowledge, one root burning in the fires of Hel, the Norse underworld, and the third being devoured by the Beast. When two roots are destroyed, Yggdrasill will fall, and darkness will overtake the Earth for ever.

Within fifteen minutes a squad car arrived with two disapproving coppers. The older male took his details gruffly, recognised the name and told Doug with obvious distaste to return to Kirkwall Police station immediately. He could pick a callous murderer at twenty paces every time. Doug.

The younger, a pleasant female looked pityingly at Doug, 'hoots mon, yer drookit, have a change and dry off first.'

Half-an-hour later a dry and changed Doug was back in the DI's office again. Rob looked silently, intently at his face for any signs of guilt.

'So, Doug, my pathologist thinks death was four to six hours before you claimed to have found the body. Again, we found no vehicle tracks or footprints other than yours. Your entry ticket to Skara Brae was timed at 1.54pm and you were the only person dumb enough to go there today in heavy rain. You say you were in the conference till lunch time. Some corroboration of that would be appreciated. This man's wallet confirms him to have been a Mexican tourist who had only been on the island for three days. A visitor from away with his female wife. She is collapsed and under sedation in the hospital while her family fly in from Mexico.'

He paused looking accusingly at Doug. 'Not gay, not unfaithful. Just a tourist come from away. A Mexican murdered by the ancient Aztec ritual of his homeland. What the bloody hell is going on here doctor. Can you explain your role and analysis of these two murders please doctor? Did anyone know you were going to either place in advance? I'm not bloody Jimmy Perez of Shetland. I can't solve this in the space of an hour's TV show!'

Doug inhaled deeply on a comforting cigarette, his first since student days. Then he swallowed some more coffee before responding.

'My personal involvement seems purely fortuitous inspector. Coincidental. Horrible. Only one lady knew in advance where I was going. Carolyn. My wife is doing a water-painting course in the south of France. I call her each night to tell her of the day's events. Well, most of them,' Doug added with a wry smile.

'I have been the unlucky person to have stumbled accidentally across two ghastly killings. There seems to be some common features. Both were found in Neolithic ruins which happen to be a great interest of mine. Both were tourists. Both had suffered an ancient barbaric form of execution strangely paired with their country of origin. Does that imply your suspect is a strong Orcadian male with an interest in ancient history, a knowledge of human anatomy and, as is not uncommon these days here, an irrational hatred of tourists.'

DI Olsen continued to survey him silently.

'Thank you, Dr. Almost a description of yourself wouldn't you say? Apart from your alibis. Your alibis that still need a little checking.'

'Yes inspector.'

'The resident population in Orkney is about twenty-two thousand. There are around nearly as many tourists at this time of year. That is a lot of suspects. Stick around Dr. Do not leave the islands. We will be seeing each other again. I presume you will have no objection to being finger-printed and having a DNA sample taken.'

'None whatsoever, inspector. Anything to point your investigation in the right direction. I don't know how you could suspect me. I am a doctor. I have spent over forty years saving lives. I could not possibly be a murderer.'

'You doctors are all so bloody saintly,' countered the detective, 'there is a saying "only the impotent are pure", CCTV suggests that does not appear to be your problem Dr! Did not Dr Hastings Banda qualify as a doctor in UK and like you work in London. His cabinet colleagues in Malawi died in strange circumstances. Suspicious circumstances. Did not President Bashar al-Assad of Syria do his specialist training in London like you, at about the same time as you? Is he responsible for a death or two? I read recently that the first person to be divorced at the court of St Pauls in the fifteenth century was a doctor. Dr William Hobbys and that my dear doctor was for adultery. Fucking and murdering beats healing for some doctors obviously!'

Doug winced defencelessly at that accurate shaft.

'We had an Orkney doctor, Dr Tallian in Stromness, a descendent of the Spanish Armada who dug up bodies and sold the corpse's heart fat as a cure-all. Don't run the saintly doctor bit past me ever again.'

A silenced Doug was a little surprised to be finger-printed and then have a blood sample taken for DNA testing. Didn't they do buccal swabs here? Perhaps Orkney still used outdated technology.

On return to the hotel he knocked on the door of room twenty to hear about the shopping expedition. He said nothing about the second body. Carolyn was carried away by the quality of the city shops. First, she bought a sweater for her husband from Annie Glue. Assuaging guilt. Then a new dress for herself from Kirsten Stewart Designs, and a handbag from Modo Accessories. Some hand-crafted Orkney jewellery from Ortak and Aurora Orkney jewellers for her two daughters. A bottle of 'Skiren' Scapa whisky and some coloured mature cheddar for Doug from Kirkness and Gorie. Dutch courage to start the night together.

She held up the sweater and the whisky. 'Doug, would you prefer the sweater, you are the same size as my husband, pretty much all over?' she said looking Doug up and down provocatively.

'Ooh no thanks, the locals believe the spirits of yesteryear live on here. When the brothers, Paul and Harald shared the title of Earl of Orkney, Harald seized a cloak that his mother, Helga, and his sister, Frakkok were making especially for Paul. The ladies said his life was at risk, but he ignored them and put it on. Immediately his flesh began to quiver with intolerable pain, and he died suddenly. No, I won't have another man's clothing, only his wife please! According to the Sagas, that is safer and much more common! And much more pleasure!'

Carolyn was surprised to find that gin was distilled in Orkney. She purchased a bottle of Kirkjuvagr in navy strength. She would need that back at home whether she was found out or not. Whether she confessed or not.

Sadly, but unsurprisingly retail therapy had only increased her remorse.

CHAPTER FIVE

Friday was the last day of the cardiology conference. It finished at lunch to enable the delegates to depart for home at a reasonable time of day before the fog or rain cancelled flights or ferries out of Orkney.

The conference dinner the night before had been most entertaining with highland and island delicacies. Scallops and smoked salmon, venison stew with red wine, orange, thyme and Orkney cheddar dumplings, Ronaldsay lamb, and finally raspberry cranachan. All accompanied by the bagpipes and Highland Park 'Voyage of the Raven' single malt whisky. The raven being a symbol of Viking victories and voyages. A full flavoured smoky whisky with aromas of cinnamon, black cherries and ginger.

Tartan-clad highland sword-dancers, pipers and fiddlers, entertaining short speeches, a roaring log fire, borderline distasteful highland jokes and bonhomie made a memorable evening. It was followed by an even more memorable night. Doug and Carolyn had discovered each-other's likes and intimate preferences. Ecstasy was mingled with tears as they appreciated this would probably never happen again.

They took their secret farewells in bed so as not to be seen together as she departed at midday for Aberdeen. They used to brand adulterers with a big letter A on their cheek in the town square in Aberdeen in the distant past. Good job that was not done today! Then on to London.

London where her husband would meet her at the airport. She hoped to be able to look him in the eye.

By lunch time the following day Doug was a free agent. He had nearly three weeks to himself to view the rest of Orkney. Again, it was raining. It was always bloody raining. He couldn't remember why a trip to the Orkneys had been so appealing. This was not the beautiful summer weather of the tourist brochures. Not the blue cloudless sunny skies. Not mutilating murders in the dim distant past, but murders today.

Doug donned his trusty North Face Gore-Tex 3L jacket, alpine gloves and powderflo waterproof trousers and set off for Maeshowe. He was still cold, yet the icy fingers of the North Sea gale could not find any hidden crevices in his clothing to inflict frost bite or discomfort. The temperature was just above zero with the windchill factor. Orkney had mini ice-age periods in the past when Finns and Icelanders came down for fishing, when icebergs floated nearby. Doug wouldn't be surprised to see them in Kirkwall Harbour today. It could be a bloody cold place!

Doug's guidebook described Maeshowe as another Neolithic stone monument nearly five thousand years old, this one being a large tomb embedded in a grassy hill. It was huge for the building techniques of five millennia ago. The mound is over thirty metres in diameter and over seven metres high. The burial chamber is a square just under five meters across and is approached by a low tunnel eleven metres long.

Amazingly the winter solstice sun shines at sunrise straight down the entrance tunnel to illuminate the far wall. Right down the middle. Doug found it hard to get his head around the brilliantly accurate astronomical knowledge and building skills of Orkney's first people, to design and construct such a huge edifice with exact precision. Some of the stone slabs weighed thirty tons. Thirty tons! They would be challenging to move today with modern equipment!

There were recesses in the walls for bodies. They must have been elite members of society for such a monument. Over a thousand years ago the Vikings broke through the top presumably pillaging anything of worth as usual. When Earl Harald sheltered in here overnight in a winter snowstorm, two of his men went insane. Perhaps the ancient

Celtic undead got inside their heads in the darkness! Others even engraved some Viking runes on the stones. Many left their names. One even wrote '*Thorni fucked*'.

Doug reflected his activities on Orkney were nothing new, but past events suggested perhaps he could be forgiven. Earl Thorfinn after many years of pillaging, rapes and murders went on a pilgrimage to Rome where amazingly he received absolution from the Pope. Perhaps Doug could find his next conference in Rome.

However, as he approached Maeshowe, he found the road blocked with a police vehicle with its blue light flashing. He stopped and alighted to see if entry was still possible. He was confronted by a policeman and Olsen's detective sergeant. He of the CCTVs. Doug was recognised and admitted across the police line. The sergeant called Larsen on his lapel CB radio to say Doug was here. The DI emerged from the gloom.

'Ah Dr, we beat you to it this time. Someone reported a crime an hour ago. A tourist for once started earlier than you in this foul weather. We will check the hotel CCTV for your departure time of course. Put these on,' said Olsen giving Doug overshoes, gloves and an over suit, 'then come and see this.'

Sitting in the entrance to the tunnel was a head. A decapitated head. It was a bearded swarthy male head with long dark hair.

'Don't touch it!' Olsen warned, 'you might end up like our first earl, Sigurd the Powerful. He was riding home after a victorious battle with the head of his recently beheaded foe, Maelbrigte attached to his saddle. When spurring his horse, Sigurd scratched his leg on one of Maelbrigte's rotten teeth, developed an infected festering sore which then killed the poor earl!'

Stepping carefully past the head and walking bent over down the tunnel, they entered the ancient chamber to see a decapitated body carefully placed in one of the alcoves. There was a large pool of congealing blood in the middle of the floor. The scene of the crime.

Doug could not believe his nightmare was continuing. He knew of Sigurd; he knew of the Orcadians' passion for their Viking history and ancestors but was surprised by the detective's levity. At least he had not discovered the body this time.

'So, Dr, here you are on the scene of a violent crime yet again, another tourist come under the eagle's claws,' commenced Olsen. 'This gentleman we have here, is from the Middle-East, bordering on the Persian Gulf. He arrived five days ago as a tourist accompanied by an attractive young lady. They are both married but unfortunately not to each other!'

Doug gasped, here was another ritual execution. Coming under the eagles claws was an old Norse metaphor for meeting a violent death. Beheading for adultery was a traditional Islamic punishment, still performed in some countries to this day. The Vikings, indeed, most ancient cultures also beheaded their opponents. Three men executed according to the ancient mores of their home country within a few days. Three tourists, their holiday brutally cut short.

'Yes Doug, we are thinking along the same lines, three male tourists murdered according to the traditional forms of execution of their home country. Your presence seems the only common feature to all three. Your knowledge of history and anatomy. The crossroads of modern crime and ancient history are horrendously brutal. I am thinking of locking you up for some prolonged interrogation. Perhaps your wife's presence might help you confess some sins.'

Doug left the chamber to head outside where he sagged to his knees and vomited violently.

On recovery he looked up at the inspector, 'you know there are Orcadians here who hate tourists, perhaps you should look at them.'

'Oh yes Dr, we are doing that too. However, there is no anti-tourist group or organisation as such. Many individual comments appeared on social media after the recent rape of an airhostess. Nearly all by women under the #MeToo umbrella. Discrete enquiries of social media have unearthed dozens and dozens of small frighteningly angry female pacifists. We may yet have to interview every able-bodied male and female Orcadian. That would take months. Plenty of time for people to come and go. There is a natural honest ingress and egress of Orcadians. Some permanent, some temporary. Also, many 'come from aways' some short term, some long term. The ferryloupers as they are known. Some here for a few weeks like you Dr. For your sake let's hope there are no more of these murders. Again, do not leave Orkney yet.'

Doug spent the next few days alone visiting other ancient monuments and the highlights of Kirkwall. The days were fascinating.

Doug entered St Magnus Cathedral and sat quietly in a pew near the back to gaze in wonder at the soaring carved columns of alternating red and yellow sandstone. The choir commenced a practice session. Pure notes from the boy sopranos floated up to the rafters. Timeless beautiful hymns of yesteryear. Music. The atheist's pathway to the heavens. God's ambience in a godless world.

He flicked through the guidebook, coming across a reference to the cathedral white stone. Mr Balkie, an early nineteenth century minister used to bring forward the delinquents of society, dressed in sackcloth to stand face-down in shame on the white stone in front of the pulpit and before the whole congregation. Fornicators and adulterers were exposed and rebuked. Ministers always seemed more concerned about the seventh commandment than the others all put together. Was that the natural human salacious disposition not absent even in God's servants or just concealed jealousy

St Rognvald, the earl of Orkney who ordered the construction of this cathedral stopped on his pilgrimage to Rome and Jerusalem, in Narbonne. There he was thought to have had an affair with beautiful Viscountess Ermengarde. He wrote her love poems. She was married and he was made a saint! It was not fair.

Doug had this sudden feeling that all the visitors in the cathedral saw him in sackcloth. He felt they were all looking at him in horror and disgust. They somehow could read his sinful heart. Eyes glued shamefully to the floor he walked out uncomfortably.

One day while walking along the pier in Kirkwall Harbour he came across a brick and glass hut labelled the "Owld Men's Hut". The glass wall on two sides gave scenic views around the busy fishing harbour. Where the green swell is in the harbours dumb, and out of the swing of the sea as the poem goes.

Doug opened the door quietly, inquisitively. Several venerable male Orcadians were sitting silently watching the world go slowly by. They reminded Doug of the ancient statues of Easter Island, sitting there in a uniform imposing stillness. Ageless custodians of Lerwick Harbour. Intrusive conversation was rendered superfluous by a lifetime of island memories shared in companiable silence. One finally nodded amiably so Doug entered and sat down. Loneliness was better shared.

After several minutes silence, a grizzled one stated, 'look there, there's a rainbow touching down on the other side of the bay on the chimney of Mrs Maxwell's house. The keeries will be bring her a baby boy. Her last two babies were girls because the keeries didn't send a rainbow. She is due about now.'

'Nay,' said another, with an alternative mythology, pointing with his clay pipe, 'you can see the other end touch down within the township, the keeries in the watergaw have come to collect a soul. Probably old grandfather Maxwell. He been dreadfully sick with the dropsy.'

Grunts around the room signified ascent.

After a few more minutes silence, a third venerable islander announced, 'look, there's another bluidy cruise liner coming in.'

Another long silence followed before an ancient crusty man leaning over a gnarled stick followed up, 'twas better in the old days before tourism ruined this place, I remember when we only had a twice weekly ferry to the south and the Royal Navy. Otherwise it was Orkney for Orcadians.'

There were a few nods and 'ayes.'

Another said, 'many of the Royal Navy men were from here, or the Hebrides or Shetlands, they are almost one of us.'

There were a few nods and 'ayes,' followed by a silence.

The first speaker announced, 'now look what has happened, somewhere loose amongst us on the islands is a murderous bastard. A come from away. I hope he gets caught soon and has his balls cut off and his heart and lungs ripped out like his poor defenceless victims.'

'Aye,' was the common response.

The cathedral bell tolled midday sonorously across the town. The five-hundred-year old bell. The bell felled by lightning over three hundred years ago. Lightning from the heavens. Sinners exposed in God's domain. Doug included. It tolls for me Doug thought, as its judgemental pulse resonated with his. He stood up, nodded to the assembly and took his leave before he was recognised. Perhaps loneliness was best suffered alone after all.

The nights were forlorn, solitary, often sleepless. The hotel was almost empty. Murders of visiting tourists equals cancellations. Restaurants and bars were little better. Few wanted to be out alone even in the half-light of the summer dim. A grim reaper, perhaps man, perhaps mythical monster stalking tourists in the ancient sites of Orkney. His only companions at night were various Highland Park whiskies and horrific dreams. And guilt. At other times he would have enjoyed the Scotch, now it papered over cracks. Ineffectively.

Doug took a day's ferry trip on the roll on-roll-off vehicle ferry to the island of Hoy, passing the amazing sea-stack at Hoy.

A kilted Scotsman wearing only a tee-shirt on his upper body in the cold wind blowing in off the North Atlantic, was leaning over the rail next to Doug. Doug hoped he had something on under his kilt as it was blowing around in the gale.

'It's a bonnie dee don't you think,' he opened, 'yon wee stone was climbed recently, ye ken. It took five days to climb it, suspended from harnesses over-night. I'd need a few wee whisky's to get to sleep up there.'

Not for Doug with his fear of heights. He murmured some agreement.

'See the seals there,' continued his sociable new-found best friend and guide. 'To us they are the selkie folk, people who drowned and now live in the sea in seal skins. Sometimes they come out, shed their skins and dance. If a man can catch them before they put their skin back on, they remain in human shape and make fine wives.'

How come the Scots found truth in these legends Doug wondered? And how come the Scots thought the summer months were warm regardless of the weather. Kilts and tee shirts in fifteen degrees? Even colder with the windchill factor.

Driving off at Lyness, Doug drove north to just short of Linksness to park his car by the road. From here there was a short walk up a barren hill to find the Dwarfie Stane. This huge mass of sandstone measuring nearly nine metres long, four metres wide and two and a half metres high was deposited in remote moorland by a glacier perhaps sixty million years previously.

Some-time in the Neolithic period a chamber was carved out in the middle. Carved with stones or antlers. No modern diamond drills. Unbelievable. The entrance is about a metre square to reveal a central chamber over two metres long with two side chambers just under two metres long.

Archaeologists believe it to be a tomb. Mythology claims that it was built by giants and inhabited by a dwarf named Trollid. The Orkney bard, George Mackay Brown believed a hermit, an anchorite may have lived there. It was a bleak lonely place. It may have suited an anchorite. One with a tolerance for solitude, cold and hunger.

The entrance-sealing stone was rolled back perhaps four hundred years ago, and more recent tourists have inscribed their graffiti. A Captain William Mounsey wrote in Persian calligraphy during a couple of nights back in 1850.

Armed with this knowledge, Doug approached this enigmatic monolith isolated in barren moorland with awe and perplexion as to its original purpose. It would be indeed be a great place for an anchorite if there was such a place. As Mackay Brown said, *"a darksome house of mortal clay the better to understand the light of the first world."* It was a long way from habitation for elite corpses. No other human being could be seen around. He clambered through the narrow opening and shone his torch around.

There was graffiti inside on the wall! New graffiti in black spray paint. DEETH TO FUCKN TOORISTS it read. Doug touched this literary gem. The paint was still damp. Oh my god, this had just been sprayed by someone who may be a murderous psychopath. Doug climbed out quickly to look around for danger. Again, he appeared quite alone thank god. He climbed back in, took some photos and texted them to DI Olsen. Then he rang the number.

'More dead bodies today Dr?' asked the cheerful detective. 'I saw your pictures, could you stand outside away from the stone till my team arrives by chopper. Come and see me tomorrow. Thank you, Dr.'

Doug sat down meditating for a while, then extracted his heavily annotated tour guide to check up on other points of interest on Hoy. The Naval Museum at Lyness looked the next place of interest.

Soon his reverie was interrupted by the sound of an incoming helicopter. Two police ladies hoped out and officiously, cautiously approached Doug. Both were armed. Pistols. One with a hand on the grip! Police accessories only worn in adverse circumstances. They demanded an imprint of his shoes in moulds, checked his story and dismissed him. Contemptuously. 'Don't forget to report to DI Olsen tomorrow for an official interrogation and don't leave Orkney,' they ordered. He was judged and convicted already in their eyes.

He drove to the water's edge in Lyness looking across the nearly empty expanse of grey water that was once the home of the most powerful battle fleet in the world. Home to up to a hundred thousand sailors. A time when local farmers could attempt to satisfy an insatiable demand for milk and eggs, fish and meat at way above local market prices.

Today it was empty apart from two garish orange tankers. Today it was calm. Mythology had a tale of Scapa Flow. It had tales of everywhere. It was the summer months when the gentle Mother of the Sea was dominant. She would ensure calm seas and abundant fish. In a few months, according to the myths, Teran, the malignant spirit of winter, would bind the Mother of the Sea in chains and wreak havoc with the weather and the seas through winter. Fierce storms and boiling sea would shatter fishing boats on the rocks and sent the sea life into deep waters below the fishing nets. People would scuttle out of their warm houses to manage their business and get back inside before the peat fire as quickly as possible. Come spring the cycle would reverse, and the Sea-mother would dominate again. These myths seemed so much more plausible sitting alone by the silent calm waters.

Gone were the destroyers, the sleek grey sea warriors of the Royal Navy. The natural successors of the Viking longboats of a millennium previously. Gone were the huge leviathans, massive battleships with massive guns.

The lyrics of Allie Windwick's song, "Lonely Scapa Flow" came to his melancholy subconscious.

*"how we lingered long upon the shore to see beloved ships
come sailing up the Flow....We saw them anchored proudly
as the sun went down, and heard a lonesome bugle from
the old Renown.....But that was yesterday, and they come
no more, among the small green isles, where oft they lay of
yore, and so we linger sadly, by an empty shore, and shed
a tear for lonely Scapa Flow."*

Doug did indeed shed a mournful tear, for his grandfather had been
here. Initially as a seventeen-year-old falsifying his age in the First World
War. He worked as a sick birth attendant on the *Iron Duke*, Admiral
Jellicoe's flagship at the Battle of Jutland. Having his appetite piqued
by medicine, he resigned from the Navy, and went to the Middlesex
Hospital Medical School after the war. The start of a family tradition.
Twelve years later he re-joined before the start of the second World
War as a Surgeon-Commander aboard *HMS Rodney* stationed then in
Scapa Flow. Granddad would be desperately sad to see not one ship of
the Royal Navy some eighty years later.

In some ways life was simpler then. Doug's life was also much
simpler before flying into Orkney. However, one could not take back
things experienced in life. Dealing with them afterwards was a problem.
He had a pint of heavy and a bridie in the local pub, before spending
the next two hours in the newly opened renovated Scapa Flow Museum.

He read about the battle fleet, the battle of Jutland, the mutiny
of the fleet, the bold German submariners who attacked the fleet at
anchor, and the scuttling of the Admiral Ludwig von Reuter's German
fleet. A site now for recreational divers. He read about the sinking of the
battleship, *HMS Royal Oak*. Hit by three torpedos from U47, in 1939,
she rolled over and sank within a few minutes with the loss of eight
hundred and thirty-four lives. A winking green light across the Flow
off Scapa Beach marks the spot where she went down.

Twenty-four graves in the immaculate and tranquil naval cemetery
outside marked the few bodies that were found. The rest went down
with the ship.

There were pictures of the battleship *HMS Vanguard* which blew up in 1917 with only two survivors from a crew of over a thousand. Unstable ammunition was probably the cause. Doug had been on the replacement battleship *HMS Vanguard* in Portsmouth Harbour on the occasion of the coronation in 1953. Number twenty-three of that name in the Royal Navy. The first ship of that name had fought the Spanish Armada. A small boy, he was overawed by the size of the ship at forty-five thousand tons and its fearsome fifteen-inch guns. A ship however, rendered impotent by naval air power even then.

There were pictures of the destroyers *HMS Narborough* and *HMS Opal* which sailed at full speed into the cliffs of South Ronaldsay lost in a blizzard at night with only one sole survivor. The ocean's blood sacrifice. There was a picture of an unnamed Spanish Galleon from the Spanish Armada in 1588 that supposedly foundered on North Ronaldsay. Another Spanish galleon, the *El Gran Grifon*, according to the caption, went down on Fair Isle. Godsends, the locals called the wrecks full of precious plunder.

He returned by ferry and drove to Helgi's restaurant in Kirkwall. Named after a great Viking warrior, it served food amongst the best in Scotland. Doug could only toy with his smoked shellfish and steak garni. He scarcely tasted his Rob Hill's Scapa Special draft pale ale or his sixteen-year-old Scapa single malt whisky. He wondered if the whole venture had been a disastrously big mistake. Perhaps he could ask Rob Olsen if he could go home. Perhaps he should confess all his sins to his wife. She was still enjoying herself in France. That could wait till she returned.

Later Doug lay in bed. Sleepless again. Thoughts floated round his head like confetti. Not colourful confetti settling or blowing away. Just confetti blowing round and around in angry circles. He worried about his bizarre predicament finding mutilated bodies. He could not forget the intimate details of exquisite lovemaking with Carolyn. Following another double scotch, he subsided into an agitated torpor.

CHAPTER SIX

After that restless night, the next morning he was admitted to the DI's office.

'Ah, the good doctor,' welcomed the DI sarcastically, 'so we are little the wiser about your graffiti. Only your footprints were found on the footpath, but there had been the usually heavy rain about two hours earlier. Obviously, the stone can be approached without going on the footpath. Was it our murderer do you think Dr Sherlock?'

Doug felt the inspector was playing with him, 'how should I know, I'm not bloody Jimmy Perez either. The spelling is not that of a person with a deep knowledge of medieval history. Maybe they are unrelated. Maybe it's to put you off the scent. I presume you have checked all the ferry bookings and the Lyness Harbour and the ferry CCTV.'

'Indeed, we have, Dr Watson. Our artist would either live on Hoy or have taken a car over. It's a long walk to the stone. The pedestrians are nearly all people who were commuting to work one way or the other or have family there. Five hundred and two cars went on and off the island yesterday. We are checking all the owners currently.'

'Did you find the empty can of black spray paint discarded somewhere?' asked Doug.

'No.'

'That suggests a more careful artist than the average vandal. How many stores sell that sort of paint?'

'Five. We are looking at their CCTV. What are you planning next Dr now your entertainment seems over? Both forms of entertainment,' he said mockingly.

'Well Inspector, partly I want to go home and get away from the whole sorry business, but partly I want to finish seeing the old Neolithic sites now I am here. That leaves me the Stones of Stenness, The Tomb of the Eagles on South Ronaldsay, Midhowe Broch on Rousay and the Brough of Birsay. Finally, I really want to do the little flight to Papa Westray and see the Knap of Howar. If you hear that I am at the Kirkwall airport, it will only be for a local flight.'

The Detective Sergeant tapped on the office door and placed a piece of paper on Olsen's desk.

The DI looked and laughed. 'Well Dr, the graffitist has been solved. First shop my sergeant went to, the Home Hardware shop told him that 'Slow Jock' had been in two days before for some spray cans of black paint. A check of CCTV vehicle registrations landing on Hoy yesterday found Slow Jock's old unlicensed banger.'

'The Sergeant went to his home; he lives with his devoted Mum and he admitted it was him with lots of tears. Now 'Slow Jock' as he is known is not a historical scholar or indeed any sort of scholar. He went to an opportunity school for a while but truanted most days. He has a record of minor crime, stealing cigarettes, beer, ladies knickers from washing lines, but is quite harmless. He is not even an accomplished liar like many young men his age. No, he had never heard of the Aztecs, or the Persian Gulf, but he thought he knew about the Vikings. He is not our murderer. You were right, Dr, it was unrelated.'

CHAPTER SEVEN

D oug had ten days left to complete his tour of ancient ruins. The size and number of these dwellings was amazing. The first people here obviously had great strength, organisation and architectural skills. Strange that they appeared to leave Orkney after a thousand years habitation for a few centuries. Experts had ascribed this to one of the natural cycles of global cooling.

Doug's first stop was the Ness of Brodgar located between the Ring of Brodgar and the Stones of Stenness. He had an appointment with one of the site archaeologists at 10.00am.

'Ah, you must be Doug,' a diminutive but exceptionally earnest young lady said to him on his arrival at the enclosed dig site. 'I'm Fiona, I am Associate Professor in Archaeology from the University of Edinburgh. Usually we have a handful of visitors, but these bizarre murders are keeping people away. Do you think the man who found the bodies did it?'

Doug shook her hand and mumbled in reply. He thought how young she appeared to have climbed so high in academia. He was nearly fifty when he was made a professor at the London University.

Fiona continued, 'this complex of buildings was only recently discovered. Excavations began in 2003. This walled enclosure is a huge area of two and a half hectares. We have found the ruins of probably fourteen buildings. Some on top of previous constructions, some replacing others. Come and look at the biggest. We call it the Neolithic cathedral as it was probably their centre of worship. Whoever they worshipped five thousand years ago. I expect it was the one true god! Lots of one true gods have come and gone since then. They all seem to have a shelf life.'

They walked along a pathway to the ruin known as Structure 10. Fiona looked curiously at Doug. 'Have I seen you before somewhere, were you at the last meeting of the Scottish Archaeological Society meeting in Dunblane?'

'No', answered Doug.

Fiona looked carefully at him, then continued, 'Amongst the numerous buildings this huge construction is the biggest. We think that it was perhaps was a temple. It is twenty-five metres long, twenty metres wide, over three metres high and walls that were four metres thick. I find the thickness of their buildings amazing. More than twice your height. It was full of bones, mostly cattle and some reindeer. It sounded a warm place for feasting.'

Under a covered area, Fiona showed him some fragments of grooved-ware pottery typical of the time, and some painted stones. 'Over there we found the skeleton of a wee bairn, carbon dated to five thousand years ago....' Fiona faltered. 'oh no I know where I've seen your picture, you're the man who found the bodies.'

Fiona looked around in panic to discover she was the only worker on the site. She backed away hastily to where there were a few stone axes.'

Doug didn't move. He spread his empty hands in front of her. 'Sorry Fiona. I did find two of the bodies. I have not murdered anyone. I was much more distressed by the horrible discoveries than you are now, please I am a harmless man. I am only interested in your ancient ruins.'

Doug paused and looked at her apprehensive expression.

'Would you like me to leave? I don't want to be killed by a Neolithic stone axe.'

Fiona looked into his eyes. 'Yes, I'm sorry too, but I think I would feel safer if you left.'

'Thank you for showing me around, could we meet for a drink or dinner and I can apologise to you in a safe environment.'

'Thank you but no.'

Doug departed feeling like a leper. He would arrange a delivery of flowers to the dig site tomorrow.

Next Doug took the ferry to the island of Rousay to see Midhowe Broch and Midhowe cairn. He hoped to have the site to himself and not be recognised. The ubiquitous dislike of tourists and the understandably increased paranoia since the murders hung over the fascination and pleasure he had hoped to experience. However, on his arrival he was greeted by another extrovert knowledgeable young lady working on the excavations.

'Hi, I'm Morag, would you like me to tell you about this place.' Morag was going to tell Doug about it regardless of his agreement. 'It's quite fascinating. The Scottish National Trust likes us to be here to tell visitors about it.' Morag stopped and peered at Doug closely. 'Don't I know you? .....Oh my God, you are the doctor with the dismembered bodies in the paper!'

Morag looked around anxiously for her colleague, 'Willy, come over here, this is the doctor in the papers with the mutilated bodies!'

Willy came over. He was a huge man. Perhaps two hundred centimetres tall and a hundred and ten kilograms. Morag would certainly feel safer with him beside her.

'Hi Willy,' said Doug looking nervously up at his tangled orange beard, 'I'm Doug, and my name is only in the papers because these places fascinate me too. Don't ask me why someone leaves dismembered bodies in these Neolithic ruins. I would be totally entranced if you would take me around. Thankyou.'

'Hi Doug,' said Willy, giving him a warning smile and a bone-crushing handshake. The pecking order was clearly established. Not much would intimidate Willy.

'Willy plays Rugby for Scotland, at number eight, they call him William Wallace because of the way he destroys opponents on his battlefield,' announced Morag standing close beside him. She came way below his shoulder.

'Well,' said Doug, 'I don't damage anything, or anyone so let's go on please.'

'OK,' said Morag falteringly, 'This is an iron age round tower built some two thousand years ago. It is a well defended structure as you see, with a steep cliff down to the sea on one side, and this semi-circular rampart and ditch on the other. There is only a narrow entry space over there,' she said pointing.

'It is still four metres high, even taller than Willy,' she reminded Doug. 'Come inside.'

Doug followed obediently. He could feel Willy's intimidating presence just a step behind.

Morag continued, her voice sounding more confident now, 'It has four and a half metre thick walls, and an internal diameter of nine metres. The inside is divided into two rooms, both of which have a freshwater spring. They would have been well equipped to deal with a long siege. The first archaeologists excavating here nearly a hundred years ago had plenty of fresh water even then. See the stones on either side of the hearth, there are sockets which we think were for an iron roasting spit.'

'One of the most interesting finds here was Roman pottery. There were multiple fragments, yet we are several hundred miles north of Hadrian's Wall, the most northern extent of the Roman empire on a permanent basis. The Orcadians of two thousand years ago must have traded over long distances, probably by sea. Skilled and courageous sailors as they are today.'

'Quite incredible,' said Doug, 'did these people have a written language, did they leave any parchment like the Romans at Vindolanda? And do we know anything about their boats, I don't suppose any have been found like the Viking longships at Roskilde?'

Morag looked shrewdly at Doug with some new respect. Maybe this man is honestly an innocent Neolithic tragic.

'No sadly. That would have told us so much more. Although written communication was developing in Mesopotamia, Crete and China in late Neolithic times, this is dull backward old Scotland. Left behind on the edge of the ancient world. Don't forget that we did discover golf, tartan, whisky and the bagpipes later on.'

Morag checked that Willy was still close by.

'Doug, would you like to see the cairn as well?'

'Yes please if I am not taking up too much of your time.'

They walked the half mile to the cairn, Morag leading, Willy immediately behind Doug. They passed a mound by the path. 'See that mound, the farmer here believes that trolls and fairies live there. He puts a little food out each night to please them. In the morning it is gone. He won't dig or farm there so as not to upset them. If he does his crops may fail, his animals may die, and they will carry off his new-born leaving a changeling in the cot. He always leaves a bible and a knife in his wee bairns' cots to ward off the trolls. He claims to have seen fairies dancing on top of the mound once when returning from the pub.'

'Are you an archaeologist too?' Doug asked Willy, rolling his eyes in disbelief.

'Yes,' answered Morag for him, 'We are both senior lecturers in archaeology at Edinburgh University doing the last year of our PhDs.'

So, Willy had a big brain to go with his big body.

'Congratulations,' said Doug, 'what will you be doing next year?

They looked at each other long enough for Doug to speculate they were in a relationship. Morag also spotted Doug's covert glance at her left hand.

'We expect to continue our academic careers. And no, we are not married or engaged. We aren't into that medieval romantic nonsense. We have an open relationship.' Morag giggled suggestively, 'Willy's appetite is as big as his body.'

Doug wondered what his wife would think about an open relationship. One in which he could bed Carolyn as well. Perhaps both together. He didn't wonder for very long. Perhaps Willie was the luckiest man on the planet.

They arrived at another stone construction. This cairn appeared to be an ancient tomb. Once roofed over it was now protected from the elements by a modern hangar roof. It had a central aisle nearly twenty-four metres long separated into twelve chambers by stone pillars.

Willy took up the well-informed dissertation. 'Howe is an old Viking word for mound or barrow, which is what this was. The walls are two and a half metres high still. Some people feel this is like a church with pillars along a straight central aisle and a sort of shrine at the end.' Morag interjected jovially, 'I'm afraid you're too late to find a body here, Doug. Or even bones. The skeletons were excavated from here nearly a hundred years ago...'

Morag faltered as Doug winced visibly.

'Gently, Morag, poor Doug has been most upset by his gruesome discoveries,' soothed Willy. Obviously, he was a gentle giant off the rugby field.

Morag took in his pained expression, 'yes sorry Doug. Twenty-five skeletons had been excavated from these side sections. Some compartments had up to four skeletons, some none. Some of them had their backs to the wall with their legs bent up. Some were skulls only.'

'There were many animal bones as well. Ox, sheep, eagles, buzzards and other birds. The fish bones found here included bream which today only inhabits warmer seas suggesting that the Neolithic period must have been at the time of a previous global warming cycle.'

Doug absorbed the pre-historic ambience. Some of the Neolithic buildings had been so specifically constructed that the ceremonies here in them could be easily imagined. As in this case. Presumably only the elite were buried here. Neolithic Orkney's Westminster Abbey.

Willy took Doug back outside to where his backpack was sitting. He extracted his thermos, poured three cups of steaming coffee and added a generous slug of whisky. 'Here Doc, really sorry we upset you.'

'Coffee like this with scotch on a cold day and I can forgive anything. Thanks so much for the guided tour. Most fascinating and informative.' Doug shook hands with Morag and Willy. He had forgotten the mangling his hand had received earlier till Willy gave him another bone crusher. They looked at him curiously as he walked back to his car.

Doug's next island was South Ronaldsay to visit the Tomb of Eagles. That had been discovered fortuitously some eighty years ago by a farmer digging up flagstones in his own land. On the way out of Kirkwall heading south on the A961, he called into the Highland Park whisky distillery to buy a couple of bottles. One was the Rebus30 to commemorate the thirty years since the publication of Ian Rankin's first best-selling novel, *Knots & Crosses*, about the irascible detective. A light golden scotch, Doug hoped it might inspire him to find some answers. The label said it was *best shared with friends or while enjoying a dark crime novel!*

What about actually living in a crime novel! Would he be able to identify a murderer before DI Rob accused him? From amongst many thousand islanders and visitors? Unlikely. The other bottle was labelled the Wings of the Eagle. It was a memento to the eagle that sat on top of Yggdrasil, the Viking tree of knowledge. Its beating wings were said to have created all the winds of the earth. Doug reckoned the bloody eagle was particularly busy today!

He drove down the A961 to South Ronaldsay over the causeways linking the islands. His first stop was at the tomb's Visitors Centre. Here Doug purchased some delicious Orkney ice-cream and wandered around the original artefacts, visual displays and explanations plus all the local craft and books. Perhaps some local jewellery for his wife might atone for his sins. Unlikely.

He then walked a mile along the path to find the tomb. It was another complex large stone building entered through a low narrow tunnel on a board on wheels. Doug pulled himself anxiously through the claustrophobic passage on the rope and rose to find himself alone in a large chamber over three metres high with several compartments. No bodies mercifully!

Here over three hundred bodies had been buried some five thousand years ago. Thank god there were none today. Doug felt some trepidation each time he entered an old ruin. Were these the elite of society, the queen bees or the ordinary drones? The brooding silence could not answer his questions. Time travel would make this his first port-of-call if he ever had such a machine.

Some two thousand years ago over a dozen complete sea eagle skeletons had also been buried here suggesting some veneration for these magnificence warriors of the air. Were these the warriors' spirits escaping from their flightless mortal coil? The darksome clay of the poet. Doug pondered and moved on.

Half a mile away was a bronze age building which included a water trough and pipes with a hearth where a fire would heat the water container. Warm showers would definitely beat a cold bath in Orkney, Doug thought. Magnus could have the lust-controlling freezing dips to himself!

On his return to the main island Doug drove to the standing stones of Stenness. He arrived in the car park at the same time as another car pulled in. Two young ladies climbed out of their combi-van. One looked at him and smiled. The other took one look at Doug and her face froze.

'Oh my god, shite, that's the axe murderer, quick back in the car, let's get out of here!'

The other said, 'he could be an Orkney fin-man or a devil selkie, oh my god, run.'

Before Doug could protest his innocence, they had left some rubber on the ground doing a frantic U-turn in the car park and were speeding down the highway. Doug was getting pretty upset by this. He wouldn't take much more, but he still wanted to finish his exploration. A swig of Scapa whisky strengthened his resolve.

Located just south-east of the Ring of Brodgar, this henge, over five thousand years old, older than Stonehenge, originally comprised a dozen stones. Four stones up to five metres high still stand. Charred remains of pottery and bones were found in the middle. Outside the circle is another monolith, 5.6 metres high, the Watch Stone marking the past steppingstones, now bridged, to the Ring of Brodgar.

Just to the north had been another separate stone pierced with a circular hole. Odin's stone. Vikings took binding oaths with their hands clasped in Odin's stone. Once couples would plight their engagement holding hands through the stone. Sadly, the farmer owning the land over two hundred years ago smashed the stone to prevent trespassers. Perhaps if it was still standing, and if Doug had been there two weeks earlier, he may not have become an adulterer. Perhaps he would.

It was hard to think a happening of such consensual intimacy, such mutual affection and intense pleasure was also so bad, so wicked. Love was an emotion that would be hard to erase now once it had clasped him so tightly. Or was it lust? Either way it would be hard to forget.

Last stop on the mainland was the Brough of Birsay. Accessible at low tide along a quarter kilometre causeway, it has an unmanned lighthouse today. In the past there were settlements there from Pictish time in the sixth century through to the Vikings. Moulds for bronze metal working and a stone carved to depict three Pictish warriors were notable finds.

In the Viking period Birsay was the centre of power. A twelfth century ruined church marks their conversion to Christianity. Did the Vikings all of a sudden become devout followers of the seventh commandment. Regretfully that would show more moral fibre than he had.

The church had a tower at one end and a circular apse at the other. Jarl of Orkneyjar, Thorfinn the Mighty lived there. The first Bishop of Orkney was appointed and construction of the first Kirkwall cathedral commenced during his reign.

The remnants of the Norse house show heating and drainage, perhaps also saunas. Small sops to the inclement climate. A howling wind was blowing off the North Sea accompanied by intermittent squalls of rain. Doug remained impressed by the fortitude of the Orcadians throughout the island's history. The Romans apparently called this place Ultima Thule. Doug suspected the title may have been of more recent origin. The English thought those who lived in this unwelcoming climate were ultimate fools!

At least there were no more bodies. Perhaps the murderer had already left the islands. Doug suddenly thought he was a potential victim. Misbehaving tourists seemed the main target. Oh my god. DI Olsen might be convinced of his innocence if his was the next mutilated body. What would the murderer's chosen form of execution for an Englishman be? Hung, drawn and quartered? Not the best way of proving your point and your innocence. He appeared entirely alone on Birsay apart from the spirits of past inhabitants. The ruins were apparently uninhabited yet did not feel entirely uninhabited. He would have to watch out for other visitors.

CHAPTER EIGHT

Doug finally was full of enthusiasm for the last place of interest, perhaps the most interesting. Certainly the oldest. The Knap of Howar. The Knap is a Neolithic farmstead situated on the little Orkney island of Papa Westray. Radiocarbon dating suggests that it was first occupied nearly six thousand years ago. That would make it the oldest preserved stone house in northern Europe.

After that he would be flying home. Home away from mutilated corpses. Home to a mutilated marriage. Why had temptation led him so astray? Why did such an irresistible desire at the time seem not so compelling now?

Accommodation was booked for three nights on Papa Westray in the Beltane House. An interesting name. Beltane, the old Druid festival on May 1st to improve the fertility of the land. Beltane in which men and women coupled with as many others as possible to spill seed on the land regardless of marriages. A tradition of fidelity for three hundred and sixty-four days a year might be easier to follow.

Doug had booked a private room, sadly all to himself, with an uninterrupted view of the sea. It had a self-catering kitchen and a well provisioned shop where he could buy some food for his dinners. A three-course lunch was provided at the local craft and heritage centre.

Doug's first night, there would be a ceilidh in the lounge-dining area. These little sparsely populated islands all concealed surprising musical talent. There was little to do through the long dark winter months for the islanders beyond honing skills on the bagpipes or the fiddle, or highland dancing or singing. Alcohol was plentiful. It was Scotland. The community shop was well provisioned with beer, wine and whisky. Woe betide the tourist asking for other spirits. Americans seeking bourbon were re-educated. English seeking gin were despised. The English were despised anyway.

He rang Olsen, 'Inspector, as I told you, I am flying to Papa Westray, so don't get worried if you hear that I am at the airport. However, once I have seen the Knap of Howar, I would like to be returning home. My sabbatical leave is almost up. I trust you will see no reason to request my company any longer?'

'That's fine Doc don't find any more bodies will you! Westray is not a safe sanctuary for law breakers. Even Lord James Bothwell, husband to Mary Queen of Scots and suspected murderer of Darnley could not hide there from Scottish Law. He spent the last ten years of his life chained to a pillar in jail. So, no more bodies please doc.'

Doug drove to Kirkwall airport. Security was ramped up. There was a hideous murderer loose in the islands. His luggage was scanned for meat cleavers. Nothing more threatening was found than his safety razor. His cabin baggage was inspected carefully. No dramas.

Doug boarded the Loganair Britten-Norman Islander. It had space for nine passengers. Doug was quite alone apart from a not very friendly hostess. Remote Neolithic monuments had apparently lost their appeal for tourists when a vile murderer was roaming Orkney. He hoped the ninety odd occupants of Papa Westray paid little attention to the local newspapers. He hoped not to be identified again. The axe-murderer! Sickening.

The small plane landed briefly on Westray to load and unload supplies. Then it took off again for the shortest schedule flight in the world. It was under three kilometres to hop from one island to the next. A flight of around one minute. There was no inflight service!

Disembarking in the rain he was partially protected descending the steps and crossing the tarmac by accepting one of the collection of umbrellas offered. It was not much good for the driving horizontal rain. Doug entered the little airport terminal such as it was, dripping wet.

A smiling young woman approached him, 'you must be Doogie, I'm Jeanie, welcome to Papa, your luggage will come shortly, there aren't many cases. Well, we have some special treats for you tonight at the ceilidh. The women here are always on the look-out for a handsome male partner, especially when the boats are out at night. I hope you have your dancing shoes in your case.'

'Had you been here a week ago, you could have come to the Fun Weekend. It's the third weekend of every July. We have a BBQ, ceilidh, games and sports and a carty race doon the New Hooses Brae. We are usually booked out, but we could have found a bothie for you. It was before all the atrocious murders. Hardly anyone has been here for a week now sadly.'

Jeanie chattered away amicably without stopping or looking closely at Doug till they entered the guest house, 'there is some lunch ready for you. We expect the rain to stop in the next hour, so you can have a nice time walking around the sights of Papa. By the way, we have given you a room with an Orkney chair.'

Lunch was a delicious lobster mornay and a couple of bottles of Orkney Gold beer. Then a wee dram of Scapa scotch. Drinking was better than thinking. Euphoria better than guilt.

Sure enough the rain ceased. Doug grabbed his North Face jacket and set off. As he walked enthusiastically out the door, he bumped into a huge figure, it was Big Willy accompanied by both Fiona and Morag.

'Well, it's wee Doogie. Hey doc, we were most unkind and judgemental last time we met. Can we show you the sights and sites of Papa Westray?' Doug kept his hand thoughtfully behind his back.

'Well, thank you. This island seems full of fascinating ancient ruins. I would be most grateful. Especially as everyone else, DI Olsen included, thinks I am an axe murderer!'

'Don't be too hard on Robbie. He's had some awful things to deal with recently, well before you arrived here. I'll tell you later maybe over a beer in the bar,' said Willy confidentially.

'Come on then,' ordered Fiona, secure now with Willy beside her, 'nowhere is especially far here. It's all within walking distance. You know Papay is Pictish for priest, all the Papays had a priest. This place is also famous because Earl Rognvald Brusisson was buried here after he was murdered. First stop the ruins of St Tredwell's chapel. It's just to the south on a peninsula in the middle of St Tredwell's Loch. Its built originally in medieval times on top of old iron age buildings and there used to be an underground passage somewhere. After that you can buy me a single malt whisky or two for frightening the shite out of me at Brodgar!'

A few minutes brisk walk brought the four to an old ruin on a mound in the loch.

Willy told Doug, 'A hundred and fifty years ago its walls were still six feet high and coins from the reigns of Charles II and George III were found. Now it's just a ruin. However, it's still a place pilgrims come to for miraculous cures, particularly for eye diseases. That idea originates with the story of a young woman called Triduana. In the 8th century AD the Pictish King Nechtan attempted to seduce her. He started hopefully by saying how beautiful her eyes were. Rather than lose her honour and virginity, she gouged her eyes out, skewered them on a twig and sent them to the king. She said he could have what he admired so much.'

Morag took up the story, 'Fiona and I think that's a bit drastic, don't we? There are other ways a girl can preserve her virginity and protect herself these days!'

'That's if you want to preserve your virginity Morag, yours didn't last very long at University!' Fiona interjected. The two girls giggled suggestively, and Willie looked a little embarrassed.

Morag continued, 'Doug, did you know Fiona has a black belt in karate. She wasn't really scared of you at Brodgar! Anyway Triduana later became abbess of a nunnery at Restalrig in Edinburgh, and subsequently was canonised as St Tredwell. The pilgrims have to walk around the loch. Some thousand years ago, Earl Harald Maddadsson of Orkney didn't like his current Bishop, John of Caithness. He had his tongue cut off. Perhaps his sermons were long and boring! Then he plunged a knife into his eyes. However, when Bishop John was taken here by a helpful lady, his speech and sight were miraculously restored to normal!

'I've been here several times, but I still have severe myopia,' continued a disappointed Morag.

Fiona laughed, 'that's because you aren't godly enough Morag! Or virginal enough! It's also said the loch will turn blood red if a dire catastrophe happens to the Scottish royal family. According to mythology that hasn't happened since Bonnie Prince Charlie's tragic defeat at Culloden.'

They turned north west to find the recently restored St Boniface Kirk.

Fiona said, 'my turn now since I threw you out of Brodgar Ness. This church was originally built in the eighth century in an immediate area of Iron Age, Pictish and Viking ruins. It was named after St Boniface, who progressed from teacher to missionary to archbishop to violent murder victim, an essential ingredient for Scottish saints. Perhaps the bodies you found will become saints. Oh, sorry Doogie, that wasn't really funny,' she continued as he winced, 'see over there is a Viking hog-back gravestone and nearby two early Christian cross-slabs. Other seventh century early Christian carved stones, found at this site are on display in Orkney Museum in the Tankerness House, Kirkwall.'

Fiona continued, 'somewhere on Papa Westray, possibly here, is the grave of Thomas Traill. He was an evil laird of four centuries ago said to be in league with the devil. He mistreated the people terribly taking their food and letting them starve. He demanded the right of prima nocte. He screwed every bride on her wedding night before the husband had a chance.'

Willie interjected, 'silly fool, the husband should have had her long before the wedding night.'

Fiona smacked Willies bum affectionately, 'not everyone is like you Willie, anyway he was cursed by one of his starving cottars. Traill's wife died and he died not long after from that curse. Two ravens fought over his coffin. It was thought to be the laird and the devil fighting for his soul. Blood poured from his coffin and he was buried with no blood in his body as predicted by that curse.

Morag pointed nearby, 'over there is the Knap of Howar, go and see that tomorrow. You will need more time and rain is coming again. Last quick trip for today is North Hill at the northern tip of Papa. See the hill up there. We will walk a bit closer. It is the local highest mountain, forty-nine metres above sea level. Many seabirds breed there. The terns and skuas are fantastically territorial. If we get too close, we will be dive bombed. The stupid local islanders killed the last great auk on Papa back in 1813. A story goes, like St Kilda in the Hebrides, that they thought it was an evil witch!'

Fiona pointed to some pretty little purple flowers as they passed, 'see them, they are the Scottish primrose, *Primula scotica,* and incredibly rare.'

Once a hundred metres from North Hill, birds started squawking around them. A few lined up for a dive-bombing run. Big brave Willy was the first to run. 'It's all very well to laugh at me, the bonxies always attack the tallest person first. It reminds me of The Birds, you know Hitchcock's movie!'

Everyone remembered that one, Doug thought.

Back in the bar, Doug brought a couple of rounds and told his life story. Except for the past two weeks. After half an hour, the three archaeologists seemed to think he was perhaps a near-normal person.

The ceilidh hour drew on. Jeanie and her kitchen staff emerged with a pile of pizzas as the whole island population filed in. Willie took a turn behind the bar filling pints. First acts were the small surprisingly talented children performing songs and dances before being escorted unwillingly to bed. An eleven-year-old lad showed amazing mastery of the bagpipes for such a young age.

Then a surprising treat. Doug's new-found friends took to the dance floor, Willy on bagpipes with Fiona and Morag dancing on the swords. Wow, they were unbelievably good. Especially light on their feet. Finally, the island dance band assembled with the dance mistress calling the moves. Doug's hand was seized by a buxom young lass without question to be taken to the dance floor. He managed a passable Eightsome reel and the Gay Gordons. He was manoeuvred through an unknown Orkney reel by both Jeanie at the side and Morag and Fiona on the floor both in convulsions of laughter.

It was time to retire breathlessly to the bar to be entertained over a whisky. Or two. He fell into a discussion with Willie about rugby, an activity where he had some skill, at least during university days. He had been fly-half when Middlesex Hospital last won the inter Hospitals cup.

After an extremely convivial three hours, all the assembled throng were exhausted, or full of alcohol or both. Willy told Doug a bit about Detective Robbie's recent problems. How he had been glassed up by an inebriated English football fan on cocaine and alcohol when he was trying desperately to keep the peace in Kirkwall. His new beard hid the scars. At least the physical scars. How one of his relatives had also been assaulted, though Willie avoided giving more details.

Willie thought Olsen was the founder of a fantastically secret group called Odin's eye. They were a few people mainly in the hospitality industry who attempted to stop English tourists visiting in favour of Europeans. Any European rather than the Sassenachs! Anyone calling a local tourist agency from England was told there were no vacancies, no car spaces on the ferry, no cars to hire or no available flights. Good job Doug booked his and Carolyn's seats and rooms through the Scottish College of Physicians.

Doug thought there was a lot more to the story that he was not being told. Slowly the room emptied, some to the bothies, most to their homes and a few to their hostel room.

The Beltane guests all headed up the stairs to bed, happy and weary. Doug was not particularly surprised to see his new-found friends all retired to the same room, the one next to his. Well the bed was probably big enough for three. He hoped they would not be too noisy.

Willy stopped at the door and gave Doug a wink. 'You know in the old days when a man became betrothed here, he was allowed to sleep with his wife for a few weeks before the wedding, but only with the bride's sister being in the bed as well. I thought that meant a chaperone to lie between them, but Morag and Fiona thought it would have been a threesome! Hmm?' Willy winked confidentially and disappeared closing the door firmly behind him.

Doug sat thinking on his Orkney chair for a while. Made with a timber frame, the padded seat was made with straw as timber was scarce. The chair legs were short, so he stretched his legs out, Apparently, this had two purposes, to keep one's head under the peat smoke from the fire and to reach one's knitting wool on the ground. The last identifying feature was a small drawer under the seat containing a bible, compliments of the Free Church of Scotland, and a two hundred ml bottle of Scapa whisky compliments of Jeanie.

Doug sipped on that giving thought to his plans for the night and morning. He didn't need to read the commandments.

Prior to finally retiring for the night, Doug phoned one of his new-found colleagues, the infectious diseases specialist in Kirkwall. She was not enthusiastic about such a late call but was able to give Doug enough information. De-identified confidential information, but most helpful and worrying.

Doug read his tour guide. He was interested to read that this island was the birthplace of a John D. Mackay. He had been a teacher and then headmaster in the schools on several of the Orkney Islands. It was John Mackay who suggested in the Times over sixty years ago that Orkney and Shetland be returned to Norway after five centuries as part of Scotland. After all they had only been pawned to Scotland as a dowry. Time for Norway to redeem that pledge many thought.

At the time the administrative powers of the island authorities were being subsumed into mainland authorities who were abysmally ignorant of local concerns. Mackay's proposal was therefore well supported by the island community.

Doug read on with excitement and some trepidation. He hoped there would be no more bodies for his last site visit. The Knap of Howar Neolithic farmstead is the oldest preserved house in northern Europe, dating from around 3500 BC. The Unstan ware pottery shards found there pre-dated the grooved ware and apparently dated the farmhouse to nearly six thousand years ago.

The farmstead consists of two adjacent rounded rectangular thick-walled buildings with very low doorways facing the sea. The two structures are linked by a low passageway. Like Skara Brae it was built into a midden for warmth. The rooms have a door each but no windows. The roof has long gone, but the walls are still over five feet high.

Like Skara Brae, the stone furniture is intact giving a vivid impression of life in the house. Fireplaces, partition screens, beds and storage shelves in the rooms are almost intact, and post holes were found indicating the roof structure.

Examination of the middens had found bones of cattle, sheep and pigs. Barley and wheat grain and shellfish remnants were also found.

Before flying to Papa Westray, a bizarre thought went through Doug's head. It was wildly improbably, but as Sherlock Holmes said, when you have eliminated the impossible, whatever remains, however improbable, must be the truth. It would explain everything. Doug drove to Kirkwall to check a few facts in the registry office. Births, deaths and marriages, and the licencing department. He contacted a friend in Amazon books to check someone's purchases. Highly illegal, but Doug had once saved his son's life when he had meningococcal meningitis.

The next morning Doug walked the short distance to the Knap and looked curiously inside. His brain suddenly went into shock mode. Disbelief. Time slowed down. There were what looked initially like lumps of meat, but rapidly Doug could see this was a dismembered corpse. There were two arms, two legs and a head. Each limb was attached to a portion of trunk. There was a fire in there still smouldering with what looked like the remnant of some intestine and maybe genitalia.

Doug phoned Olsen. It was some moments before he could say anything. 'Come to Papa Westray, the Knapp of Howar now! Please!' he begged croakily. Then Doug hung up. He looked again at the body. He recognised the form of execution suffered by this oh so unfortunate man.

This victim, the fourth, and the third he had personally discovered had suffered the unbelievably cruel, unbelievably painful fate so beloved by the tyrannical and brutal Tudor monarchs of being hung, drawn and quartered. Hung till not quite asphyxiated, the cut down, castrated and eviscerated while still conscious, guts, cock and balls went onto the fire in front of the victim, then finally mercifully beheaded before being dismembered. Quarters of the body were then displayed around the country at the corners of the compass.

A not-so-subtle message to the community to support whatever may be the belief-set of the current homicidal Tudor monarch. Retaining the current religious variety, be it Catholic or Protestant, absolute regal power and the throne being the predominant absolutely ruthless demands for all of them.

The remnant of the corpse's neck showed rope burns, the still glowing fire on closer inspection also did contain the half-burnt remnant of cut off male genitalia and the gastro-intestinal tract. It also contained the charred remains of a red football jersey. The club logo was still discernible. It was Manchester United, an unpopular team here. They had knocked Rangers out of the EUFA Cup twice.

Doug sat down in the drizzly rain. He vomited several times and wept until a chopper sat down nearby. He was in trouble now. Olsen and his sergeant emerged. They took one look at Doug and peered into the ruin. Both reeled back. The sergeant sagged to his knees and began to vomit.

Olsen was quicker to react. He got onto his mobile. 'Close all airports and harbours immediately, take details of every boat and crew arriving in any harbour here. Call Inverness and Shetland for back up. I want at least two dozen extra squaddies now.' he ordered the police headquarters in Kirkwall. Olsen turned to the helicopter pilot, 'get up in the air and scour the area. Photo any boat in the water nearby.'

He went back to Doug. 'Another ritual execution doctor. Hung drawn and quartered! Edward Longshanks liked that one. Many Scots, true patriots, suffered that in the War of Independence, including one or two of the Bruce's brothers. I expect we will find this poor bastard is a Sassenach! Unless it is the bloodless corpse of Thomas Traill come to the surface.'

'So, Doug, you have been here since yesterday? Presumably you do not have an alibi this time. I believe your lady friend left you a week or more ago. Unless you have found another. Douglas Larsen, I arrest you on suspicion of murdering four innocent male tourists.'

Olsen then leaned over to Doug and whispered confidentially, 'and by the way, should you confess honestly to these frightful murders, then your little sordid affair may not need to come out. You just might have a marriage when you emerge from jail, should you ever emerge from jail,' Olsen added mirthlessly.

CHAPTER NINE

Susan was admitted to visit Doug. As a murder suspect they were separated by a perforated perspex partition. Physical contact was not possible.

'Look at this darling, this jail was created with stones from the original Kirkwall Castle. It's not every day you can stay in a historic monument with free board and lodging. My soul must live in this darksome house of clay briefly. Isn't it fascinating? My trial will be in the Victorian courthouse near the Bishop's Palace. I get to see the inside of some ancient building.' Doug announced with false bonhomie.

Susan just looked at him with silent tears rolling down her face.

'OK,' Doug continued, 'this looks serious, but it isn't. I'm not guilty and they only have awfully poor circumstantial evidence against me. I'll be a free man in three days.'

Susan sniffed and tried to stop weeping. 'I have something to confess to you.'

Doug amazed, responded slowly, sadly, 'I do too.'

'It's about my French painting lessons. Our teacher Henri said I was the only one with talent. I was too. He offered to give me some private tuition one evening. Well what the soft fading light, the bees buzzing soporifically in the honeysuckle, the warm summer breeze and a bottle of Chablis, we offered to pose for each other for life drawing. Sorry Doug, but one thing led to another, and........we ended up in bed together for the next four nights.

'I'm so sorry and so ashamed, but I'm also, yes, sorry, I have to say, glad because it was a most pleasurable affair. It was exciting abandoned guilty pleasurable, not loving comfortable relaxed exciting pleasurable like with you. I was terrified his wife would walk in. She was supposedly at a big company meeting in the states. Henri said the French don't get too worked up about these things anyway.'

'It was something I have never done before and will try never to do again. Hopefully I have that curiosity out of my system now, having never slept with anyone else in my life. I'm so sorry to tell you this when you are in so much trouble yourself.'

'My darling, my confession is sadly similar. Sorry. You know Carolyn, my colleague at work. She came to the conference and we spent four nights in bed as well. She is one of my alibis. It's also something I've never done before, like you I'm happy-sad about it and hope not to succumb again. The pleasures are different. Her husband does not know about it but will probably have to be told before she appears in the witness box.'

'When you leave here this morning Susan, make sure you go to the Reel in Kirkwall, it has the best coffee and often some beautiful live music. How do you like the West End Hotel? I had a drink there one night. It was built some hundred and fifty years ago by a William Richan who made much of his money from smuggling. It was a centre for incredibly rich businessmen in their fancy outfits to consume prodigious feasts of meat and ale, and to gamble ferociously, beyond their means, at whist and brag.'

Doug paused and looked at Susan. Tears ran down her face. She wasn't listening to anything he said. 'I'll be acquitted don't worry. We will both go home in a few days.'

Three days later Doug was indeed led into the packed Victorian courthouse near the Bishop's Palace. Handcuffed. Humiliated. Suspended from his hospital position pending the outcome of the trial. Blinded by the paparazzi's flashes. His picture already on the front page of all the London newspapers.

The trial was fairly short. Doug pleaded not guilty. He declined legal representation believing it to be unnecessary. The Government forensic pathologist detailed the mutilation of the four bodies and confirmed that the injuries and dismemberment were copies of past modes of execution. He informed the court that Doug's blood had been found on the corpse in Howar. Or a DNA match with a probability of six million to one.

As Larsen suspected, that was an unfortunate Englishman. One who had spent his first night in Orkney four days ago in the police lock-up for being drunk and disorderly at the front in Kirkwall. One strangely with the surname Longshanks.

Doug was most surprised to hear about his blood being found on the dismembered body, but a piece in his jigsaw puzzle fell into place.

Olsen detailed the discovery of the bodies and the failure of Dr Larsen's alibis to stand up. He dismissed Carolyn's testimony and alibi as the fire escape was easily accessible through the window of room twenty. He described Doug's interest in history and his medical knowledge of anatomy. His supposed discovery of three of the corpses.

The judge instructed the jury in their duty. The jury returned within two hours to announce Doug guilty as charged of all four murders. Even the one in Maeshowe somehow.

'Dr Larsen, you have been found guilty of the most heinous crimes I have encountered in all my years as a judge and in the legal profession at an earlier stage of my career. When I come across murderers like you, I sometimes wish we had not abandoned the death penalty. Do you have anything to say before I pronounce sentence? Don't expect to ever be a free man again!'

'Your honour, I do indeed have something to say now. I have not raised these facts before. I am totally innocent. I thought there was only limited circumstantial evidence against me. I had not been informed about my blood on the fourth corpse before. I can explain that.'

'I became quite fond of Detective Inspector Olsen during our brief acquaintance in-spite of his attempts to stitch me up for these heinous crimes. I am sorry for the misfortunes he has met. I hesitate to pull an otherwise excellent detective down. I know he has been through difficult times.'

'One of his colleagues has noted with sorrow that he is a recently changed character. Full of hatred. She loved him dearly, she said he had been a most brilliant detective, a great boss and a marvellous role-model. Some six months ago he changed beyond all recognition. He became bitter and twisted. The lion king had become the rogue elephant. Inspiring brilliant team leader to one intent on destroying all around. Sadly, she felt she had to tell me this as she thought I was being stitched up for the murders.'

'Yes, I admit to adultery. My wife and I will have to deal with that shortly. That does not make me guilty of murder and infidelity is not against the law of Scotland fortunately for both of us, your honour.'

There was a little titter and indrawing of breath in the court room. His honour was strongly suspected of non-professional relationships with some junior female lawyers.

'I am sorry to say DI Olsen is your murderer. I have undeniable proof.'

A gasp of disbelief went around the courtroom.

Doug continued, 'firstly he has an antipathy to tourists. He was sick of the gratuitous violence among the football thugs in Kirkwall. He was sick of being spat upon by the detritus of society. I hear he was glassed up some months ago while trying to control a riot in Kirkwall. Three cruise liners arrived in the harbour at the same time. One from London, one from Amsterdam and one from Hamburg. Unfortunate or probably stupid planning.'

'They were full of drunken football louts. The inevitable fights followed. Olsen was glassed up by a spaced-out hooligan full of cocaine and alcohol. A current HIV positive intravenous drug addict wielding a blood-stained broken bottle. Olsen's beard dates from that event to conceal the scars.'

'Rumour states that he too is now HIV positive as a result of that injury. His hospital tests confirm this. He is on treatment in the HIV clinic. The disease and its treatment can both cause psychotic episodes.'

'The Orcadian airhostess who was raped and bashed six months ago in the Kirkwall airport carpark was the DI'S natural daughter. Yes, Rob Olsen has not been faithful either. I checked birth certificates in

Kirkwall Town Hall. He was totally outraged by this assault and set on revenge against all tourists. Olsen is the proud possessor of a PhD in Icelandic literature and the Sagas. A high degree gained in his own time with mainly online studies. His Viking predecessors gave him the tradition of inviolable family honour. Olsen's honour had been traduced and like the Earls of Orkney, he would have his revenge. He had had enough.'

'Secondly, there is the issue of my blood being found on the dismembered corpse on Papa Westray. Nobody found any laceration on my body. Nobody looked. No source of where the blood could have come from on my body. When Olsen requested a sample of my DNA, he arranged for a blood sample to be taken. Not the usual buccal smear. I discussed my suspicions with the same member of the Orkney police before I flew to Papa Westray. She subsequently confirmed that my blood sample which still should be refrigerated has disappeared. Disposal of all DNA samples should be documented. She confirmed that every other DNA sample taken by the police for several years was with a buccal smear.'

'Thirdly, I know Olsen has an extensive library of medieval history. Amongst other similar books he has on his shelves, there are *The History of Torture and Execution: From Early Civilization Through Medieval Times to the Present* by Jean Kellaway, *The Book of Execution: An Encyclopedia of Methods of Judicial Execution* paperback by Geoffrey Abbott, and *Medieval Punishment and Torture (The Library of Medieval Times)* by Stephen Currie. Online orders from Amazon. DI Olsen is as well acquainted as I am with the most horrendous forms of execution performed in the past.'

'Fourthly he needed someone to hang his crimes on. A doctor would be a good start. Someone staying a month to visit Neolithic ruins, someone with a knowledge of ancient history and of anatomy. Me'

'Fifthly he told me there is no organisation opposing tourists from England, yet he is the founder of a secret group called Odin's eye who do just that. A prophecy stated that Earl Ragnald would die after a slip of the tongue. Apparently, he once said, 'we shall have aged enough when this fire burns out' when he meant to say 'baked'. He died soon after according to the prophecy that he would die. Detective Olsen made a slip of the tongue telling me there was no group opposing English tourists when he started one. His fall will come shortly.'

'The most damning evidence is that of my own eyes and my camera. Olsen has a microlite plane. I checked plane and helicopter licences in Kirkwall. He would have been able to land on Papa Westray at night undetected when the airport is closed. Who else would have been aware of my plan to visit Papa Westray? I told nobody else. My visits to other archaeological sites were not a secret. Olsen's contacts could have informed him in advance of my plans. This was his chance to finally provide evidence to convict me.'

'I started wondering about Olsen after discovering the third body at Skara Brae. It seemed the only alternative to my own guilt. I landed on the commercial flight to Papa Westray during the day. I watched the airport from my room having set up a GoPro camera on the edge of the runway just outside the secure enclosed area. At two am Olsen landed by moonlight. His plane lights were off. He was carrying a huge bag.'

'My movement detector on the GoPro alerted me to his arrival. He dumped the bag in a car he keeps there and drove off. I followed on a hired bicycle to see what he was up to. The roads are few and short. I could see his headlights. He drove to the Knap of Howar, emptied the contents there and lit a fire. I have an infrared camera and have pictures of the DI.'

'He then returned to the airport and flew out with his lights still off. He never logged the flight with Kirkwall Airport. It was only when I returned after daylight that I discovered what had been done. Only in daylight did I see that he had dumped a dismembered body. The fire, still alight, was to burn the guts and genitalia.'

'Your honour I have a folder of these pictures and can show these pictures to the jury if you would so allow. However perhaps DI Olsen may save you the trouble by confessing to the murders.'

The courtroom sat in dumbfounded silence for at least half a minute before a deafening babble developed. Fiona, Morag, Wee Willy, Susan and Carolyn sat looking totally stunned. Susan and Carolyn burst into tears. The judge viewed the pictures and ordered Doug's release. Larsen nodded at the judge and surrendered to police custody. A psychiatric assessment as soon as possible in confinement was ordered.

The entire town had packed the courtroom and surrounding area. They headed to the town hotels to digest the astounding turn of events over a few pints and a few more wee drams. Willy, Fiona and Morag slapped Doug on the back. Willy said, 'I never believed it was you. Rugby players are not murderers. They take out their aggression on the field. I did hear you had been an unbelievably naughty boy though! Tch tch Doogie!'

Susan and Carolyn were chatting together surprisingly amicably about Doug's failings. Sheer relief and surprise overwhelmed jealousy and resentment. Neither could be too critical under the circumstances. However, after a couple of large glasses of Highland Park, they both agreed he was not really a bad person, an exceptionally good doctor, a pretty good detective and certainly a great lover!

BOOK THREE

THE SHETLAND ISLANDS

....

Sheenagh Pugh – From '**Visitor**'

Sometimes, after a storm, sand shifts,
stones are flung aside, and a skull
stares out, or a framework of ribs
startles with its whiteness. Whole villages
have come back: hearths, stone tables,
even the shelves built into their walls.
The neighbour who called in just once
And whom we never got to know.

CHAPTER ONE

I t was supposed to be more exciting than reading about another dumb arse corpse. The great Scottish football team.

However, Detective Inspector Lachlan McKenzie turned off the TV in total disgust and drained the remnants of his last glass of Highland Park single malt. Scotland had lost yet again. Mainly because of the bluidy rubbish referee. That was also the end of his single malts.

After his divorce settlement it would be cheap blends from the supermarket from now on. At least not the bluidy rubbish whisky from China. The vivid swirling hues of the Northern Lights on the horizon last night, the bright blues and greens, the pinks and purples, contrasted with the blackness of his emotions.

They were called the merry dancers in Orkney. Mythology thought them to be the souls of the dead dancing for joy, a joy not transmitted to Lachie. Lachie's mood owed more to the current winter seasonal Shetland sunshine. Or lack of it. Sunset before three in the afternoon and just under six hours sunshine maximum on a good day. Many days black thunderclouds obscured the sun for hours.

He rubbed his two-day-old grey stubble. At first, he thought it was growing blonde like the hair of his childhood. A Viking beard like his youth. Reality check, he was well into middle age. It was grey. Lachie's good days were sadly all in the past.

Christmas had just passed. Lachie sat in his fully mortgaged flat alone. After his divorce in the summer, his ex took off with their kids, the car, and nearly all their money to join her boyfriend in London. Her so-called business trips there for the last two and a half years turned out to be with side-benefits. He was some sort of celebrity photographer, an A-lister. Bank balance and balls bigger than courtesy and intelligence.

She left last summer solstice. Lachie returned from working really late just after 3.00 am to find an otherwise empty unit for the first time in years. The Shetlanders were proud sole owners of the British summer sun for nearly half an hour at that time in the June morning before sunrise in Orkney. That was about all Lachie possessed now after she cleaned him out.

She made the mistake of leaving the kids old toothbrushes behind. A mate in the forensic pathology laboratory doing some DNA testing as a favour had the sad task of informing Lachie that the seven and five-year old boys were his, but his three-year old daughter was another man's child. Not so surprising now. At least she would have a richer father.

However, he would continue to be as good a father as he was allowed to be to all of them till someone confessed to the poor wee girl! Not so surprisingly, like many men in Shetland, he discovered his Y-chromosome was Scandinavian. A Viking from a millennium ago! His maternal side mitochondrial DNA dated back to the original Celts.

Solving difficult crimes and putting societies malefactors away was worth fifty times less than being a celebrity. Unless you were Jimmy Perez, the detective in 'Shetland' on TV. One hour to solve all crimes. Easy. The Lerwick police station was on minimum staff for the Christmas week. Lachie was unpaid on-call, but the islands were quiet apart from the usual drunks. He looked forward to returning to work, even on his minimum salary.

Some days Lachie wondered why he stayed on these barren windswept remote islands. Even summer was often cold and wet. Maybe the south of France or costal Norway would be nicer. Maybe some warm sunshine and turquoise seas. Maybe some buildings made of warm colours rather than the ubiquitous dull grey granite.

An inexplicable entity in his DNA and in the islands' historical mystique tied him here, home to his family for thousands of years as far as he knew. Home of his job, his friends, the only culture he knew. Further south would take him nearer the bitch-ex and her A lister lover. No thanks. His roots were too deep here. Better on the edge of the world with real people rather in the middle with its worship of money and celebrity.

The football had nearly been so glorious. Nearly. Scotland led Germany 1-0 in the final round of the European Championship qualifying section at Hampden Park till the eighty-eighth minute. Famous battles flitted through passionate Scottish crowd consciousness. Stirling and Bannockburn. The shade of William Wallace wearing the nine-jersey, scoring a goal and wielding a broadsword. The ghost of Robert the Bruce in five organising the schiltrons in mid-field.

Then Germany was erroneously awarded a corner when the last touch over the Scottish line was clearly by a German. The corner bounced of the head of an unsighted Scottish full back into the top corner. Brilliant goal. Wrong end. Scotland would still qualify for the finals with a draw. They deserved a win having dominated the game with skill and passion. One goal was a poor reflexion of the game. Three strikes on the woodwork, one rejected controversial penalty and one missed hand ball in the German penalty area kept the Scottish score to one only.

In the fourth and last minute of extra time a German striker took a theatrical dive in the Scottish penalty area and writhed on the ground in apparent mortal agony. An Oscar winning performance in Lachie's assessment. The nearest Scot at least two yards away raised his hands in horror and innocence. Penalty! The referee was mobbed by irate men in blue and sent two off to restore peace. He refused the video replay. The wounded striker made a miraculous recovery from his apparent life-threatening injury and slotted the penalty easy as shelling peas. Lazarus with golden boots!

Depression. Disaster. Daylight robbery thought Lachie and fifty thousand Scottish spectators. Falkirk and Flodden. Oh well there's always the World Cup in two years thought Lachie. Was it Einstein who said something like the definition of insanity was supporting the

Scottish team over and over again, but expecting a different result, a win, next time? Something like that.

Many of his friends on Shetland supported Iceland or the Faroes or even Denmark and Norway as their home team. They saw themselves as part of Europe not Scotland. Certainly not a part of Great Britain. Their tradition was Scandinavian. The War-time Shetland bus linked them to Norway in that country's dire hour of need. The inviolable fidelity of comradeship in arms against evil. Family.

Brexit was the last straw. England might want to go back to being little England again. Protected from the frog-eating peasants by the English Channel! Bread instead of pork and garlic in the sausages.

Not Scotland. They had always recognised a higher civilisation in Europe compared with England. Dutch art, French cuisine and wine, German music, Greek philosophy, Roman architecture. Better than warm beer, tasteless curry and cold chips. Better than retarded so called rock stars and pompous egos in Westminster. They had an independent liberal-Democrat member of Westminster. They would not be voting for either uncaring mainstream party, Labour or Tory. However, they still preferred unfashionable democracy to trendy violent activism unless severely provoked.

The devolution and opening of a Parliament in Edinburgh was still seen from a Shetland perspective as busy-body ignorant people somewhere down south telling them what to do. Scottish Lowlands or London made little difference. They felt unrepresented and misunderstood. Better to go back seven centuries and be part of Norway again was a common opinion.

Lachie unenthusiastically picked up the dry coroner's report into the death of Lance Corporal Thomas Smith of the Wessex Regiment. He had been deferring reading it till the last minute before returning to the office.

Smith had been holidaying in Shetland having just completed his second term in Afghanistan. He had been drinking and boasting in the Queen's Hotel bar for a couple of hours. Boasting about his success as a sniper. He claimed a few kills at the two-kilometre mark. Boasting that the Afghanistani women told him that Scots were better lovers than their locals. They loved looking up his kilt he maintained. Especially at what they found there. He announced that he would keep all their names secret, so they didn't get stoned for adultery. Secret because he was a perfect gentleman according to Smith. An up-himself dumb bastard though Lachie.

Many witnesses said he was unsteady with slurred speech. The publican had refused his previous request for the last beer and whisky chaser.

Three young female primary school teachers were celebrating the end of term. The end of the school year. Four weeks without bluidy rude lazy kids and aggressive parents. They expected the teachers to make a silk purse from a sow's ear when most of their kids were the sow's arse!

Smith approached them to have a drink with him, and to join him in his top room where he could still get another snifter. He wanted then to share his bottle of Highland Park Valkyrie single malt. And more. Lucky bastards Lachie thought. Well at least for the Scotch. Nectar of the Gods.

Once upstairs according to the girls he had bragged that he would be doing mountain training in Skye on the Blue Cuillins next week but was already brilliant at it. Shooting, screwing, mountaineering, he was the best. To prove his points, he said he would climb out one window and back in the other of his hotel top floor apartment if they would all go to bed with him afterwards. Predictably he fell three stories. The slab in the morgue, not a foursome in bed. His suspect prowess was never tested.

Post-mortem showed catastrophic head injuries. His blood alcohol was 320mg per 100ml. Four times the legal limit for driving. He wouldn't have felt much Lachie thought. He might not have managed the sex either.

Death by misadventure was the coroner's verdict. There did not seem much to cause concern. Though why women went to lecherous men's rooms defied Lachie's logic. They probably thought the three of them could fend off any amorous advances. Or that he was too drunk to perform.

Mind you that was a fantastically good Scotch. In fact, where did the bottle of Valkyrie go? It was not mentioned again in the report and not noted within the room examination. Bet the girls took it. Lucky bastards!

Chanting outside drew him to the window. A mass of belligerent females, maybe five hundred or more were marching down the street. They carried placards bearing illuminating statements such as 'no soldiers on Shetland', 'ban all British troops', 'reclaim the islands', 'same sex marriage for lesbians', 'stop climate change' and 'Oslo + LerwicK = OK'. Lachie recalled when women wanted men to behave like the gentle sex, now they wanted to be more aggressive than the worst of men. Frightening, intimidating!

Some waved Shetland flags. Like all the Scandinavian flags, the vertical part of the cross was shifted toward the hoist. A potent symbol of a shared heritage. A potent symbol of their preferred current allegiance. Some were waving Norwegian flags and singing the Norwegian national anthem. Something about "armed to guard our peace." That seemed appropriate as so many now had gun licenses.

Lachie made sure his front door was locked. They wanted separation from Scotland. Shexit. Ex with shit round it. Like Lachie's ex.

They wanted Norway to redeem the pledge of some six centuries ago when Norway pawned the islands to Scotland instead of cash for a dowry for Princess Margaret of Denmark. She was betrothed to James III, but her father King Christian of the newly combined Denmark and Norway was stony broke. Stony broke for a king, not stony broke for a policeman. A quick whip round today for twenty thousand marks should suffice. The Shetlands were only held by Scotland in pawn.

That female group outside, the OsloLerwicK OK group, arose nearly a year ago after a Shetland teenager, a local beauty, outstanding dux of the high school with a recently awarded academic scholarship to Oxford University, was raped and murdered, while two other girls were brutally raped. A life of limitless possibilities was brutally cut short. Two others perhaps mentally scarred for life.

These horrible events occurred while a thousand men from an English regiment were on a training exercise on the islands. Under political directions from some 'high-ups' in London, the investigation was taken over by the regiment's military police No convictions were laid. The perpetrator apparently could not be identified despite a claimed so-called thorough investigation which left no stone unturned. The press conference was delivered by pseudo-sympathetic bigwig administrators from London. People with a silky tongue, all the jargon words, but no expertise as detectives. Soothing words for the dumb islanders! Politically correct saccharin.

Deep regrets. Most soldiers appalled. Never happened before with this regiment. Maybe a local Shetlander. Horrendous crimes. Investigations on-going. DNA samples carefully collected in Shetland from the victims either lost in transit or unfortunately contaminated in the forensic laboratory in London. Sorry! Thorough internal enquiries. Strategic strategies. Continuing up-to-date information for Shetlanders. Perpetrators brought to justice. Government doing everything within its powers. Bullshit coverup! Forked tongues!

Lachie's unit covertly continued forbidden investigations. A couple of English soldiers were strongly suspected by his unit as the probable villains, but interrogation of any of the soldiers by the local detectives was not permitted. They were flown out rapidly. A whitewash was generally believed. Local anger was widespread. The events would not be forgotten. Not by the island men. Nor by the women. Not ever. One sergeant was severely bashed by some fishermen in Lerwick. Shops and pubs refused to serve soldiers. Or pissed in their beer behind the bar.

Shetlanders suspected their local detectives had discovered the truth. Lachie was a local legend to a few of them who had come into contact with him and his unflinching unceasing search for the truth. Lachie appeared not to care if he upset those in authority. The locals figured out that non-experts, the 'high-ups' in the south were making the decisions. The whole military unit was withdrawn early.

Lachie heard the next day about the subsequent progress of the women's gathering outside his window from one of his colleagues. The island women would certainly not forget the murder and rapes either.

The demonstrators loaded onto a dozen buses parked brazenly on yellow lines in the main street. No parking inspectors came anywhere near. Wisemen. The convoy headed to the Neolithic ruins of Stanydale Temple where they filled the small interior oval measuring only twelve metres by six metres. The remainder stood two deep all-round the top of the four-metre thick walls. Three glowing braziers scarcely challenged the freezing North Sea wind. The wind on Shetland was always cold. North-east or north-west, summer or winter. However, these women all were warmed by fire in their souls.

A speaker stood on the wall to talk to her sisters. Few were publicly identified beyond calling themselves the vestal virgins of vengeance of Shetland, though not just a few were known to hold important roles in the islands. Many leading professionals and an increasing number of senior administrators and successful businesswomen.

'Friends, sisters of Shetland, we know what a real man is on Shetland. He is not some egotistical psychopathic national leader from America or Russia or China who threatens nuclear Armageddon if he can't have his juvenile way. A tyrant who thinks having the biggest bomb will solve the problems of global poverty, malnutrition, clean water supplies, global warming and human rights. No. Not some juvenile twit who continues to pollute our earth and contribute to climate change. He is not even the poor bastard who fights his fellow man on the battlefield at the whim of some arrogant narcissistic dictator who is hiding way below ground in his six-star bunker.'

'It's time wars were fought as a personal duel between such tyrants, not that any of them would have the courage to engage in fighting personally. He is definitely not some British squaddie who rapes and murders our innocent teenagers. They destroyed one of the brightest and best of our young women and scarred two others for life. The ancient spirits of Shetland, our foremothers expect revenge. We don't like toxic masculinity; we don't like the typical male emotional void.'

'A real man on Shetland is the one who goes to sea fishing to feed his women and children, who fights the elements and sometimes loses his life in the process. A man following in the footsteps and seaways of his ancestors over five millennia on Shetland. A man who learnt communication skills and anger management from his parents and primary school. A man who is not afraid to cry, a man who can change nappies and cook a meal. A man who accepts a woman's decision and sees her as an equal in their partnership.'

'It is only a few months since two of our fishing trawlers were lost at sea with all hands. Here amongst us are the wives and lovers, mothers and sisters and daughters of these brave men. You have our deepest sympathy and support. That is a real man on these isles.'

Thunderous cheers greeted the orator.

Fiona Sutherland, Lachie's detective sergeant was part of the group. All activists' speeches were applauded, English and English regimental flags were burnt, and an effigy of a male was castrated and beheaded. Its balls and head were thrown into a brazier while the women laughed, chanted and danced. Life's useless garbage tossed casually, no, vindictively into the rubbish bin. Fiona wondered if their ideal male was one castrated at the altar after pledging to obey, saving a sperm sample and buying a vibrator for his spouse!

A couple of women commenced playing their fiddles, bouncy Shetland style similar to the Norwegian folk music while all the women danced with enthusiasm. Many as intimate couples.

Fiona spoke to Jean, one of the speakers, after the meeting. 'The OK women's group is full of firebrands protecting women in trying situations. I work in a difficult stressful position. How do I join this group?'

'Oh, there is no membership, you have joined already, anyone can come along, well any woman. Preferably one in a same sex relationship even if they have a trophy husband as well.'

'Oh,' replied Fiona, 'who is the president or secretary or whatever?'

'We don't have anyone in charge or anything like that.'

Fiona was getting nowhere, 'who organises the speakers?'

'Oh, that just happens, anyone who wants to talk gets up.'

'When do you have meetings?'

'When anyone feels like it, usually Saturday around 3.00pm when the brain-dead men are watching boganball and getting pissed. Pigskin ball for male pigs. Fiona, someone told me you are a police detective. Am I being interrogated? Do you think one of us peace weavers is a shield maiden in disguise? Do you think one of us is a mass murderer or something?'

'No, no, certainly not. I just feel awfully vulnerable as a gay policewoman dealing with extremely violent men every day. I was looking for some spiritual and moral support. Sorry to sound like a detective, but it's what I do all day.'

CHAPTER TWO

New Year's Eve passed. Lachie consumed half a bottle of cheap blended whisky alone. it didn't make him feel better. He now understood the Orcadian Dwarfie Stane poem by George Mackay Brown about the soul having to live in a darksome house of mortal clay.

He re-read some Christmas thank-you letters emailed by his kids. Brief, lacking affection, duty. His ex-wife had told them he was a bad man. What hypocrisy! Said he was an alcoholic. Said he was a serial womaniser. He wished. Fiona looked more attractive each day of celibacy.

An attractive fiery redhead, Lachie had idly wondered if she could keep his bed warm. It had been cold since the ex departed, mind you it had not been convivial for a while before. However, Fiona was his junior. Lachie knew an undisclosed sexual affair across a police chain of command would probably end his career should it be discovered. He was aware that Fiona already had a partner. Another female. It remained no more than an idle fantasy unfortunately.

Lachie's mobile phone rang. Hopefully it would be work. Something to do. Better a juicy murder than repeats of juvenile American sitcoms with canned laughter and cheap scotch.

'Hi boss, put the scotch down and come in there's been a murder.' It was Fiona.

Thank God, thought Lachie, better even a dull murder than the best of American TV.

Fiona was waiting for him at Lerwick police station.

'Hi boss, another dead soldier, another Sassenach. He was with a tour group at Jarlshof when he was found in the ruins very dead. Nasty injuries I hear.'

They drove down to the south end of the main island to the Neolithic ruins. A popular spot for tourists. Pottery found in a midden there dates back to at least 2500 BC. A continuous sequence of stone constructions fills the site linking the Neolithic era to the Stewart kings via the bronze and iron ages, the Picts and the Norsemen, and finally Scottish ownership of the Shetlands. One building would be demolished to build the next. The bronze age smithy advanced to his iron age replacement. Animal bones included those of red deer, wild cats, seals and the extinct great auk.

A crime scene had been established. A bus full of tourists sat waiting impatiently, selfishly.

Lachie entered to a chorus of protests about the delay.

'Quite please! Are you aware one of your group has been murdered? I am sure he would appreciate your amazing concern and sympathy. My God, I am disgusted! OK, you can go back to your hotels once we have taken everyone's names, passport details, phone numbers and addresses. No one leaves the islands yet. No one. Remember you are all witnesses to a crime scene, a murder. That puts you all on the list of suspects. You are all subject to the law of the land and its officers. Me!'

'Present yourselves, all of you at Lerwick police station between 0800 and 1200 tomorrow. Your names will shortly be known at the ferry terminal and the airport. Do not attempt to leave please.'

Lachie dismounted and turned to Fiona.

'Lead on and tell me about the victim.'

'His name is Captain Brian Riggs also of the Wessex regiment like Thomas Smith our climbing Casanova. An expert in military history. He was one of a group of twenty being conducted round the old buildings here. After an hour's tour and some souvenir collecting in the shop, they returned to the bus. A head count found nineteen. Should be twenty. Checked again, still nineteen. The tour guide returned to search the ruins and found the body. He is the pale one leaning against the wall over there smoking a cigarette.'

An ashen faced man shivered under a bus company cap as a few snow-flakes floated around him. Shocked or cold, probably both.

'A phone call to Lerwick had a PC here to close the site within ten minutes. He did not go near the body since death was obvious and he knows your methods.'

Lachie and Fiona entered the Neolithic ruins to find a policeman standing at the entrance of a subterranean roundhouse with thick stone walls. Beyond in the ruined broch bathed in a pool of blood lay a nearly naked very dead corpse. His throat had been cut and he had been castrated. Judging by the blood loss around the pelvis his throat had been cut after his balls were chopped off.

'Jesus,' said Lachie, the cheap scotch hovering uncertainly in his stomach for the moment, 'you could have given me a heads-up on the injuries. A bit more than nasty! This could only have been done by overpowering him. There must have been at least two or three perpetrators, probably strong men.'

He looked around. There were footprints everywhere. 'OK pictures from all angles, picture of all footprints.'

Interrogation of the grumpy tourists the next day added little. Some had exchanged pleasantries with the victim during the tour. None had ever seen him before the tour. None had seen him for a quarter of an hour before boarding the bus. None could recall seeing him in the souvenir shop. They had not seen anyone else visiting Jarlshof apart from the group. They all had alibis in the souvenir room. They all had made a few friends within the group. The guide had been giving advice on locally made jewellery. The only CCTV was in the souvenir shop. None in the ruins. More important to protect the jewellery than people or priceless unique ancient ruins. Money rules, mused Lachie. Thirty pieces of silver.

Most of the group had identifiable footprints in the ruins when their boots were subsequently matched with the pictures.

Back at the Lerwick police station, Fiona mused, 'funny finding him in the broch, it used to be a secure stronghold, but not for poor Brian. You know the OK women's group see symbolism in brochs. They liken them to a woman's body. They are the fortress at the heart of the stone-age village. A central cylindrical cavity for intimacy and security. Security for a baby in the uterus, intimacy for a man in the vagina. Entry most definitely only with permission.'

Lachie wondered if there was any significance to the idea or just the wild ramblings of the anti-men brigade.

The autopsy showed the expected. An exceedingly sharp knife appeared to have been used. One cut through the scrotum, one through the neck. No weapon had been found. A bruise on the back of his neck. If he was lucky, he would have been knocked unconscious before the knife-wielder got to work. No other marks. Nobody else's DNA. No witness. No CCTV. No weapon found. No clear motive. An unsolved case so far.

CHAPTER THREE

The women's OK group had another meeting to commemorate next week's Up Helly Aa festival and the New Year. It was down the south end on the main island. Another of the police station's young female PCs, a new recruit, took a covert recording of events with a wire from the office. She was not sure if she was impressed by the organisation as a career woman, or suspicious it was a front for violence. The recording was played back in Lerwick police station.

The first unidentified speaker arose near a log fire. Warmth was a privilege of leadership. They never seemed keen, however, on announcing their names.

'Welcome sisters of Shetland to Old Scatness. It is with great sorrow we record the unfortunate but violent death of another British soldier in Jarlshof this week. The presence of English soldiers here has been a total disaster for several centuries. Oliver Cromwell sent his victorious army here after the English Civil War. All that did for Shetland was to introduce venereal disease amongst the women they raped or seduced.'

'A hundred years later the English sent three hundred soldiers nominally to protect us from the Dutch. The Dutch never came, but we would have been safer with them than the perverted debauched English who forcefully deflowered our women'

'If the English warmongers did not send their soldiers to Shetland, the unfortunate man found in Jarlshof would still be alive. His family in England would still have a husband and a father. Desperately sad. The death remains unexplained. Many wonder if the spirits of our stone age ancestors or even the little people still live amongst us, to protect us from invading armies and seek revenge for us. I expect we will see the merry dancers tonight; our old Shetland ancestors will be pleased.'

'These ancient sites in Shetland date back from medieval times to the Iron Age. We women played important roles from the Iron Age to the Viking settlements. Women were the power on the home front. Decision making on homes, health, food, families and marriages were in our hands. Men were sent out to hunt for the families' food and some ill-advisedly played their silly war games against our better judgement.'

'Unfortunately, in the medieval period Norman culture and concepts of power spread up here and altered the political landscape. The Normans claimed to put women on a pedestal of virtue, but it was in fact a pedestal of disempowerment. We should choose if we wish to be virtuous or not, not men choosing for us.'

'It was part of a planned brutal suppression of Anglo-Saxon and Celtic men and women. The Norman influence brought only one good thing. It gave us our wonderful cathedral in Lerwick but sadly nothing else of benefit to women. We are only starting to repair our loss of control of the last thousand years. We still have less pay, less political representations and less assets than men. Equality within two decades in Shetland is one of our aims.'

'We meet at our heritage sites in Shetland to acknowledge the strong women who preceded us and to stiffen our resolve for greater equality. This site was only unearthed in the 1970s when the Sumburgh Airport was extended. The earliest building is this one where we are gathered, the iron age broch.'

'It is a cylindrical refuge at the heart of the settlement. Like our womanly bodies. Bodies we should control. We should decide how and when they are used. Contraception, intercourse pregnancy and terminations should be our choice. Only ours.'

'Like women the broch went through three stages. Virgin, mother, respected elder. Outer tower, second wall and inner cells. There are some twenty other structures clustered around including three round houses up to two metres high and twelve metres across. One structure is subterranean, a characteristic of the Picts building. This broch is the most important. The most central. These buildings were a home for a large village, maybe a hundred or more stone age dwellers. A village controlled by the women.'

'It was such a sound set of structures that it was used by the Vikings and as a barn and corn drier in the seventeenth century.'

A second female stood up and initiated some rather fearsome chanting. Again, a Union Jack was burnt, and a male effigy was beheaded, castrated and thrown on the fire to loud cheers. Again, the fiddles emerged, and all danced around in gay abandon.

Lachie thought it mostly sounded fairly harmless. Maybe he wouldn't want to have intruded on the gathering. His balls may have ended up on the fire or he may have been burnt at the stake like a heretic of yesteryear! Maybe he was better alone rather than living with such fierce feminist opinions around the clock! Better keeping relations with Fiona purely, or impurely as wishful thinking. Not that his ex was a feminist like these women. She was just a user.

CHAPTER FOUR

Before the impending big 'Up Helly Aa' festival, a new sporting event had been arranged. The Shetland triathlon, the *'Up To Hell Yes'* Triathlon! A tragically prophetic name as it turned out. It was not like the triathlon Lachie had run with the ex a few years ago on holiday in southern Queensland. A good year, a good relationship he mistakenly thought then, warm hopefully shark-free canal water and a flat running track. This one in Shetland was to commence at 9.00am when there was enough daylight. Swimming in a near-freezing sea inlet. Cycling would be into fierce winds at least one way. It would end with a steep run to Ronas Hill, the island's highest point four hundred and fifty metres above sea level over rough moorland. There was not clearly a track. The top was usually in cloud, occasionally the locals could say, Ronas has his cap off today.

Land and sea would be cold, bitterly cold. It would, however, be infinitely preferable for the locals to the island games last held in Guernsey where many Shetlanders suffered heat-stroke when the mercury crept past thirty degrees! They hoped Hades would not be that hot. Next year's games were planned for Bermuda. Few would go there from Shetland.

When the triathlon was announced, not only the local athletes and fitness fanatics decided to compete. The local football team and other sporting groups would be surprisingly challenged by ace men and women of the army Highland Volunteers. This was composed of the famous fighting warriors from regiments with battle honours going back over a few hundred years. Proud teams boasting of magnificent past victories. At Blenheim and Waterloo, at Balaclava and on the Somme.

Three men and two women each came from the Black Watch Company in Dundee, the Seaforth Highlander's Company in Wick, the Queen's Own Cameron Highlander's Company in Inverness, the Gordon Highlander's Company in Aberdeen, and finally the Argyll and Sutherland Highlander's Company in Stirling. No Campbells or McDonalds. Too much residual hatred. Over three hundred years since the massacre of Glencoe had not softened traumatised memories. Not even as far away as Shetland.

These were the toughest and fittest men and women from a regiment of hard men and women. Fighting men and women grudgingly respected by the Taliban and in Iraq. Feared and respected like their regimental predecessors. Inter-regimental rivalry and clan feuds hundreds of years old would ensure only the strongest and most determined would win. The origin of some clan rivalries was lost in the mists of time. Others were only too vividly and bitterly remembered. Clan tartans would identify them to spectators and their rivals.

Then surprising late entries came from south of the border. Four of the toughest from each of the Paratroop Regiment, three Commando Brigade and the Special Air Service had heard boasting amongst the Scottish Regiment and would certainly not be intimidated by man nor weather nor terrain.

The local women's activist group, OK, were equally not intimidated. They wanted the event cancelled or at least outsiders, especially military outsiders rejected. The town council ignored them. Money could be made from such events. Money trumps social issues, especially ones important only to women.

Many OK young women then enrolled for the event. Ones with muscles honed by hours in the local gymnasia. If you can't stop them, beat them!

The 1.5km swim commenced at high tide in Voe village for 750 metres up the gulf, around a buoy, then back again. The water temperature was a refreshing, bracing, challenging seven degrees. Warmed by the Gulf Stream so the geologists claimed. Most wore wet suits. A few hardy souls were covered in a thick layer of grease. The leading pack emerged within twenty minutes to cycle 40km to North Roe and back to the transmitting station below Ronas Hill. Voe to Roe into a forty-knot wind from the Artic. From here it was a five km run up the steep hill to the high point of the Shetlands, the site of an old Celtic Chapel. Then another five kms down to the finishing line

Snow commenced to fall as they emerged from the water to transition to cycling. Eighty minutes passed before the first cyclists completed the ride into an arctic gale. The Olympic record was under the hour but in much easier circumstances.

The visibility was down below a hundred yards as a leading group of five men and two women dropped their cycles and started to run uphill. The English men of Three Commando and the Paras, the women just behind were Gordon Highlanders.

The snow now became really heavy. Ronas was wearing a white balaclava! Visibility was down to thirty metres or less. Fortunately, there were path markers every ten metres.

The leaders were expected back within thirty-five to forty minutes. Money exchanged hands amongst excited spectators supporting their favourites. Hands warmed by several braziers scattered amongst the crowd. Thirty-five minutes passed. Another three dozen competitors had finished the cycling and set off running.

After forty-five minutes the two Gordon Highland young ladies emerged from the dense snow to run together through the finishing tape hand in hand. Arms raised. They were given thick warmed blankets and a slug of Muckle Flugga blended scotch beside a brazier sparking in the freezing wind.

They appeared a unit as they hugged and kissed each other to supportive cheers from the OK female spectators.

Another ten minutes passed. The first two men out of the murk were local Shetlanders. Climbing hards who set a record ascent time of the Old Man of Hoy a few months ago. Heavy formidable men not built for running, but able to cycle powerfully into an Arctic gale for as long as it takes. They were greeted with euphoric applause and a slug of Muckle Flugga. One rejected the tot. Instead he grasped the bottle and downed half of it before passing it to his mate who downed the other half. More enthusiastic applause.

Other men and women emerged to rapturous applause. The first five men to set off up the hill over an hour ago had not emerged inspite of a handy lead at the end of the cycle race. Organisers started to become concerned. It would be easy to get lost up there. These men were survival specialists but not without cold weather clothing. Heavy snow was still falling.

By this time, all the event supervisors and assistants from along the course began to gather at the finish line after the last competitors passed them back down the track. They were all wearing thick Gortex jackets, gloves and beanies. Many had CB radios. The fit younger ones went in a group of twenty up to the top and back. They found no trace of the missing men.

The Black Watch Helicopter was in Lerwick having ferried in their general to distribute prizes. He had told his troops that he expected them to win both the men's and women's events. The honour of their regiments demanded that.

It was summoned to fly over the hill with its ground following radar and sonar. With its heat detecting sensors. After ten minutes searching in the minimal visibility, they announced they had detected five still warm objects and were lowering a paramedic to check.

There was then a ten-minute break in transmission. No further details followed to the increasing apprehension of the officials, spectators and finished athletes. Five minutes later a request for a police presence and three ambulances was received. Anxiety increased.

Ten minutes later a police car with fog lights on high beam and siren blaring arrived. The helicopter landed, embarked a police sergeant and a detective, Fiona Sutherland, and took off again into the continuing thick snowstorm.

The chopper continued to fly in and fly out. Bodies were disembarked first two, then another two, then the last. They were all extremely dead.

They had all had a bullet hole right in the middle of their forehead. Silence and deep shock overwhelmed all those at the finish line.

Lachie was summoned and arrived by road as the snow continued. He surveyed the bodies and abused all and sundry for removing the bodies from the sites of their murders. Fiona approached Lachie. 'sorry boss, the temperature up there is now minus fifteen with the wind chill factor. We would have had more corpses with hypothermia. I took pictures of all of them. By the time I got there, there were numerous footprints everywhere from the search party and paramedics. I have a videoclip of the whole place. They need post-mortems to identify the weapons.'

Lachie looked at them sadly, 'well the locals will be hard pressed to blame our stone age ghosts for this, I don't think they carried guns, or indeed razor-sharp steel knives.'

The bodies were transported to the Lerwick Hospital morgue. The forensic pathologist in Aberdeen decided to fly to Shetland in view of the number of bodies. Once they were stripped and placed on the autopsy room slab, they were also found to have all been castrated.

Bullets were removed from all five brains and subsequently found to have come from Glock 17s, the standard British army issue. The standard side arm of half the world. A police search of Ronas Hill once the snow had melted with metal detectors found five ejected cartridge shells. Firing pin analysis suggested three different pistols were used as did examination of the rifling striations on the bullets.

Instructions from the Ministry of Defence to the Police Service of Scotland demanded that this would be investigated again by the London based Defence Department Military Police. Scotland's Chief Constable rejected this. Not again. The last time was a whitewash. A cover-up. Under the terms of devolution this was an internal Scottish affair. Words were exchanged between the British Prime Minister and the First Minister of Scotland. Not harmonious words. The first said a team would be sent to investigate, the other that they would be rejected. The former promised an open and competent search this time to find the murderer. The later rubbished that as only being interested in solving a murder of English men, not detecting rapists and a murderer of Shetland women.

CHAPTER FIVE

I t was three days after the triathlon murders. Local rumours said the soldiers had ascended an old execution site. Many summits became the site of gibbets in the past. Hanger Heog, they were called. Tradition claimed that any condemned criminal ascending a hanger would never come down alive. Any English soldier was a condemned criminal in local eyes.

Another rumour prevalent in the rural areas was that soldiers had previously used a troll mound for target practice. The bullets were simply being returned. It was only a short run from Ronas Hill down the A970 to the Kames, a lonely hilly area north of Lerwick where most of the trows lived according to local mythology. A mythology publicly disclaimed, but privately, quietly, the older inhabitants wondered. Never underestimate the spite of the little people, the first people of Shetland they thought.

It was starting to get light, though the streetlights still provided most of the illumination. The council garbage trucks, and an army of councils workers arrived at 7.00am to clean up the city. It had been the town's once-a-year day last night. Up Helly Aa. The parade of a thousand men dressed as Vikings led by their Guizer Jarl. The ceremonial burning of a replica Viking longship.

The OK group had demonstrated silently in the crowd. Their placards read 'Women in the Parade', 'Women were Vikings too', and

'No sexism in Shetland.' 'we sew Viking clothes; we should wear them.' Even the Scotsman was reporting the ban on women participating in the parade. As always, they did all the work in the background. All guts and no glory!

The detritus of Up Helly Aa was all along the sea front. Empty whisky bottles and beer cans. Burger cartons. Cigarette buts. A few used condoms. Enthusiastic indiscreet but careful young lovers in spite of subzero temperatures. The trolley conveying the galley was now cool enough to approach and remove.

Jock surveyed the ashes of last night's torching ceremony. He peered at them; his curiosity aroused. Then recognition dawned on him. He was looking not just at a buckled carriage metal frame and ashes of a longship, but a charred human skeleton. He summoned his unit director who peered as well.

'Oh my God, you're right Jock. I'll call the police, there is probably one nearby.'

Within ten minutes the local bobby had been supported by a forensic investigation team. Fiona and Lachie arrived shortly afterwards. Statements from the clear-up team added little to what was obvious. The Viking team dragging the Viking ship were all interviewed over the next few days. They saw nothing untoward. There had been no body visible on the trolley during day light hours. They all threw flaming torches at the ship as they had many times before in previous years.

The autopsy was limited by the damage caused by a partial cremation. Dental wear suggested a young adult. DNA analysis revealed a male Caucasian. Skeletal examination detected a posterior skull fracture of serious magnitude, possibly adequate to cause death.

Enquiries did not match with any missing person of the last year. Police press conference was not followed by any matched missing person being reported.

The data was forwarded to security headquarters in London, ultimately to MI6. Word came back officially from a high level of government that the victim had been identified and to cease further investigation. Unofficially whispers crept back that the victim was an anti-terrorist operative working underground in Shetland to detect covert Iranian or Chinese interference in the island infrastructure or backing for the women's movement.

Eight British soldiers had now died violently in a few weeks.

CHAPTER SIX

T wo days later three members of the investigative arm of the British Military Police arrived at Sumburgh Airport. Perfectly pressed uniforms with razor sharp creases. Shiny medals and shiny boots. Self-confidence and self-importance. A colonel, a sergeant and a corporal.

'Sergeant Smith and Corporal Brown, go and collect our luggage from the carousel. I will fix a car and accommodation,' snapped the colonel. A member of the upper classes. Minor nobility. Born to rule. The enlisted men saluted rigidly. 'Yes SIR!' Members of the peasant class. Born to obey.

The colonel, a detective chief-inspector in equivalent civilian terms, approached the first car hire desk.

'I am Colonel Lord Ponsonby-Bohun, I'll have a saloon car for two weeks in the first instance. I may need a four-wheel drive shortly. I am here to investigate the cruel murders of our brave soldiers.'

'And I'm the Queen of Sheba. I'm sorry your lordship, all our cars are being repaired at the moment. One of our new staff filled all our vehicles up with diesel by mistake. It's twenty-five miles to town, quite a nice walk once the rain stops. The bus has just left, it will be back tomorrow for the day's incoming flight. The taxi is out of action. Poor Jock the driver is in hospital with a broken hip. He was so pissed at the final Up Helly Aa town party that he didn't feel a thing, when he fell over, silly bastard. And by the way you need Isaac to find your killer.'

'And also, by the way, your lordship, wearing regimental insignia is unlucky here. Always has been. A thousand years ago, Earl Sigurd was about to fight Finnleik. Sigurd's mother, a sorceress made him a banner decorated with his tribal emblem and said whosoever follows this banner will win, but whosoever carries it will die. That is what happened. Sigurd won the day though his standard bearers died. You carry your tribal emblem on your uniform, as did your unfortunate runners in the Up Helly Aa triathlon. I fear for you. The Celtic and Viking undead live on here and should not be offended.'

'Bah, such superstitious rubbish,' the colonel barked and stalked off.

At the second desk, the response was, 'sorry Milord, an old fellow hired one of our cars three days ago, had a medical event in the car park and drove round and around in circles smashing our whole fleet. They are all at the panel beaters. We should have some back in five days. Isaac would find your killer, he's incredibly smart.'

The third desk response was little better, 'are you after the killers? All our cars are out after the problems the other two dealers had. We will have one back by next week-end sir lordship. My old dad has a spare tractor on his farm if that would help. He could introduce you to Isaac, he's our best detective'

The irate and frustrated colonel headed to the accommodation desk. 'I am Colonel Lord Ponsonby-Bohun, I'll need three rooms for two weeks in the first instance. One room needs to be an executive suite with an office and Wi-Fi. I am here to find a killer.'

'Have you booked ahead your Lordship?'

'No, you stupid idiot, that is why I am talking to you.'

'Hm, it's a bad time of year, your lordly eminence, sir. After Up Helly Aa all the hotels close for a week or so for repairs and maintenance. The tourists get a bit wild with the festival and all. Too much alcohol. Bit of damage you know. Innocent fun though. You should come next year. Not in that uniform though. We don't like uniforms here. They bring bad luck. It's now the end of the tourist season till spring. I should have a room for you all in a week, it would mean two of you sharing a double bed.'

'There is a better alternative for you. Your flight leaves again in twenty minutes for Aberdeen when it finished refuelling and servicing. Aberdeen has plenty of accommodation and rental cars at this time of year. No one visits Aberdeen even in summer unless they have to. Mind you, you could go to the football, Aberdeen play Rangers tomorrow. Should be a great game. That might be your best bet. Also you should contact Isaac to nail the killer.'

Ponsonby-Bohun bristled, 'you know I heard a myth about the origin of your pathetic islands, a giant walking across the North Sea from Norway to Scotland stopped to open his bowels. The myth says he 'shet lands'. It doesn't seem a myth to me anymore. This is a shitty place full of turds! Bloody Isaac!'

Then the colonel stormed back to the carousel. All the other passengers had left with their cases. The army bags had yet to appear. A baggage handler emerged and approached Corporal Brown. 'Your Lordship. I am sorry, your luggage has been left on the plane by mistake, sorry. But we have heard you are leaving on the same plane in fifteen minutes, so we left it there for you. If you come ever back, you should contact our detective Isaac about the murders. It might have been our little people getting revenge.'

A tactical withdrawal with little grace appeared to be the only military option. The suggestion of staying in Aberdeen was not appreciated. Nor was the idea that some Isaac idiot could solve the case. The three left on the next flight from Aberdeen to London, his Lordship furious because he had to travel economy with the enlisted men. Economy! With the peasant class! Whispers suggested that a stronger team would be following to Shetland under the covert guise of academia or tourism or other business. Their suspicions had been increased.

CHAPTER SEVEN

Fiona knocked on Lachie's door. 'There an er "gentleman" who wants to speak to you sir.'

A tall thin middle-aged man walked into Lachie's office. He had two days greying stubble above a ragged Fair Isle fisherman's sweater and faded jeans with designer knee holes. Cold Shetland nights usually removed that dumb fashion idea for thick denim with no holes. Common sense. Fashion's antonym! He was not a local in spite of the rest of his appearance.

'Inspector McKenzie, thank you for seeing me. My name is John Smith...'

'That's funny,' said Lachie sarcastically, 'that my usual alias as well!'

'Well in my case it happens to be true. I am with the British Military Police. A captain underneath this,' he said waving his hands at his attire, a disguise to appear a local fisherman, and then displaying his ID badge. Lachie perused it carefully. 'One of the victims, Brian Riggs was a very close friend and colleague of mine. We both had an interest in military history.'

'I must start by apologising for the clumsy approach in sending a unit last week without permission and notification. My boss, his Lordship does not believe tact is necessary for the peasant class! His opinion of the Scots. About the same as old Longshanks seven hundred years ago. Obviously, we are concerned at the deaths of eight of our soldiers, one in an undercover operation. We are afraid our organisation in London may have been penetrated. We are concerned also that there may be a covert Russian, Chinese or Iranian unit operating in the Shetlands.'

'So, inspector, I am seeking your permission to work under you, alongside you in this investigation. To be kept informed of your progress, but not to be directly involved unless our fears are realised. I have access to sources of information not available to you. I have a high security clearance in London.'

'The Ministry of Defence have decided that there will be no more military exercises on Shetland. No service personnel will be posted here unless there is some international incident demanding the defence of these islands from foreign interests.'

Lachie surveyed the new arrival thoughtfully. 'Thank you, Captain Smith for coming to see me. Sit down. Thank you for your honesty. I like your disguise. Different from his lordship! We will work together on this. Currently we have several lists and lines of investigation to discuss with you.'

'I have a list of all gun owners and members of the shooting club. I have a list of all those who left the island within twenty-four hours of the shooting. I have a list of the probable OK women's organisation members who want union with Norway and exclusion of British Armed Forces. I always have a list of all overseas passport holders on Shetland at any one time. That is a lot of possible suspects.'

'The investigation is complicated by the five hundred odd Shetland women who took out gun licenses after your troops murdered one of our girls and raped two others. At least a hundred have become crack shots. They flogged our best police team at a recent island shooting championship. We were coerced at a high political level not to be involved with that investigation. The people of Shetland will never allow that to happen again. Working together the islanders have a lot of political muscle as your Lord Poncy-Bone discovered.'

'If we are to work together there will be no protection for your soldiers from the processes of the law.'

'Agreed,' responded Smith.

'So,' began Lachie, 'let me tell you of my progress. Five Chinese men arrived five days before the triathlon murders and flew out to Edinburgh, London and onto Hong Kong six hours after the murders. You will have heard of the recent high-level Chinese defector who claims the Chinese have inserted political assassins in many foreign countries. The Chinese said he was a convicted fraudster, but they would, wouldn't they.'

'So, these five men were also in Shetland when Brian Riggs was murdered. They paid for everything here with cash. They never used a credit card. CCTV picked up images of them taking pictures around the airport and the docks and of the transmitter towers. They appeared healthy young men. Smart charcoal suits, white shirts and red ties. They kept communication in their apartment with staff to an absolute minimum. They ate only in one Chinese restaurant in town. The owner has been there ten years and claims to be a Shetlander. He said they were just normal Chinese tourists.'

'We thought they were probably active members of their communist party working for the Chinese government, though that seems to apply to all their tourists these days. A secret power-grasping agenda behind an inscrutable face and superficially friendly official denials.'

'We wondered if they were doing something to the Ronas Hill transmitting tower, taking pictures, leaving monitors, even inserting a sleeper virus into the computers there, a Trojan horse. They may have been disturbed by the Highland regiment runners and so they shot the five victims.'

Smith replied, 'we picked them up too. Customs spotted them arriving in Edinburgh initially and notified us. Five impeccably dressed young Chinese males aroused suspicion. We planted a taxi driver on them. Chinese national. He swore loyalty to the Communist Party to them, but actually lost his father in the Tiananmen Square massacre and knows where he is best off. He reckons the best hope for the Chinese is another civil war, one to throw out the dictators and replace them with a true people's republic.'

'He drove them everywhere. Around the coast, photos of every inlet and port for their proposed harbour controlled by China. A home for their new aircraft carrier. Photos of the airport and ferry terminals. Photos of communication sites. Photos of sites for the Buddhist temple as a front for the communist party. Plans for Chinese Europe part one after Chinese Pacific islands, Chinese Africa and Chinese Australia.'

'We contacted the Chinese embassy in London. They said they could not trace anyone by their stated names and home addresses on their national database. They disappeared shortly after arriving in Hong Kong. The embassy thought they may have been on false passports. They say Hong Kong is full of bad people. Legacy of the British occupation of course. The recent riots in Honk Kong were caused by British infiltrators. Fortunately they have all been eliminated after the military crack-down to protect the true Chinese patriots.'

'The Chinese displayed all the fake indignation you expect from communist dictatorships when they are caught out with their nose in other people's business. Straight from Stalin's manifesto, deny the truth, deflect blame, obfuscate, procrastinate and actively obstruct or delay justice. So no, how could you ask, how could you think ill of the Chinese, no Chinese men had been sent to spy on Britain or anywhere in the world. They want to live in harmony with other countries. They only want peace in the world. Like hell! Why are the political communist leaders telling their generals to prepare for war? Why do they spend a fortune on so-called defence when millions are still living in poverty? How can they claim to be a developing nation still?'

'After getting away with murder for several decades, the world is beginning to see through them. The invasion of Tibet and the re-education of the Uighurs in prison camps. The hushed-up deaths of several thousand Uighurs with untreated coronavirus. All this bonhomie with small countries is only to tie them to Chinese interests. I expect every dollar we spend on Chinese goods will one day come back as bullets. Our IT experts, civilians of course, are checking essential Shetland systems for computer hacking. They are fairly sure some attempt has been made to corrupt your computers.'

'Lachie, next you should expect to see Chinese couples buying key real estate. Migrants who profess to love Shetland. Happy families wanting a little home and a little business. Migrants with shitloads of money courtesy of the Communist Party and all their poor exploited factory workers on a pound a day. One site from each real estate agent over a long period. Potential harbour sites the most important. China's long game'

Lachie was thoughtful. 'Sounds as though our demonstrators wanting separation from UK may end up with China not Norway as the controlling power. Chexit! We will watch out for that.'

'So definite suspects if they were caught on Ronas Hill.' mused Lachie. 'Next, we found three Iranian men who spent three days here and took the first flight out the morning after the Up Helly Aa festival. Again, all cash, no credit cards. CCTV and subsequent enquiries showed they went to three real estate agents looking for a large block of land near the middle of Lerwick. Cost was no object. The real estate agents took them in rapidly and quadrupled asking prices. Two agents were business types from Glasgow. Never going to miss out on a few good Scottish pounds from gullible tourists with deep pockets! The Iranians bought an acre of empty land in an outer suburb with a lot of cash and left once that was done. We suspect they were planning an Islamic centre for Lerwick. God, John, we once thought we were under the world's radar here. Now some really bad bastards are wanting into our island paradise!'

Smith continued, 'we picked them up too. The Iranian consulate in London denied all knowledge of them, though we think CCTV picked them up entering the consulate there before they flew to Lerwick. The official we contacted said they did not reveal details of any individual on their data base to infidels. And of course, everyone knows Islam is a peaceful religion and murders are against their beliefs.'

Lachie summarised, 'so more suspects, perhaps hostile to UK military forces, careful not to reveal personal data and left immediately after the crime.'

The detective looked at the captain, 'the Glock 17s used in the shooting of five men, correct me but I understand these are sold all over the world. There are five or six million out there. The British army has been using them for some six years. The bullets forensic experts thought three weapons were used.'

'Yes,' responded the captain, 'you probably are not aware of unaccountable losses. There was a probable theft from the armoury in Aberdeen of five Glocks two months ago. They could not account for the deficiency. Allowing for service commitments in Afghanistan and Iraq perhaps a hundred pistols have been mislaid.'

So, Lachie thought aloud, 'the use of a Glock 17 tells us nothing. It could have been used by anyone, from any country, even members of other Scottish military companies to settle ancient clan feuds.'

Lachie continued, 'we have eight dead British soldiers, one maybe an accident. Maybe. We have no clear suspect, no witness, no weapon, no useful footprints, no DNA from suspects, no useful CCTV. There are possible motives. The Shetland people for the rapes and murder. Hostile foreigners caught doing something inappropriate. The Iranian group. Probably not the Chinese, they have alternative nefarious interests.'

'The OK women's group are dreadfully anti-British soldiers but claim to espouse peace. They describe themselves as peace weavers not shield maidens. Old Anglo-Saxon terms. A demonstration marched past here recently. Some of them look bloody terrifying! Perhaps they hired a Norwegian hitman. Rumours circulate here of a medieval Norse custom called holmganga in which men with a dispute engage in trial by combat. They say the shades of the Vikings were in dispute with your five triathletes and they were all killed in combat. Old beliefs live on here in the land, but I don't know of any Vikings with modern pistols.'

'What about all the castrations, does that suggest sexual revenge to you, Shetlanders seeking revenge for the murder and rapes?' Lachie asked.

'Yes and no,' Smith, the military historian, responded, 'castration has been used in war from the mists of time. The Normans were said to have done that to the corpse of Harold Godwinson after the Battle of Hastings, and to other Anglo-Saxons in the next two centuries of Norman tyranny and oppression. Simon de Montford had his balls chopped off after the Battle of Evesham in 1265. The Chinese chopped the balls off prisoners of war for centuries and did the same to all the poor eunuchs in the palace in Beijing. Again, that is not a factor that limits suspects.'

'One more question from my boss, Lachie. Who the bloody hell is Isaac?'

Lachie laughed and laughed. 'That is an old Shetland wives' tale John. Isaac was an old, old man said to be able to pick a murderer from some suspects. He tells them that his cat is the super sleuth. All the suspects are put in a totally dark room with an old sooty cooking pot placed upside down in the middle with the cat underneath. Isaac says they must all place their hands one at a time on the pot and when the guilty man does that, the cat will screech. The cat doesn't screech at all, but when they go back out into the daylight to be examined, one man does not have soot on his hands. He had not touched the pot for fear of being detected by the cat. Isaac had found the guilty man. A canny Scot. Smarter than Lord Poncy-Bone!'

'First find some suspects for Isaac.'

The two were unable to progress any further.

CHAPTER EIGHT

Two days later there was more work for the pair. John Smith's mobile rang.

'John, Lachie here. We have another dead body. It has just been found by a tourist at the Broch of Clickimin.'

'Oh God, that's awful but also interesting. I was wanting to visit Clickimin. The broch there dates back to the iron age, perhaps seventh century BC. It used to be in the middle of a loch approached by a causeway. It is unusual because it sits in an outer walled enclosure and entrance to the broch is through an outer blockhouse. It has a couple of other entrances higher up in the wall. There are a pair of footprints carved in stone there marking the site where Pictish kings were crowned.'

'Archaeological digs found Roman glass. The ancient Shetlanders must have been amazing sailors long before the Viking longboats came.....sorry Lachie, I'm drifting off on a tangent.....tell me about the body.'

It was another similar story. A pair of tourists from Taiwan had found a mutilated body. A middle-aged man found in the ruins with his throat cut and his balls chopped off.

Lachie and Smith surveyed the sorry corpse with a mixture of anger, frustration and revulsion. Smith slapped his face. 'Your bloody midges drive me crazy. I'll be glad to leave them behind. Where do they all come from?'

'Ah,' replied Lachie, 'that's the Skerry Giant.'

'Oh yes, more Shetland myths? Tell me.'

'Well there was once a skerry giant who would wade to the mainland villages, seize a child and disappear. Presumably it ate the child. The men all gathered to make a plan to kill it. One day a boy, a fantastically fast runner led the giant into a trap. All the concealed men caught the giant in a net, tied it up and killed it. But it said, 'I am going to eat you!' So, they cut of its head, but it still said, 'I am going to eat you!' So, they chopped it into little bits, but the voice said, 'I am going to eat you!' So, they made a big fire and burnt all the bits of flesh till they became into little flecks of ash. The villagers danced around saying, 'we have killed the giant, we have killed the giant!' Then the wind blew all the little bits of ash into the air. Still the voice said, 'I am going to eat you!' All the little bits of ash had turned into midges and the skerry giant is still eating you!'

The detectives drove to the crime scene. Another unfortunate traumatised tourist shivered next to a wall, endeavouring in vain to shelter from the chilly North Sea wind, endeavouring in vain to light a cigarette in the light drizzle, awaiting their arrival. His statement added little beyond the awful discovery. The other tourist had collapsed and been taken to hospital.

There was no weapon, no footprints in the stone floor, no identification on the corpse. No CCTV at the site. Forensic pathology noted the body was rain-soaked and had been out overnight. Death was at least twelve hours before. Again, there was a large bruise on the back of his head.

A Lerwick motel phoned the police station while the detectives were at Clickimin. One of their guests had not been seen for twenty-four hours. He appeared not to have slept in the bed overnight, nor been seen in the restaurant for dinner or breakfast. His name was given as John Smith. His given residential address in Leeds did not exist. He was paying his bills with cash. He had not paid for his room yet. He arrived in Shetland three days previously. He appeared to have no birth certificate or other evidence that he existed on preliminary police investigation.

A check at the airport revealed two Afghanistanis had flown to Edinburgh on the first plane out that morning and were already on a flight to Kabul. There were not many tourists from Kabul these days. Apparently, according to their motel, they professed an enthusiasm for ornithology. It was the same motel that John Smith had stayed in. Coincidence? There were only two motels currently open. Ornithology? That sounded a plausible cover. For true birdwatchers or for villains.

When the detectives returned to Lerwick, Smith phoned his base. Yes, the 'John Smith' was a special agent from the Ministry of Defence also evaluating the possibility of Shetland being infiltrated by any opposing interest and the cause of so many British soldiers being murdered.

Lachie was unhappy, 'so, John, the real John Smith, how come there are so many of you investigating events in my territory? So many John Smiths. How come someone seems to know fairly rapidly about the identity of covert operators here and murders them, but no one touches you?'

'Good questions, ones of concern to me. I am unhappy the office appears not to have confidence in us working together, I worry that I may be a target, though being with you may increase my safety. The other two guys came from a different branch of the office which appears to have been infiltrated. One hand is not communicating with the other. There will be a lot of internal evaluation going on back in London.'

The coronial inquiry concluded one death by probable misadventure and eight murders by person or persons unknown, possibly overseas visitors. An open conclusion with the recommendation of ongoing investigations.

CHAPTER NINE

The decision not to send any more British soldiers to the Shetlands went around like wildfire. Ecstatic wildfire amongst the OK women. A special celebratory extra meeting of their women's group was called to be held on Mousa, one of the smaller islands.

They were called to attention by a fiddler playing Neil Gow's lament to his second wife, a soulful tune of astonishing beauty and sadness. After a reflective pause, Aileana, a resident of Leebitten, the site of the ferry connection across to Mousa, addressed the group, several hundred strong.

'Welcome to the island of Mousa sisters, vestal virgins of vengeance. Thank you Struna for that hauntingly beautiful tune. If all men esteemed us women as much as Neil Gow loved Margaret Urquhart we probably would not need to be here. I am sure she hears that in heaven. However, in the year Neil Gow wrote that music, 1805, the stupid bastard English were fighting the battle of Trafalgar. Always bloody fighting! They still celebrate Trafalgar Day, not Neil Gow Day.'

'You have known me as Aileana, from tomorrow I will be known as Aileana Birka after the fairly recently excavated grave in Birka, Sweden. The grave was that of an elite warrior, a leader of the men. Two horses and a mass of weapons were found in the grave. Arrows and a spear, A battle-axe and a sword. It was obviously that of an elite warrior. A war hero. A leader of men. For a few decades the men just assumed arrogantly that it would be a male warrior. Obviously. Self-evidently as far as men were concerned. Wrong again men! Obviously!'

'In 2017 a female archaeologist from Uppsala University, Charlotte Henenstierna-Jonson discovered with DNA testing that this elite warrior was female! In the times of our Viking ancestors in Scandinavia, and we should return to being part of Scandinavia, women could be warrior-maidens. Shield-maidens, not peace-weavers. A person could be judged on the strength of their character and leadership, not on the size of the balls between their legs. Go Charlotte!'

Laughter and applause from the audience.

'Today we celebrate women power. The British have announced a complete withdrawal of their troops from our homeland. We have won a major victory. No more bastard English soldiers. No more toxic military masculinity on Shetland.'

'It is often asked; how many rapists have to be killed to stop men raping women. The answer here now appears to be no more. The little folk of Shetland have had their revenge. They have succeeded!'

Tumultuous applause followed.

'You may wonder why we have come here, a twenty-three-kilometre journey by boat from Lerwick. I will come to that shortly. Our feminist interests do not prevent an interest in our history and culture. A pride in our heritage. A pride in women's roles in Shetland's history.'

'This is a truly amazing building, just over two thousand years old and the finest iron-age broch in the world, the tallest still standing and the best-preserved prehistoric building in Europe.'

'Many sense the shades of the long-dead stone-age people flitting around the ruins at night. The ghosts of yesteryear protecting the women and removing the dangerous soldiers from our midst. Across the water at night, in the middle of the night I sometimes see flickering lights in here from my house. Flaming peat torches. Nobody lives here as far as we know. I would not come here at night ever.'

'Mousa Broch was mentioned in the Icelandic Egill's Saga as a refuge for a couple eloping from Iceland. The Orkneyinga Saga tells of Margaret, the mother of Earl Harald Maddadsson who was abducted by Erlend the Young and held here till rescued by her son. Erlend had wanted to marry Margaret. An unusual man who mixed a little honour with a lot of lust. Harald besieged this place but as you see, it's not an easy place to attack. Eventually Erlend agreed to be Harald's liegeman in return for his mother's hand in marriage.'

'A half-useful pair of males, not many of them who care for women's safety. Today it is a home for some seven thousand breeding Storm Petrel pairs. They are the living reproducing representation of my next allusion.'

'This building is symbolic for women. It is symbolic of the female body. It is a hollow cylindrical construction over thirteen metres high, which has always provided intimate hospitality for pleasant guests. It has a single narrow entrance for welcome visitors. The entrance passage is five metres long, bigger than the average male appendage or ego.'

She smiled coyly at the assembly who soon caught her drift. Pretence coyness. She continued, 'perhaps for a refreshing new one longed-for over many years, perhaps a delightful regular caller. There is an internal spiral staircase to take the visitor to the top. Men like getting to the top!'

'It is never never to be entered forcibly or violently! It is not for unwanted undesirable males, especially vicious powerful soldiers!'

The audience cheered and cheered.

A voice from the back yelled, 'can I have my husband and my secret lover alternating at the entrance?'

A raucous voice added amid laughter, 'what about both at the same time?'

'If the men can deal with that, that would be fine with me!' replied the first interjector.

More laughter.

Aileana raised her hand for quiet and continued. 'I have something else to tell you. Something symbolic. A pair of sea eagles have been seen flying around here for a few months and may be nesting on Mousa. They were extinct here for nearly a hundred years but have recently been reintroduced in the north of Scotland.'

'There are two things special about our eagles. They were thought by our ancestors to represent the souls of our departed heroes, men and women. That is why so many eagles bones were found in the Tomb of Eagles in Orkney. This pair are the souls of our ancestors come to protect us women in our hour of need.'

'The other special thing about the sea eagle is that the females are bigger and stronger than the males, as we must be mentally stronger than the men who oppress us. We will drink a toast shortly to the female sea eagle.'

Struna played some captivating highland jigs to enhance the celebratory mood as many danced joyfully and others raided a box of drinks for the toast.

Numerous bottles of Norwegian Brennevin, Norway and Iceland's signature liquor, a mere 40% alcohol, were consumed before the return ferry took the participants, all overflowing with glee, back to their homes and maybe, unsteadily, back to their jobs. After union with Norway there would be less tax to pay for Brennevin. Bring it on!

The women reckoned they had not had as much fun on Shetland since the Dutch East Indiaman *Kennermerland* was wrecked on the Skerries in 1664. The sixty barrels of spirits and wine that floated ashore kept both the men and women drunk for three weeks.

CHAPTER TEN

Fiona went to the next OK meeting at Scalloway Castle. Most stood in the ruins of the central tower, while the rest overflowed into the attached gallery. Novels and history texts centred on the islands past leading womenfolk authored by members of the group and paintings by local talented female artists were on display in the covered area. New flags flew displaying the female sea eagle with a large 'OK' in the corner.

Isla, one of the group's leading personalities stood up first.

'Welcome women of Shetland. Welcome my sisters. We have come to Scalloway Castle to mock a historical figure who is all the things we deplore and hate in men. This castle was built for one Patrick Stewart, Earl of Orkney in 1600. He also built a palace in Kirkwall for himself. Over the door he had engraved, *that house whose foundation is on a rock shall stand, but if on sand it shall fall.* Remember that.'

'He was a tyrannical bastard, himself the son of a bastard, Robert, Earl of Orkney, an illegitimate son of King James V. Like all former noble families in steep decline, he retained a false memory of his current status and importance. Delusions! Hubris! Black Pate Stewart was in fact the most evil man in the whole known history of the Shetlands.'

'Infamous for his godless nature and tyrannical rule over Orkney and Shetland, he was extravagant beyond his means and oppressed the unfortunate populace. He didn't even pay the poor beggars who worked long hours summer and winter for seven years to build this bloody castle.'

'In 1594 he attacked a merchant ship from the Baltic port of Danzig but was absolved by the courts. Presumably by bribing a judge. He ordered the people of the Northern Islands not to assist wrecked mariners so he could claim the valuable shipwrecked cargoes personally. Too bad about sailors dying for want of aid. Patrick didn't care.'

'That year he thought his younger brothers were trying to poison him, sensible fellows. I would have done so. Patrick arranged the torture and execution of his brother John's servitor and an Allison Balfour for being a witch involved in the conspiracy. We all know anyone killed as a witch was usually of superior intelligence to the man. We all know they were usually unjustly accused.'

'He married Margaret, a wealthy widow, spent her considerable fortune on himself and left her to die in poverty. They had no children, but Patrick screwed around and had at least three illegitimate kids. He was executed for treason in 1615, I hope it was slow and painful! His execution actually was delayed briefly because his chaplains found him so incredibly ignorant he could barely recite the Lord's Prayer. Perhaps smart enough though to become a British soldier or member of parliament!'

'They wanted time to educate him and give him communion before he was beheaded. Turns out the rocks were in his brain and his character built on shifting sands. That may not have altered his IQ much! Like most men he obviously thought through his balls.'

'So that is the original owner of this castle. A dumb philanderer. A tyrannical spiteful spendthrift who became an earl. How easy life seems for such men. I spit on his soul and his memory. If I had been Margaret, his wife, I would have cut his balls off!'

Loud cheers followed. Other speakers talked about a Shetland assembly, more devolution, compulsory child maintenance, equal pay for women, home economic classes for men at the TAFE and other topics.

Fiona approached Jean after the meeting. 'I hear you now have an official membership. Can I join?'

'I gather you are in a relationship with Cairistiona, that is one requirement. Cairistiona hates men, she is one of our best members. However, you cannot become a full member with your job. You have a conflict of interest.'

'What do you mean?'

'You have a job working with men for the British Government.'

'Well strictly speaking my job is with the Scottish Government.'

'Will you resign?'

''No.'

Jean stood in front of Fiona, hands on hips. 'Then I can't tell you what full membership entails. It would have to be secret, secret especially from Lachie, even if you are in bed together. Mind you I wouldn't mind a screw with him, he's quite good looking in a rugged neglected way. I think Lachie is the best friend we women have. He's been responsible for getting more than one violent Shetland male behind bars. Rumour has it that he identified the murdering raping English soldiers but was prevented from being involved by the high-ups in England. So, the bastards got away that time. Never again.'

'My mother told me that his father, a trawler captain, was lost at sea when Lachie was a little boy. His mum was expecting her second, a daughter. She remarried a couple of years later. Apparently, his stepfather used to bash Lachie, his mum and his sister. Rumour is that he sexually abused all of them. Rumour is that his little sister committed suicide when Lachie left home to join the police and get married. She had no one to protect her from that bastard. Lachie's first case as a policeman was then to nail his stepfather. The bastard got knocked in jail years ago. The cons sometimes dish out more appropriate justice than the law. No wonder he wants to nail such violent bastards. He deserved better than that two-timing bitch of a wife who pissed off to London with some celebrity photographer.'

'So, there it is now. Secret from the police. Secret from you while you wear that uniform. Punishable by death if you inform!'

Fiona gave a rueful smile. 'I have never been to bed with Lachie, he is my boss and sex across a chain of command would see us both sacked. Also, I have a female partner and he's totally off women since the ex shot through. Totally. That doesn't mean I don't fantasize about Lachie. I am interested in joining OK. I am a woman and always will be. I won't always be a policewoman. Tell me once I resign.'

'OK. One other suggestion is that you should change your name then to Inghen Ruaidh, you have the most vibrant red hair of any of us.'

'Why? Who was she, I have never heard the name before?'

'Over a thousand years ago, she was a red-headed Viking leader. She led a Viking fleet to Ireland and was said to have been a fearsome warrior. Fiercer than the men under her command.'

'Maybe a good idea, I am already a fearsome police warrior for law and order!'

CHAPTER ELEVEN

The next night in a light snow fall, Fiona knocked hesitantly on the door of Lachie's flat at nine o'clock. She bore a burning peat, sparking in the cold wind, on a pitchfork. An old Shetland tradition to light your way and add warmth to your host's fire till you left for home. Then you took a peat off the fire to light the walk home. Fiona was in tears. Not the traditional greeting for your host.

Fiona sobbed out, 'they all hate men more than I ever could. Lachie, I have just separated from Cairistiona. I can't hate all men as she does. I quite like some men, one more than anyone. You! So, Lachie, I have only one request for you tonight. Can I share your bed tonight? Please! Please! I know I am being a bit of a floosie, perhaps even a shameless hussy. Totally shameless. Feel free to say no if you don't want me. I can cope with rejection even though I have completely bared my soul to you. We can worry and work out the police chain of command tomorrow. Please Lachie.'

Lachie smiled. His first warm smile for a couple of years. All his Christmases had come at once. Tonight would be the greatest pleasure since the ex left, and indeed from long before she 'fessed up about the London photographer. Lachie drew her in and placed the peat on his fire. Then he gave her a long intimate kiss while holding her tight, then picked her up light as a feather to carry her to his bed.

The next morning, they smiled at each other and said simultaneously, 'I have an idea, another idea.'

'You go first Fiona,' said Lachie.

'Well since we have been naughty police officers last night, naughty but unbelievably nice, we must do something before we are both sacked and humiliated,' she cuddled up to Lachie and exchanged more kisses, 'I've been in bed with a few men before. They were only interested in having a quick screw for their own satisfaction, as many women as they could. The quicker the better. No interest in whether I was enjoying it, no interest in me as a person. Hence, I sought other women. You Lachie, you're different. You're a better lover than Cairistiona in how you make me feel. Last night was the best two hours I have ever had in bed. Emotionally and physically. How do you manage such a long time? Your ex was an idiot to lose you!'

A few more kisses were exchanged before Fiona continued.

'I thought we should resign and set up our own private detective agency. There is not one in Shetland or Orkney. Many of the OK women have approached me to do some private detective work checking on their kids and husbands. We will make more money than the meagre government salaries we get here.'

Lachie nodded in agreement, 'I was going to suggest just the same thing. Some men have asked what goes on in the OK meetings. They think their wives are having lesbian affairs. Let's type up our resignation letters now, well perhaps in quarter of an hour, or perhaps longer. Then let's go to the Peerie Shop café for breakfast to celebrate! It's so bloody cold I fancy their mutton and tattie soup for breakfast, followed by eggs and haggis with lots of coffee. Last night's exercise has left me totally famished, and fairly exhausted you naughty girl!"

CHAPTER TWELVE

'OK, Jean, I resigned my job yesterday and would like to become a full member with all its responsibilities and secrets. Here is a copy of my resignation letter and the superintendent's regretful acceptance. I am out of the force. Tell me!' announced Fiona.

'OK, we need some of your skills and knowledge. One of our individual obligations was to each remove a British soldier from Shetland. Dead or alive. The more shocking the better. The end justifies the means. Actually, it was the main purpose of the organisation. Should they ever return we will go back on the offensive. Rapes and murders of our innocent young women will take our peace-weavers down never previously anticipated roads to protect us women and as shield-maidens to exact revenge. Half an hour later they are back to being peace-weavers scarcely able to believe what they have done.'

'One of our group lives in London and is the mistress of a high-up in MI5. He is discreet in what he tells her but is unaware she checks his phone once he is fast asleep. Sex two or three times in an evening and he is literally completely fucked. He doesn't stir till morning. We know who and when they sent a secret agent up here.'

'Others of our group work in hotels, restaurants, travel agencies and with the airlines. We know when tourists from middle eastern countries or China will be on the first flight out for the day. You can be pretty sure that a group of young brainwashed Chinese men will be up to something for their communist dictator and totalitarian government. Perhaps planting a Trojan horse somewhere in our computerised systems or organising a sleeper in the community.'

'We think that provides the police with false clues. It draws attention away from us.'

'Every three months we had a draw, three black balls and two thousand white ones. our membership is large. The three women drawing black balls have three months to do the job. Removing a soldier that is. After the draw, the three chosen ones meet at a preordained place and time wearing balaclavas and stockings over their faces, so they don't recognise each other, and arrange the job.'

'Usually two distract the man while one knocks him unconscious with a baseball bat. The first poor bastard was distracted with a possible sex orgy, a threesome while he was pissed. The other blokes in the ruins, the military historians, had the usual British middle-class attitude to sex, not today thank you. We had to ask if they had seen the test match cricket scores! That caught their undivided attention.'

'The five who were shot was a fairly impromptu event, but the weather forecast of abnormally heavy snow alerted us to the possibility of getting a few at once. Several women moved the track markers to lead those five men astray and a long way in the wrong direction before they were eliminated. As soon as they went past the markers were replaced in the original position'

'If caught all two thousand of us will plead guilty. It is impossible to know who. We all alibi each other. None of us know who did each elimination.'

Fiona returned to Lachie's flat and sat down having a cup of tea with him. She sat pensively.

'Penny for your thoughts,' enquired Lachie.

'Well, I have been told what is happening now I am out of the police. I will tell you if you also see this as confidential. It is not our job any more to tell everyone now.'

Fiona repeated the story she had been told.

'So, Lachie, that is the full story. The Iranians were here only to buy a block near town to build an Islamic centre with a mosque and school.

All part of their plan to eliminate Christianity and impose Sharia law in UK. That won't help employment in the distilleries! All part of the plan to increase the percent of Muslims in the Shetlands from today where it is less than half a percent to a controlling majority. They hope to open the mosque within two years. If they succeed you and I might get stoned!'

'The Chinese didn't murder anyone either. They were here to fund the OK women's group expenses to separate Shetland from UK. They will pay for anything to diminish the power of the west, particularly USA and UK. Also, they were spying on the infrastructure here of the military and communications networks. Anything to infiltrate and exert covert control. Anything to buy essential infrastructure in the west so they can shut it down whenever they want. Every penny we spent on cheap Chinese goods will come back to us as Chinese bullets.'

'The women's group murdered everyone. Even Private Thomas Smith was thrown out of the window by the girls. They will all deny this. You will not pin anything on them individually. They will all take collective responsibility if under suspicion and duress. They have hired the sharpest female lawyers in Scotland. They all alibi each other. None of them know who did the other killings. They will all go to jail together or not at all.'

'As long as there are no more soldiers here, there will be no more murders. So, Lachie, can we get on with organising our private detective agency. But not quite yet. I have a better idea for the next hour or maybe two!'

'Me too.' agreed Lachie, 'I'll text John Smith to tell him that you and I have resigned from the police force to set up our private detective agency. I'll tell him he can be our first customer at the considerable expense of the English taxpayer. Alternatively, he can continue the investigation alone.'

'I will tell him that the murders were perpetrated by person or persons unknown to us. I will tell him we are sure that there are no foreign agencies responsible for murdering the soldiers and to reassure him that security has not been infiltrated by a foreign power. At least not over this problem. I might suggest we meet at the pub for a farewell drink.'

'OK if I tell him one of his high-ups shouldn't take his phone to his mistresses flat for his regular unfaithful nightly trysts? Adultery seems to get found out sooner or later perhaps unfortunately. And yes, I am divorced Fiona! In this case in London with considerable loss of face, eminent responsible position and generous salary. Silly bastard!'

Lachie paused and continued, 'One bit of some different news first, I see in the local rag that the A-lister photographer is in police custody for bashing my ex. Apparently, she caught him in bed with a couple of his models! One male and one female! He likes a bit each way evidently. She didn't appreciate that. Don't concern yourself, if she rings feeling sorry and asking to come back. My little sister warned me not to marry her, said she was a two-timing selfish bitch before she she....' Lachie stopped and shed a tear before he gathered himself and continued, 'I shall tell her that I am in a much better relationship!'

Fiona hugged him and whispered in his ear, 'I heard about your family, I am so so sorry Lachie, I will never let you down. I will try to fill the empty spaces in your life every day with lots of love.'

After holding each other for several minutes in which both shed a few more tears, Lachie replaced the tea with some single malt Scapa whisky, and they shared a toast.

'What goes around, comes around! Stupid pair of A-listers. She needn't call asking to come back to me. I have other plans.'

Lachie dropped to one knee, and hopefully offered Fiona a diamond engagement ring.

'And Fiona, will you marry me?'

The remote Scottish Islands. Beautiful wild bleak friendly isles cloaked in mist and ancient history. And the little people. Beautiful islands of bizarre brutal murders, a promiscuous academic on St Kilda, tourists executed by ancient barbaric rituals in the Orkneys, British soldiers castrated and murdered in the Shetlands, all in the ruins of an ancient civilisation. A fascination for historic ruins may be a dangerous occupation.

ABOUT THE AUTHOR

Peter Stride is a recently retired consultant physician living in Brisbane. He graduated MB BS from the Middlesex Hospital, London in 1970 and migrated to Australia in 1975. He is a Fellow of the Royal Colleges of Physicians of Australia, Edinburgh and London, and has a higher medical doctorate, D.Med, from the University of Queensland.

History has been a passion since primary school days in the birthplace of Sir Francis Drake and attending the same public school as King Alfred, though some years later. Growing up in England and overseas as a child of a physician in the Royal Navy one is surrounded by living and ancient history on land and at sea.

Peter has some hundred publications, some medical, some relating to aspects of the medicine of history, and some political satire in bridge magazines. After thirty-seven years working for Queensland Health and the University of Queensland, he resigned to spend the last five years working as a peripatetic locum physician in every Australian state becoming familiar with the 'outback'.

Peter has been married to Rosemary, a former nurse and English teacher, for fifty-three years and enjoys the company of his three children and eight grandchildren who all live nearby. He has published one previous historical fictional novel, 'William Hobbys, the promiscuous king's promiscuous doctor', about a doctor during the Wars of the Roses, and one murder mystery novel set in Scotland, 'The Islands of Death' and appreciates travel, friends, wine and duplicate bridge.